The Wrecking Bar

*Book II from the
Inspector Lambert Trilogy*

David Barry

The Wrecking Bar
First published in 2012
This revised edition
Published in 2022 by
Acorn Books
acornbooks.uk
an imprint of
Andrews UK Limited
andrewsuk.com

Copyright © 2012, 2022 David Barry

The right of David Barry to be identified as the author
of this work has been asserted in accordance with
the Copyright, Designs and Patents Act 1988.

All rights reserved. No reproduction, copy or transmission
of this publication may be made without express prior
written permission. No paragraph of this publication may be
reproduced, copied or transmitted except with express prior
written permission or in accordance with the provisions of the
Copyright Act 1956 (as amended). Any person who commits
any unauthorised act in relation to this publication may be
liable to criminal prosecution and civil claims for damage.

All characters appearing in this work are
fictitious. Any resemblance to real persons,
living or dead, is purely coincidental.

To Henry, Alan, Robert, Paul and George

Contents

Author's Note v
Acknowledgements vi

One 1
Two 5
Three 11
Four 17
Five 24
Six 28
Seven 33
Eight 38
Nine 42
Ten 51
Eleven 56
Twelve 63
Thirteen .66
Fourteen .71
Fifteen 77
Sixteen 95
Seventeen 101
Eighteen 116
Nineteen 125
Twenty 130
Twenty-One 142
Twenty-Two 149
Twenty-Three 161
Twenty-Four 173
Twenty-Five 184
Twenty-Six 191
Twenty-Seven 195
Twenty-Eight 199

Missing Persons Preview 203

Author's Note

Apart from the first chapter, *The Wrecking Bar* is set in 2010. I mention this because there have been a few changes in the UK since then. Flybe, the mainly domestic airline, filed for administration and ceased operations in March 2020 – although there have been recent talks of a re-emergence sometime soon, and perhaps by the time this book is published the airline may well be operational again. There were seven regional police forces in Scotland, including Borders and Lothian, and these have all merged and became Police Scotland in 2013.

Acknowledgements

I am deeply indebted to South Wales Police for providing me with information and setting me right on details of police procedure. Any deviation from police practice or procedure is either an error on my part or appears for reasons of dramatic licence.

The Wrecking Bar

One

As he neared the familiar terrace house, Keith slowed his steps. Thoughts of turning back and going home weighed on his mind but he was committed now. He'd promised his friend, and he *would* go through with it. Besides, in a strange way, the thought of what was about to happen fascinated him – like being drawn to the scene of an accident.

To calm his nerves, he tried breathing deeply, inhaling the overpowering smell of yeast from the local brewery. Streets away, he heard voices rising in anger, and then a bottle smashing. He walked faster, conscious of the slap of his shoes on the wet paving slabs, slick from a recent shower.

He paused in front of the shabby front door, pulled a pair of woollen gloves from his anorak pockets and slid them on. Then, glancing nervously over his shoulder, he stared into the shadows, eyes straining for any sign of movement. After eleven o'clock the pubs would turn out, or stragglers on their way home from the cinema would be on the streets; but at 9:15 people were where they wanted to be and the street behind him was deserted.

The muffled sound of a television set came from the living room. Keith knew Con's father spent most of his time glued to the set, chain smoking and swilling beer, all provided by state benefits. He rang the doorbell, keeping his finger on the button for a good couple of seconds until footsteps pounded down the hall. The door swung wide open, exactly as he'd expected. Mr O'Sullivan looked down at him, his eyes hard and cold, mouth clenched tight. When he recognized Keith, a glint came into his piggy eyes and an ugly smile tugged at the corners of his mouth.

'He's not home. I thought he was at your place.'

Keith tried to keep his voice steady. 'That's why I came round. To see if he wanted to come over and see the rest of *Goldfinger* on TV.'

O'Sullivan shook his head, puzzled. 'Well, if he's not with you...'

As if remembering how stupid he'd been, Keith raised his performance a notch. 'Oh, of course. I forgot. He arranged to go to Pete's tonight.'

'Who the hell's Pete?'

'New boy in our class.'

O'Sullivan nodded as he assimilated this information. Keith waited nervously, wanting to glance over his shoulder. The longer he waited in the street, the greater the chances he'd be seen. And what if Con's father didn't ask him in? Their plans would be ruined. Keith shifted his feet and gave O'Sullivan a weak smile. 'Well, I suppose I'd better head home. Don't want to miss too much of the film.'

Unable to suppress a crafty smile, O'Sullivan glanced furtively up and down the street, and Keith knew he'd taken the bait. 'You can watch it with me if you like. And I'm sure a youngster like you could handle a beer.' He stood aside, holding the door open, his huge body filling the entrance.

This was it then. Taking a deep breath, Keith squeezed past O'Sullivan, his arm rubbing against the man's enormous stomach. It disgusted him, but he tried not to show his feelings. O'Sullivan slammed the door shut and led the way down the hall to the living room. Keith had been here twice before and remembered the stink of cat's piss, and tonight a curry smell also hung in the air. In the living room, his eyes were drawn to the TV set, a scene where James Bond was strapped to a bench and was about to be sliced up the middle by a laser cutter. As the deadly beam neared Bond's crotch, O'Sullivan giggled.

'Ouch!' he exclaimed, closing the living room door. 'Make yourself at home. I'll get you a beer.'

Keith sank into the sofa, looked up and noticed O'Sullivan eyeing him suspiciously.

'What's with the gloves? It's not cold out.'

Keith had an explanation ready. 'I'm having piano lessons. And just the slightest drop in temperature...' He left the sentence open-ended, hoping this was enough. Con's father shrugged, bent over the coffee table, prised a can of beer from a six pack and handed it to him.

'You can take your gloves off now. You're inside where it's warm.'

Keith stared at the beer can in his hand, trying to think of something to say. His nerves were jarred by pounding music from the television set, and he gripped the can tighter.

'What's wrong?' O'Sullivan asked.

'I'd sooner leave the gloves on. I've been having skin problems.'

'I thought it was something to do with the piano.'

'I need to cure the skin problem so I can get back to playing the piano.' As he lied about his hands, Keith stared at the television screen. Inside he burned with fear, waiting to hear Con enter the front door. Thankfully the volume on the television was turned up high.

'How you gonna open your beer?' Con's father demanded.

Keith paused. He hadn't expected this. 'I'm sorry,' he said, placing the unopened can on the coffee table.' I don't know why I took it. I had a beer once before and it tasted like medicine.'

As he stretched forward, glancing at his watch, he saw four minutes had elapsed since he'd entered the house. He and Con had agreed they'd be just five minutes apart. One minute more and it would be over. Something throbbed in his calf, a spasm he couldn't control. He wanted to change his mind. But it was too late for that. He'd reached the point of no return.

O'Sullivan laughed and eased himself onto the sofa. 'Boy like you – not liking beer. Bit of a wimp, if you ask me. Still, you're a nice looking young wimp.'

Keith focused on the television, trying to appear calm. It took a moment to register something crawling like a spider along his thigh. Then, as he felt warmth through his denims, he realized it was O'Sullivan's hand. Praying the minute was almost up, Keith looked round, and the stench of rancid sweat overwhelmed him as O'Sullivan shifted his bulk closer and squeezed his leg. Keith had the awful feeling the man was about to kiss him. The booze-red face and double chins, the revolting fleshy lips puckering in anticipation, loomed closer, and Keith felt sickened by breath so bad it actually smelt like shit. Now he knew exactly why Con had to destroy his own father. But where was his friend? Had he changed his mind at the last minute?

The grip tightened on his thigh. 'Hey, come on! I thought we were gonna have some fun.'

Squinting at the living-room door behind O'Sullivan, Keith thought he saw the doorknob turn but couldn't be certain. Suddenly, the father made a lunge for him, reaching for his crotch.

'Get off me!' Keith sprang off the sofa and stumbled against the television set as the living-room door swung open. Feeling a blast of cool air, O'Sullivan stopped and began to turn round.

He never saw what hit him. The metal bar came down with a sickening crack on the top of his head, like a rock being split in half.

Shocked, yet fascinated, Keith watched Con raise the club again. This time the blow split the skull open and he could see the father's brains spill. He felt sick and looked away, swallowing saliva to control the queasy feeling.

Numbed by the horror of what he'd done, Con stared at his father's enormous body slumped across the sofa, the head a repulsive broken ball, oozing blood on to the sofa. Then he stepped back and let the metal bar slip from his fingers.

Keith grabbed at Con's jacket and saw the stream of blood that was splattered across his friend's trousers and shoes. Knowing Con was about to panic, he tightened his grip, but Con slipped out of his grasp. 'Wait!' Keith shouted. 'Don't run! We have to walk back to my place.'

The front door slammed and he stood rooted to the spot, praying no one would identify Con on the streets. He was shaking and sweating with fear, his clothes soaked as if he had a fever and there were great spots of blood on his shoes. He had to keep his cool and finish their plan. Working quickly, he grabbed a plastic shopping bag that had contained the six-pack and thrust the murder weapon inside it. He almost gagged as he saw bits of bone clinging to the blood smeared on the club.

O'Sullivan's body was on its stomach, so Keith fumbled in the back pocket of the man's trousers and removed his wallet. He took two five pound notes out and shoved them into the inside pocket of his anorak. Then he pocketed O'Sullivan's wallet, intending to drop it somewhere in the neighbourhood, making certain it wasn't in the direction they were heading, and hope the police would see this as a robbery gone bad.

As soon as he left the living room Keith felt his legs give way. He ran a hand against the wall of the hallway as he staggered towards the front door. But his head was clear and he remembered what to do. He clicked the front door lock on to the latch, as they'd arranged. Con would deny ever owning a key to his house, would get rid of it, and explain his father sometimes left the latch on so that he could let himself in.

Stepping out on to the street, Keith spotted a man with a dog on a lead walking on the other side. He eased back into the doorway, waiting in the shadows until the man passed by. As soon as the coast was clear, he walked briskly from the house in the opposite direction, holding the bag with the murder weapon beneath his coat. The further he got from the scene of the murder, the easier his breath came. Within a few minutes he felt a soaring sensation in his chest; the same thrill he experienced when listening to a Black Sabbath track. Everything was clear now. He was in control, and this was just the start. He was going places. One of those places was a quiet spot on the river, not far from the park on the Isle of Dogs, where he'd hurl the metal bar into the River Thames.

But an idea came into his mind, cunning and audacious. Instead, he'd take the murder weapon home with him.

Two

Driving from his flat in the Mumbles along the sea front towards Swansea Marina, Lambert experienced the initial nervousness he invariably felt before visiting a murder scene. His temperature rising, he wondered if wearing his leather coat had been a mistake, because it was unseasonably warm and sunny for mid October. He toyed with the idea of turning on the air conditioning, but the unnatural blast of cold would irritate, so instead he let window down, breathing in good sea air mixed with car fumes. The dazzling autumn sun was low in the sky and he squinted and lowered his windscreen visor. Stopping at a set of traffic lights he felt a sting of cold air coming in from the mouth of the Bristol Channel, a reminder of how cold the nights were becoming.

A trickle of sweat ran from under his arm and he realized it had little to do with the temperature. He'd always had an aversion to violent crime and sometimes wondered if perhaps he should transfer to another division. But his CID record was a good one, unblemished in fact, and he drove such thoughts out of his mind, hoping his squeamishness wouldn't show at the crime scene. He felt a weak stomach was a shortcoming in a police officer and tried to hide it by appearing blasé. But he could never switch off his feelings. The only time he'd let it show was when the victim of a particularly brutal slaying was a pre-pubescent girl. He'd needed counselling after that one. But he hadn't been the only one affected, and it seemed perfectly normal at the time to see tough, grown men weeping because they found it difficult to cope with what they'd seen.

A quick blast on a car horn disturbed his morbid thoughts and he realized the lights had turned green. Raising a hand to his driving mirror to acknowledge the driver behind, he took his foot off the brake pedal, pressed hard on the accelerator and the Mercedes automatic darted forwards. He smiled, inwardly pleased with his new toy. The two-year-old Mercedes was a

THE WRECKING BAR

compensatory gift for himself, bought when he received the decree nisi from Helen's solicitor.

Once he had turned off the main road towards the marina, it didn't take long to locate the crime scene. The yacht basin in the middle of the marina was surrounded by luxury flats on one side and a pub, shops and restaurants on the other. He parked near the crime scene vehicles and walked to the police cordon. Opposite, on the other side of the basin, customers lined up outside the pub, joking and laughing as they watched crime scene officers search for evidence on the deck of a small launch.

Detective Sergeant Tony Ellis stood on the quayside near where the boat was moored, his receding hairline drenched in sweat. Beside him stood Detective Constable Kevin Wallace, nervously pulling on his moustache, an adornment he'd grown hoping to give his boyish, chubby face a touch of authority. The two men were already kitted out in crime scene outfits.

Standing a little way off, near another SOCO van, was Debbie Jones, and Lambert saw her talking to someone he couldn't see, on the other side of the vehicle. He liked Debbie. She was part Welsh, part Asian, and correctly guessed the Asian was on her mother's side. She was slim, attractive and elegant in a trim-fitting, charcoal-grey trouser suit, her black hair centre-parted and falling into neat curves, ending just below her chin. Because she hadn't changed into crime scene coveralls, Lambert mentally gave her extra Brownie points for anticipating the way he intended to work the investigation.

He gave the detectives a cursory wave before changing into protective clothing. A wolf whistle came from across the yacht basin as he walked towards the boat, followed by raucous laughter from the drinkers. When Lambert reached the steps leading down to the boat, he stopped and spoke to Ellis.

'The incident took place inside the boat, I take it. Have you been down there yet?'

'Got here just minutes before you did, sir.' Ellis wiped his forehead with the back of the blue surgical glove he wore.

'It's extremely cramped down there.'

Lambert turned as he recognized the broad North Wales dialect of Dave, the crime scene manager.

'Hello, Dave,' Lambert acknowledged with a nod. 'Bad, is it?'

'Not a pretty sight, this one.' Dave looked pointedly at Ellis and Wallace. 'Like I said, Harry, it's small and cramped, and Hughie John's down there. And you know what he's like about wanting his space.'

6

CHAPTER TWO

'Bloody prima donna,' said Lambert. 'Still, he does a good job. Where would we be without forensics? Okay. Thanks, Dave. It was never my intention for the troops to go swarming all over the joint.'

'Fair enough. I'd better prepare myself. Press office is sending someone over and pretty soon we'll have reporters and the telly people swarming all over the marina.'

As Dave returned to his vehicle, Lambert acknowledged Debbie Jones with a brief nod and slight smile, before talking to the three of them.

'I'm going to take a look down below and have a word with Hughie. Incidentally, who discovered the body?'

'Emergency call came through over an hour ago,' Ellis said. 'Man named Gordon Mayfield. He has a boat moored in the next basin. Seems he'd borrowed a boat hook or something from the victim and was returning it.'

'Where is he now?'

'On board his boat. There's a female PC with him. Mandy Goring. Got her job cut out trying to calm him. Apparently he was very shocked by what he found.'

It took Lambert a moment to deliberate. He realized the other detectives probably had a morbid curiosity to visit the crime scene, a compulsion to see the awful reality of human viciousness, even though it was something they hated doing. But he knew any potential witnesses need to be interviewed promptly, while small details are fresh in their minds.

'Right,' he said decisively, glancing briefly at the boat. 'Let's give Hughie the space he needs.' He turned towards Ellis and Wallace. 'Tony, Kevin, you can both get changed, quick as you can. Tony, I want you to question this Gordon Mayfield. On second thoughts, take Debbie with you. See if you can find out whether the victim had any visitors to his boat.'

'I'm onto it.' Ellis hurried towards one of the police SOCO vans to remove his protective clothing. Before following him, DC Debbie Jones hesitated, staring at Lambert with an expression of motherly concern, sympathetic yet reproachful. Her boss's dark hair was greying fast, his rugged features looked unhealthily drawn, and his once slim physique had become flabby.

'Well?' he snapped, irritated by her ambivalent manner. 'Something wrong?'

She shook her head and walked off. He immediately forgot about her and pointed out the apartment block to DC Wallace.

'Kevin, I want you to start calling on the marina apartments to see if anyone noticed anything unusual happening in this vicinity. Anything, however trivial it might seem.'

7

'You don't think a quick dekko of the actual crime scene might help—'

Lambert interrupted him. 'No, I don't think it's necessary for you to view the corpse. You can see the photos. I want you to find out if anyone visited this boat.'

DC Wallace nodded, looking slightly shamefaced. 'I'm onto it.' Immediately regretting using the same words as Tony Ellis, he turned sharply and walked away, relieved his boss couldn't see the beetroot colour of his complexion.

But Lambert was already on his way down the steps at the quayside to where the boat was moored. Stepping gingerly aboard the narrow edge of the launch, which he noticed was named *Narcissus,* he held the rail with a gloved hand to steady himself onto the deck at the stern. Below the bridge of the boat was the entrance to the cabin, and he took a deep breath to prepare himself for what he had to confront. He nodded to a couple of SOCO officers who were examining the deck closely, and then turned to begin his descent, but stopped to give way to a crime scene officer carrying a video camera.

'I hope that carries an eighteen certificate,' he said.

The officer chuckled. 'These days this sort of thing would get by with a PG.'

Lambert stepped cautiously onto the steep steps, ducking under the sliding hatch, and descended into the cabin. As he entered, he saw Hughie John move back from the corpse to give the photographer a clear shot. The bulb flashed, and that was when Lambert observed that the corpse was naked, lying on its back on the cabin floor, wedged between a wicker chair and a long bench seat, awash in a pool of blood. The battered head had something thick and black across the lower part of the face. It looked like a strip of gaffer tape, used to silence the victim. Lambert stepped cautiously into the cramped cabin and felt a crunching beneath his feet as he stepped on shards of glass.

Hughie turned to greet him. 'Harry, good to have you on board.'

Lambert acknowledged Hughie's joke with a grim smile. Then, as his eyes were drawn along the man's naked body, they widened at the horror of it. Hughie watched his reaction.

When Lambert spoke, his voice seemed to be cloaked in some dark and forbidden past. 'What happened to his penis?'

'Looks like he had acid poured on it.'

Lambert exhaled slowly. 'Jesus!'

'No,' Hughie said, smirking. 'That was nails through hands and feet, but no acid on the genitalia.'

'Please, Hughie! Spare me the gallows humour and tell me what happened here.'

'Well, the victim's hands are bound behind his back. I'd say he was killed by three blows to the head, mainly to the side, as there's not enough room to swing a cat in here. Looks like the killer tried to get a good hard blow from above and came in contact with the light above, which explains the broken glass everywhere. Looks like it's nearing the end of rigor; putrefaction hasn't set in yet, in spite of the heat, so my rough guess would be time of death approximately ten hours ago, but I can't be certain until John Jackson's done the post mortem. There's also a small bruising at the back of the neck, indicating a blow to knock the victim unconscious. He was probably stripped, had his hands bound behind him, was sat in the wicker chair, and had acid poured on his penis. Something like sulphuric acid, I should think, and that would have eaten away at his privates. Mustn't make assumptions, but it looks like he'd been playing fast and loose with someone else's chattels.'

Lambert nodded and stared at the body. 'How old would you say he is?'

Hughie pursed his lips thoughtfully. 'At a rough guess, I'd say late fifties, early sixties maybe.'

'Any sign of the murder weapon?'

Hughie smiled and pointed towards Lambert's foot. 'You're standing next to it.'

Lambert looked down. Sure enough, his foot almost touched a steel bar about three feet long, lying in a pool of blood and broken glass. He stooped and stared at it closely, looking to see if it had the manufacturer's name on it.

'I think that's called a wrecking bar,' Hughie informed him, and couldn't resist adding, 'Appropriate name, eh?'

Lambert peered at the blood-stained shaft of the bar. He saw tiny letters near to the curved claw end of the bar, squinted and read aloud: 'Made in China. Well that narrows the field.'

Hughie chuckled as he watched Lambert. 'They reckon China's now the world's leading exporter. GDP growth at the rate of more than nine per cent over the last twenty-five years. Up until less fortunate times, of course.'

Rising from his stooping position, Lambert said, 'Enough of world economics, Hughie. D'you reckon once the weapon's dusted we'll find a set of prints?'

Grinning, Hughie shook his head.

'Yeah, you're right,' Lambert agreed. 'Still, it's got to be done.' Looking towards a bench seat, he stooped and peered at the recess under it. 'This glass looks different from the broken light.'

'I think that's a smashed bottle of Beck's beer.' Hughie said. 'And there's another bottle behind it, unbroken and unopened.'

Lambert straightened, and stared at the untidy bundle of clothes on the bench seat. 'The victim's clothes?'

Hughie nodded. 'They seem to be the right fit.'

The cabin was again filled with a blaze of light as the photographer took a shot of the murder weapon. Lambert examined the clothes. There was a rugby shirt, but not aligned to any particular club, more of a fashion statement, boat shoes, and a pair of khaki chinos. Seeing a bulge inside the back pocket of the chinos, Lambert inserted his hand and drew out the wallet. When he flipped it open, he saw maybe a couple of hundred pounds in it. That would rule out robbery. Then he saw the bank debit card and the name on it. 'My God! This bloke's name.'

'What about it?'

'It's unusual. You couldn't make it up. It's like a character from a Charles Dickens book.'

'Come on,' Hughie said. 'Hit me with it! I'd like to know the victim's name.'

Lambert raised his eyebrows and stared at Hughie. 'You ready for this? Lubin Titmus.'

Instead of laughing, Hughie stared at his feet, frowning thoughtfully as he searched his memory.

'What is it, Hughie?'

'I don't know. Name rings a bell. But where from?'

Lambert sighed deeply. 'Yes, as soon as I saw the name, I thought I recognized it. But I haven't a clue either. All I know is: I've come across the name before.'

The wallet had a display section inside, just big enough for a credit card, with a clear plastic window showing a senior citizen's rail card.

'At least we know he's in his sixties. He's got a senior railcard.' He removed the railcard from its display section and turned it over. 'This makes life easier. It's got his postcode on the back, in case of loss.' He stuck his hand in one of the leg pockets of the chinos, pulled out a bunch of keys and rattled them in front of Hughie. 'I'm off Hughie. I reckon I need to move quickly on this one, get to the victim's home address. And if there's no one home...'

Lambert paused, and Hughie finished his sentence for him. 'You can let yourself in and have a snoop around.'

'I'll see you tomorrow, Hughie, when hopefully you'll have something for me.'

As Lambert moved towards the stairs, Hughie called after him, 'When you find out who he is, give me a bell and put me out of my misery. Otherwise it'll bug me all night.'

Three

Having inserted the postcode into his navigation system, it took Lambert less than twenty minutes to get from the crime scene to Port Talbot, near the victim's home. The house was somewhere in the middle of a narrow one-way street, and the postcode offered him a choice of four or five houses. Lambert found a space to park and walked towards where he thought the house would be.

Most of the houses were terraced, with small gardens at the front, some of which had well-tended gardens, proudly displaying flowers and potted shrubs, but most had been paved over to accommodate a car or motorbike. But there was one house that stood out like a sore thumb. Not just because it looked neglected and decaying, with its dirty net curtains and a broken window pane which had been temporarily repaired with a sheet of plywood, but it was the door that was conspicuous. It was spray-painted with the word 'SCUM' in deepest red.

Lambert stared at it for a moment, frowning hard and searching his memory for something that had been on the regional news recently. Suddenly it came to him in a rush, and he remembered the television pictures: affronted mothers standing in the street, waving banners and shouting abuse; angry talking heads; rage and fear of living near men who were a danger and a menace to innocent children. It had happened after the *Sun* had named and shamed convicted paedophiles living in South Wales, causing members of the community to start behaving as vigilantes.

Right away Lambert was certain he had found the victim's house. He swung open the creaking metal gate and walked down the paved path, grass growing between the cracks, adding to the deserted feel of the place. He felt in his pockets for the victim's keys and was about to see which key fitted the lock when his attention was distracted by a movement behind him. He

THE WRECKING BAR

spun round and found himself face to face with a pugnacious-looking man of about fifty, standing rather too close and invading his space, poised and ready to attack with a head butt. Bloated and red-faced, and sweating profusely, the man reeked of alcohol and tobacco.

'Can I help you?' Lambert said, easing back.

'You a friend of that bastard?' He spoke with a strong Glaswegian dialect.

'I take it you mean Mr Titmus?'

'I asked if you were a friend of that dirty bastard.'

Lambert shook his head. 'I'm a police officer.'

'Oh aye?'

Lambert fumbled in his back pocket and brought out his ID. The man stared closely at it, and then locked eyes with Lambert.

'So what's the bastard done this time?'

Ignoring the question, Lambert regarded the man calmly, taking his time before speaking. 'The house looks deserted. Has Titmus been back here lately?'

The man pursed his lips and shrugged. 'How would I know?'

'Well, you were quick enough to intercept me. So I naturally assumed you must be keeping an eye on the place. Why would that be, I wonder?'

'We don't want scum like that in the neighbourhood. This is a respectable area.'

Lambert inclined his head towards the door. 'Presumably it was you who sprayed the message on there.'

'You can presume all you like. Proof's another matter.'

'There are worse crimes than graffiti.'

The man's glassy, alcohol-sodden eyes suddenly blazed with anger. 'Exactly! Like interfering with children. Dirty fuckin' bastard.'

'So you decided to take the law into your own hands?'

The man sniffed noisily and swallowed. 'We have a right to protect our children.'

Lambert took out a pen and notebook. 'And just how far would you go to protect your children?'

'Oh, I'd go all the way. Believe me. I'd do anything to protect my children.'

'I think I'd better have your name and address.'

'What for?'

'Because I'm asking you for it, sir.'

The man jerked a thumb back. 'I live two doors away from the bastard. Number thirty-three. Name's Norman McNeil.'

'Well, Mr McNeil, we'll need to talk again soon. But for now I've got these premises to search.'

CHAPTER THREE

McNeil rubbed his chin thoughtfully, passing a hand across his mouth, a gesture the detective noted as the action of a man reluctant to speak. Of course, it could have been police phobia. McNeil struck him as the sort who thinks the police are useless and do nothing except hound poor motorists.

McNeil leaned forward conspiratorially and Lambert got a blast of putrid tobacco breath. 'If you ask me, you guys are too busy chasing the wrong people.'

Lambert jangled the keys in front of him. 'I have to get on and search these premises. We'll be round later to ask you a few questions.'

'What about?'

For now, Lambert decided not to tell McNeil about the murder. He wanted to find out if McNeil had known the victim had a boat moored at the marina. If he did know, he could be a prime suspect, and even if he turned out to be innocent, it was always possible he could have told someone else.

'Just some routine questions and information about Lubin Titmus,' Lambert said. 'Like, for instance, how often did he come back to his house?'

'Hardly at all during the day. I think he sneaked back late at night to collect things. My wife saw him one night – about two in the morning it was. Her friend from work was getting married and they was coming back from a hen night. Jackie – that's the missus – shouted out what sort of scum he was. She might have woken some of the neighbours. She was a bit bevvied, like.'

'Mr McNeil, did you happen to know where Lubin Titmus went to from here? Whether or not he had other accommodation?'

McNeil stared at Lambert, an inward struggle showing in his face. 'How the hell am I supposed to know that?'

It was on the tip of Lambert's tongue to say, 'You could have followed him', but he thought better of it. That could wait until later.

'Thank you, Mr McNeil. That'll be all for the moment. We'll be in touch with you later today. We would appreciate it if you'd make yourself available.'

McNeil shrugged. 'I wasn't planning on going out.'

He turned, staggered slightly, and then lumbered out of the gate. Lambert slid the key into the lock and pushed open the front door. A musty, stale smell confronted him as he entered the airless house. He closed the door behind him and stood for a moment surveying the hallway.

The walls were decorated with rose-motif wallpaper so ancient it was difficult to tell the colour of the roses. Lambert smiled wryly as he stared at a grey art-deco mirror hanging from a blackened silver chain that closely resembled the hideous one in the living room of his grotty flat. A hat stand, containing several golf umbrellas slotted into its base, stood next to the mirror. Lambert pushed open the door leading to the front room and entered, coughing as he felt the dust tickling the back of his throat. Although it was still sunny outside, the room was gloomy, the heavy damask, maroon curtains half closed, blocking out most of the light, except for a stream of sunlight forcing its way through drab net curtains in the centre gap, highlighting a shaft of dust motes and coming to rest on a patch of threadbare carpet. The furniture, which consisted of a sofa with wooden arms and an easy chair that may have been the latest 'contemporary' feature in the late 1950s, contrasted sharply with the latest HD flat screen television set and DVD player. Scattered around it were dozens of DVDs, which Lambert saw were predominantly pornographic. He flicked his way through a selection. They seemed to be of every persuasion: everything from teenage sluts, to anal and oral sex between hetero and homosexuals. Incongruously, beneath a film about gang rape, he found *The Wizard of Oz*, the cover showing Dorothy walking arm-in-arm with the Scarecrow, Tin Man and Cowardly Lion along the Yellow Brick Road.

Lubin Titmus appeared to have eclectic tastes, Lambert thought sourly.

In an alcove next to the tiled fireplace was a roll-top desk. Lambert slid it open and searched the various compartments, finding nothing but odds and ends of stationery, but when he slid open one of the drawers he found a photograph of a thin-faced man with white hair and a black moustache – late fifties, he guessed – unsmilingly staring at the camera as if he was reluctant to be photographed. His arm was draped about a boy's shoulders. The boy looked to be about twelve or thirteen, and there didn't seem to be any family resemblance to the man. Lambert turned the photograph over. Written in ink were the words: 'Gordon and friend'.

He pocketed the photograph and was about to call Tony Ellis when his mobile bleeped. He clicked the receive button and saw there was a message was from Hughie.

'No need to call me. Victim *Sun* exposed pervert. C U 2morrow.'

Lambert clicked off the message and continued to call Ellis.

***

If anything, Gordon Mayfield's boat, *The Amethyst*, was even smaller and more cramped than the victim's. It was stifling and claustrophobic, and PC Goring, who had been solicitously plying the witness with words of comfort, sat squashed into a tight corner, feeling the start of an excruciating pain in her back as she was hunched into an uncomfortable position in the stern. She had had to make room for the two detectives, who sat on a bench seat across from Mayfield, who was sitting on another bench seat opposite them.

CHAPTER THREE

Mayfield was thin and angular, his cheekbones jutted out like carved marble, and his sunken eyes were green. His hair was thick, wavy and pure white, but his moustache was jet black, giving it a dyed appearance. He was clearly distressed at finding the body as there seemed to be a permanent tremor in his voice, and his hands shook like an alcoholic's.

'Can you remember what time you found his body, sir?' Tony Ellis asked.

Mayfield frowned deeply, staring at the floor as he tried to remember. He cleared his throat gently before speaking. 'Yes, I remember looking at my watch just before I went over there. It was just after 12.30.'

Ellis exchanged a brief look with DC Jones before continuing. 'The emergency call came through at 2.30 from your mobile, two hours after you discovered the body. Any reason for the delay, sir?'

Mayfield's eyes flickered briefly as they made contact with Ellis, then he looked away again. Jones stared at him intently, wondering if he was about to break down. While they waited for him to respond they could hear beery laughter coming from the pub across the basin, followed by a girlish squeal. Ellis was about to prompt Mayfield, when he suddenly stammered a tearful response.

'It was so… shocking… f–finding him like that. I felt sick. I wanted to hide.'

Ellis frowned. 'Hide? Why would you want to hide, sir?'

'His head… the way he'd been beaten. It was awful.'

'But wouldn't most people, on experiencing such a dreadful thing, telephone the police immediately.'

'I told you: I felt sick.'

'Yes and I think you said you wanted to hide.'

'I just meant… it was so awful, I wanted the earth to swallow me up. I was in a state of shock.'

'You mentioned how sick you felt. Were you physically sick at the crime scene or anywhere near it?'

'I may have been. It was just so terrible.'

Sergeant Ellis looked towards DC Jones, hoping she was on his wavelength.

'Mr Mayfield,' she said, 'the crime officers found no traces of any vomit on his boat or on the quayside nearby.'

It was a lie. She couldn't possibly have known about him not being sick as she hadn't visited the immediate crime scene. But Ellis was satisfied she had picked up on the way he was leading the inquiry and carefully studied Mayfield to see how he would respond.

'I suppose I just felt sick. I came back here and I was in a state of shock. It took me a while to recover.'

The Wrecking Bar

'Two hours. And then you telephoned the police. Did you know the victim well?'

Mayfield shifted position on his seat, and then seemed to brace himself so that he could look Ellis in the eye. 'Not well, no.'

'He wasn't a close friend then?'

'More of an acquaintance.'

Debbie Jones studied him carefully. She knew he was lying, the way it seemed a great effort for him to hold Ellis's stare.

'How long had you known him?' she asked.

Mayfield shrugged and thrust out his bottom lip as he thought about this. 'Not long.'

'*How* long?'

'Oh, I think it might have been about three, four months maybe.'

'How did you meet each other?'

'Here at the marina. We just got talking one day.'

'You just got talking!' she echoed, combining astonishment with doubt.

'Yes, that's what it's like with boat people. We all have a common interest and we like to talk about boats.'

A blaring noise in the cramped cabin startled everyone, which after a brief disorientation Debbie Jones recognized as the saxophone in Gerry Rafferty's 'Baker Street', which was Ellis's chosen ringtone.

Ellis fumbled for his Nokia then checked the display. It was Lambert. 'I'd better get this.'

Irritated by the interruption, Debbie Jones glared at Ellis's mobile, but as soon as she heard him saying, 'Yes, boss,' she listened carefully, trying to catch some of the conversation.

As Ellis listened to instructions, he studied Mayfield carefully, but his expression gave nothing away. After a short one-sided conversation, he said, 'Right away, boss. I'll bring him in.' He pocketed his mobile and stood up, stooping under the low ceiling.

'That was DI Lambert, and my boss would like to talk to you, Mr Mayfield. I hope you don't mind coming with us?'

'Where are you taking me?'

'There are some questions he'd like to ask you.'

Mayfield tried to stand up but his legs seemed to fail him. He was weak and frightened, a rabbit caught in headlights. As DC Jones watched him struggling to get up, she knew he was trying to hide something. Something which Lambert already knew. And she couldn't wait to find out what it was.

Four

As Lambert drove back along the short stretch of the M4 towards Swansea, he thought about the victim with the unusual name, whom he now knew was a convicted paedophile; and it also seemed likely that Gordon Mayfield was one, the two of them belonging to a group of sex offenders in South Wales. There had been a documentary about it on Channel 4, but the paedophiles were not identified because it was felt they had paid for their crimes, and they might not re-offend. But following a leak from the offices of the production company, the *Sun* had no such qualms about publishing the photographs and names of the six men involved.

Lambert was glad to be out of Port Talbot. Not that he had anything against the town, it was just that it brought back memories of his father who had died just over a year ago.

After his father had separated from Lambert's mother more than twenty years ago, he had left to go and live in the steelworks town where he'd been born and bred. Lambert rarely saw him. He could never forgive him for the appalling way he'd treated his mother. Lambert was at Bristol University, reading law, and he'd come home one weekend to find his mother nursing a blackeye and broken nose. Lambert went crazy when he found out what his father had done. The boozy father was no match for the fit, rugby-playing young man he was in those days, and ended up cowering and pleading for forgiveness. But Lambert never forgave him. It wasn't just the domestic rows and the violence towards his wife: there was something more, something much worse. Something which Lambert had tried to deny all these years. And it was something which now surfaced like scum on the water as the likes of Titmus and Mayfield brought it home. But instead of confronting it, he swept the disturbing thoughts of his father from his mind and turned the radio on.

THE WRECKING BAR

***

Sergeant Ellis and DC Jones were waiting outside an interview room when Lambert arrived at Swansea Central Police Station. Ellis had copies of the victim's and Mayfield's criminal records, which he handed to his boss.

'How long's he been on his own in there?' Lambert asked Ellis.

'Good fifteen minutes.'

Nodding his approval, Lambert asked about DC Wallace. Ellis shrugged and said, 'I think he's still doing the rounds at the marina flats. We took two cars to the crime scene so he should be able to make his way back here, no problem.'

Lambert suspected Wallace of skiving off but kept the thought to himself. 'Right,' he said. 'I'll question Mayfield. Debbie and Tony watch him and listen carefully to his answers, see if you can pick up on any inconsistencies. Let's go.'

Mayfield looked up as Lambert entered, his face strained and anxious, eyes shifting from one detective to another. Lambert sat directly opposite him, with the table between them, and Debbie Jones sat next to him. Ellis picked up a chair and slid it into a position slightly to the left of Mayfield, so the witness was unable to look directly into the detective's face but would feel his presence and know he was being closely scrutinized.

While Debbie Jones switched the tape recorder on and gave the time and date of the interview and the names of everyone present, Lambert slowly read details from Mayfield's criminal record sheet. After Jones had done the announcement, he took his time reading, letting the silence unnerve Mayfield. When he eventually spoke it was with restraint, deliberately keeping any emotion out of his voice.

'Mr Mayfield, you served five years of a seven-year sentence for sexual offences with children and you were released two years ago. When you were released they found you accommodation in Cardiff. Yet here you are in Swansea, of no fixed abode. Can you explain why that is?'

When Mayfield spoke, his voice was tremulous and rasping. 'The place I was living in was terrible. A sort of halfway house, and I had to share a communal lounge and kitchen with alcoholics and down-and-outs.'

Lambert glanced down at the information sheet. 'It says here that you owned a small house in Merthyr Tydfil. Why didn't you go back there to live?'

'Because the neighbours knew all about me. About why I'd gone to prison.'

'So what did you do?'

'I managed to sell the house. Not for very much. Not now there's high unemployment in the valleys and house prices have fallen. I got less than sixty thousand for it, but it was enough to buy the boat.'

'But under the Violent and Sex Offenders Register, the terms of your release dictate that any change of address must be registered with the police. If you haven't done so, you could end up back in prison.'

Mayfield was deathly still, his eyes cold as glass marbles.

'I wrote to the police, to the headquarters at Bridgend. I explained about the accommodation and selling my house. I told them my boat would be moored at Swansea. I've kept a copy of the letter.'

'That means nothing. You know damn well you're supposed to visit a police station in person.'

They had to strain to hear Mayfield's reply.

'I'm sorry. I didn't think.'

In contrast to Mayfield's mumbled apology, Lambert raised his voice. 'Why did you decide to live on a boat?'

'I've always liked boats. It was something that has always appealed to me. Also...' Mayfield struggled to find the right words and rubbed his hands nervously. 'I needed a home in which I could move to another location if people found out who I was.'

'Yet here's a great coincidence: a friend of yours is murdered. Another convicted paedophile who also, like you, decided to live on a boat.'

Frowning hard, struggling for words, Mayfield looked down at his clammy hands. Lambert glanced at Ellis, who picked up the signal.

'You lied to me, Mr Mayfield,' Ellis said sharply. 'You said you had only known the victim for a few months.'

'I was confused. In a state of shock.'

Lambert fumbled in his pocket and brought out the photograph of Mayfield with the young boy. He slammed it onto the desk and pushed it towards Mayfield. 'I expect you recognize this photo. I found it among the victim's possessions at his house. You and the victim go back a long way, don't you, Mr Mayfield?'

Mayfield stared at the photograph and nodded, his eyes dark and sunken, his pallor sickly.

'How long had you known the victim?' Lambert demanded.

Although he had the details in the criminal records, he wanted to hear it from Mayfield.

'Well?'

'It was almost thirty years.'

THE WRECKING BAR

'He was in charge of a youth custody centre, wasn't he? And you worked for him. You and he took advantage of your positions and abused the younger, most vulnerable inmates. Tell me about the boat hook.'

Mayfield caught Lambert's eye briefly, the sudden change of tactic confusing him. It was a trick Lambert often used when questioning suspects, telling them something they already knew, and then asking about a detail they might have forgotten.

After a pause, Mayfield stammered, 'I'm… I'm not sure what—'

Lambert interrupted harshly. 'Didn't you tell the uniformed officer that the reason you went over to the victim's boat was to borrow his boat hook?'

'Yes, that's right.'

Lambert stared at the suspect and smiled humourlessly. 'Or did you say you were returning his boat hook?'

'I… I can't remember.'

'No, of course you can't. It was another lie, wasn't it?'

Tears suddenly trickled down Mayfield's cheeks and he shook uncontrollably. He looked up at Lambert helplessly, as if the emotion was a demonstration to gain sympathy. But Lambert's eyes were frosty. He despised Mayfield and wanted him to know that.

Eventually, Mayfield sniffed, wiped the back of his sleeve across his nose and started to speak hurriedly. 'When I found Lubin like that, I was scared. I thought it might have been someone out for revenge, someone who had a grudge against him. One of his…'

'Victims?' Lambert prompted. 'There must have been plenty of those over the years. And were you and Titmus up to your old tricks? Is that why you have a boat now, so that you can move to different areas and evade the law? Isn't that the real reason?'

Mayfield shook his head rapidly. 'No, it isn't like that. I felt I'd done my time… paid for what I did. But when that newspaper printed our names and pictures, someone must have recognized Lubin and come after him.'

'You mean they just happened to see him on the marina one day and decided to kill him?' Lambert stared pointedly at one of the sheets in front of him. 'Quite an ordinary-looking bloke, your friend Titmus. But you are quite distinctive-looking, almost striking, I would say. White wavy hair and a jet-black moustache. It seems odd that it was he and not you that may have been recognized. But of course we are talking hypothetically here, aren't we?'

Lambert glanced at Ellis, who immediately picked up his cue.

'Why did you quarrel with Titmus?'

CHAPTER FOUR

'Quarrel?'

'Yes, quarrel!' Ellis snapped. 'You made up the story about the boat hook. Why did you visit his boat?'

'Just to see him. No real reason. We were friends.'

'Friends can still fall out. What was your argument about?'

Mayfield's mouth opened but the words stuck in the back of his throat. Then his attention was diverted to the door opening behind Lambert and he seemed almost relieved by the distraction.

A uniformed sergeant entered and handed Lambert a sheet of paper. Lambert studied it carefully, his brow creasing into a slight frown.

'Thank you, Sergeant,' he said.

The uniformed sergeant threw an expression of loathing in Mayfield's direction before leaving the room. Lambert stared at Mayfield for a long while as he deliberated. Ellis and Jones felt the tension growing, and knew by the interruption there had been a further development in the case.

'Now then, Mr Mayfield,' Lambert spoke slowly, carefully choosing his words. 'Does the name Jarvis Thomas mean anything to you?'

They all stared at Mayfield, carefully watching his reaction. His face was now drained of all emotion and his body was as still as a graveyard statue.

'Mr Mayfield,' Lambert repeated impatiently, 'does the name Jarvis Thomas mean anything to you?'

Almost inaudibly, Mayfield croaked, 'I think he's another one who was exposed by the newspaper.'

'And did you know him?'

Both Ellis and Jones noticed their boss's use of the past tense. But if Mayfield had noticed, he didn't show it.

'I know Jarvis – yes.'

Lambert put on a grave expression as he anticipated the revelation. 'I regret to inform you, Mr Mayfield, that Jarvis Thomas has been murdered. Killed with several blows to the head with a metal bar. It looks as if a killer is targeting the sex offenders who were exposed in the *Sun*.'

Lambert stood up and Mayfield watched him, his eyes begging for understanding and sympathy.

'What's going to happen to me?' he asked.

'I and my colleagues are going to visit the crime scene in Carmarthen, where the second victim lived. But, of course, you would know that, wouldn't you, Mr Mayfield? Oh, one other thing.' Lambert tapped the photograph of Mayfield and the young boy. 'What's his name?'

'He doesn't live in this country now.'

THE WRECKING BAR

Lambert leant forward, trying to catch Mayfield's eye. 'That's not what I asked you. I asked you for his name.'

'His name was Tom.'

Lambert picked up on the tense. 'Was?'

'Yes, I told you, he no longer lives here. He went to live abroad, permanently. Spain I think.'

'When was this?'

'Sometime in 2000.'

'What's his surname?'

'I can't remember.'

Lambert slammed a hand down so forcefully on to the desk, it startled DC Jones as much as Mayfield.

'Don't lie to me, Mr Mayfield. I want his name. Now!'

Trying to control the tremor in his voice, Mayfield said quietly, 'His name's Tom Thorne.'

Lambert glanced at DC Jones, who asked Mayfield as she scribbled on a notepad, 'Is that with an E on the end?'

Mayfield nodded and asked, 'What happens now?'

Lambert said, 'What happens now is we are about to take a look at another gruesome murder. We won't need you for the moment. But please don't think about setting sail from Swansea. We'd like you to remain at the marina for further questioning. But for now, you're free to go.'

Lambert gave DC Jones a nod and she terminated the interview, gave the time and clicked the machine off.

Mayfield looked as if he was glued to the chair.

'You're free to go,' Lambert repeated.

'But my life might be in danger. What about police protection?'

While Ellis and Jones rose hurriedly, Lambert looked at Ellis and said, 'What do you think, Sergeant? Have we got the resources for that?'

Ellis sucked in his breath and shook his head. 'How many people were in that tabloid exposé? Six of them, I believe. That's an awful lot of our manpower twenty-four-seven. We couldn't spare that many coppers to watch all them blokes.'

'Correction, Sergeant, there's only four of them now.'

Ellis shrugged. 'Even so, it's still a lot of manpower.'

With enormous effort, Mayfield managed to get to his feet. His lower lip quivered as he spoke. 'You can't just leave me like this.'

'I tell you what,' Lambert said. 'We'll send a patrol car to cruise the marina at odd intervals. That should offer you some protection. Meanwhile, I'm sure

CHAPTER FOUR

you appreciate we have to get our skates on to get to Carmarthen. Friday evening traffic can be a problem.'

Lambert opened the door and gestured for Mayfield to exit. As he shuffled reluctantly out of the interview room, Mayfield asked if he was expected to walk back to the marina.

'We can't spare a vehicle now there's been another major incident.' Lambert said. 'But it's only a short walk from here to the marina. Oh, and we'll check to see if they received that letter of yours at HQ.'

'Because if they haven't,' Ellis added, 'it could mean up to five years inside.'

They turned away from him dismissively, and Lambert spoke to Ellis for Mayfield's benefit. 'He'd better pray that letter's not got lost in the post.'

Five

Before leaving for Carmarthen, Lambert drove Ellis and Jones to Cockett Police Station where the incident room was situated. Detective Chief Superintendent Marden had driven over from HQ at Bridgend, and they found him waiting for them, perched on the corner of a desk, reading from an open folder.

Sitting at one of the desks, typing information into a computer, was DS Roger Hazel, and Lambert guessed he would be office manager, responsible for running the incident room. Hazel looked up briefly and caught his eye, and Lambert acknowledged him with a wave. Hazel was a sallow-complexioned man, thirty-five years old, with cropped dark hair, and a face of enormous gravity which belied his pleasing manner and sense of humour. He was good at his job, thorough and detailed in all his inputted information, and Lambert was pleased he'd been recruited to run the incident room.

Marden gave it a beat to finish what he was reading before standing, tucking the folder under his arm. He was an imposing man, six foot four and muscular, as if he pumped iron regularly, with a broad face, and a large hooked nose and thin lips, and eyes that shone like buttons. Whenever Lambert stared into his hawk-like face, he almost expected to find Marden had talons instead of hands.

'Harry,' Marden began, 'according to police in Carmarthen the murder sounds like a carbon copy of the one on the marina. I suggest you get over there right away – traffic's really bad – and you'll be met by Sergeant Mark Sweet. But before you dash off, give me a brief account of the marina homicide and the witness you brought in for questioning.'

DC Jones interrupted and suggested she get details of Jarvis Thomas's criminal record. Marden nodded his approval, and while she sat at one of the computers and logged on, Lambert told him about the *Sun* story, suggesting that someone could be targeting paedophiles, and gave him a quick rundown on the Mayfield interview.

'And what's your opinion of this Mayfield character?'

'I don't think he killed Titmus. Okay, he lied to us, but I think that's because of his sex offences – offences which he and the victim were in all likelihood still committing. He gives the impression he's running scared, knowing he could be next in line.'

Marden turned towards Ellis. 'And is that your impression, Sergeant?'

'Absolutely, sir. I think he fears for his life. With good reason.'

Like a bird of prey seeking its quarry, Marden's eyes settled on Lambert. 'So now you've let him go back to his boat on the marina, knowing there's a killer on the loose.'

'I was going to suggest, sir,' Lambert said after an awkward pause, 'that a patrol car cruises the marina at intervals.'

The door of the incident room burst open and DC Wallace marched in, breathless and looking slightly dishevelled from his afternoon of knocking on doors.

'Where have you been?' Lambert grumbled.

Wallace gave him a self-satisfied smile. 'I think I got a result. One of the women in the flats is a real nosy type, and she says she saw the victim spending a lot of time with another bloke. It sounds like it was the bloke who found the body. And these two men often spent time on each other's boats.'

Lambert was about to tell Wallace they already knew that, when Marden cut in. 'Well done, Constable. Good work.'

The chief superintendent started to leave, then turned at the doorway and addressed Lambert. 'I'll sort out the patrol car for you.'

'Thank you, sir,' Lambert mumbled grudgingly, but felt like saying, 'Big of you.'

'This'll hit the nationals tomorrow. It's going to be a big story. I'm afraid your weekend's up the spout – all of you. Hope none of you have any plans for tomorrow. If someone *is* targeting all the paedophiles listed in the *Sun*, we need to act fast on this. I know some of you might think of this as wild justice, and they might well deserve to die, but we can't let anarchy and vigilantism take over. The law must be upheld.'

He swept out, leaving Lambert wondering why the chief super could never make a clean exit, and always had to make a speech from the doorway, usually stating the obvious.

'And there's me thinking I could go after the sex offenders with a machete,' he said.

DS Hazel snorted and said, 'Unusual weapon that. Any machete murders and you'll be first to come up on a profile, Harry.'

Lambert smiled as he turned towards Hazel. 'Good to have you running the office for us, Roger.'

'Keeps me out of the rain.'

Turning back towards Wallace, Lambert thought he detected a strong peppermint smell on his breath, and suspected the detective constable of having spent some of his foot-slogging inquiry time in the pub. But now that smoking was banned in public, it was more difficult to tell if someone had been for one or two drinks. So short of actually catching Wallace skiving off, Lambert couldn't actually prove it. Instead, he thought he'd wipe that smug look off the young detective's face.

'Sorry, Kevin, but we already knew about the relationship between the two men from the marina. I hope you haven't wasted the entire afternoon.'

The sting showed in Wallace's eyes briefly, and then he bounced back. 'Oh, I think it's been far from wasted, sir. Know what else this nosy neighbour told me? She's got a balcony that looks out over the yacht basin, just about where the victim's boat was moored. She's an insomniac and she often sits out at night on the balcony. She wraps herself in a blanket when it's chilly. On several occasions she saw the victim leaving his boat about one o'clock in the morning and return about an hour or so later.'

'Was this on foot?'

'When he returned, it was in a car. She thought, because of the restricted parking, he probably collected it from a car park nearby and drove to wherever he was going. And when he returned, he came back and left it on yellow lines because it was in the middle of the night, shifting it first thing in the morning. But here's a peculiar thing she noticed: about three weeks ago he went out and came back around half two, and she could have sworn another car was following his.'

Lambert was suddenly alert. 'Did she tell you what gave her that impression?'

'As he was parking his car near where his boat was moored, she saw the other car ease quietly to a stop the other side of the marina and switch off its lights. She felt someone was inside the darkness of the car watching him, seeing where he was going. Then, as soon as he'd disappeared below in his boat, the other car switched its lights and engine on, reversed, and went off the way it came.'

'Did she manage to see what sort of car it was?'

'It was too dark and too far away. She couldn't even make out the colour.'

CHAPTER FIVE

'What about the type of car? Four-by-four, saloon, hatchback?'

'She thinks it could have been a medium-size saloon car but can't be certain.'

Lambert tugged his lower lip thoughtfully with thumb and finger. 'Hmm. Thank you, Kevin. Now that is interesting. So what about last night? Did she see anything from her balcony then?'

Wallace shook his head. 'Last night she was staying at her sister's in Cardiff. Didn't get back until just before the police arrived at the scene earlier today.'

'That was a bit thoughtless of her. If she'd stayed at home we'd have our killer in the cells by now.'

'Not necessarily,' Wallace said.

'I was being ironic, Kevin.'

Kevin tugged at his moustache and stared at the floor. Feeling guilty, Lambert said, 'But well done for the info about the car. Very useful.' Then he told them about his meeting with McNeil outside the victim's house.

'You think he could have followed Titmus from his house, to find out where he was going?' Ellis asked.

'It's distinctly possible. And McNeil struck me as an angry vigilante with too much time on his hands.' Lambert checked his watch again. 'Here's what I'd like you and Kevin to do. Go and interview McNeil, see what you can find out about him. I didn't tell him about the murder so you'll be able to see if it comes as a genuine surprise.'

'Unless he hears about it on the six o'clock news,' Ellis said.

Lambert frowned thoughtfully. 'I almost wish I'd told him now. But at the moment, because of what we've recently learnt from both Mayfield and Kevin's witness at the marina, McNeil would appear to be top suspect. Debbie and I will be on our way to the crime scene at Carmarthen. First thing tomorrow morning, Kevin, go to the harbour master's office and get the marina CCTV. And, unless we have any other sensational incidents tonight, we meet here at nine sharp tomorrow. It'll have to be a brief meeting because I have to be at Cardiff for the post mortem by ten.'

'Both post mortems, probably,' Ellis said.

Lambert pulled a face. 'Oh, I can't wait!'

As they were leaving, he told DC Jones to bring the criminal records on the three sex offenders with her, so that she could read to him while he drove them over to Carmarthen.

'Every so often I like a nice horror story,' he said.

Six

As soon as they reached the M4, Debbie Jones opened the folder and took out the first few pages on Lubin Titmus. She unscrewed a cap on a plastic bottle and took a long drink of water.

'In your own time,' Lambert said.

She looked in his direction to see if he was joking, and the smile told her he was. She screwed the top back on the bottle, held the page steady in front of her and squinted.

'I can't see in this light.'

Night was smothering the hills like a dark curtain, and the rear lights of the slow-moving cars gave the dusky gloom unnatural warmth as they coasted along in the rush-hour traffic. Lambert reached up and switched on the interior light.

'Won't make any difference at this speed,' he said. 'Okay? Can you see to read?'

'Yeah, that's fine,' she said. She cleared her throat gently and began reading. 'Lubin Titmus was the only son of Gabriel and Merle Titmus, and he was brought up in the Forest of Dean, Gloucestershire. His father made his living as a psychic and faith healer. Lubin Titmus attended a village primary school, and in 1956 his father suffered a severe stroke and died soon afterwards. When he was sixteen-years- old, he was accused of raping a girl of thirteen, but her parents feared the shame attached to such a crime and the charges were dropped. He left home soon after and nothing more was known about him until he was fined for a consenting but indecent act in a cinema with another man.

'His mother inherited her parents' house in Port Talbot and moved back to her home town. With the money from the sale of the Gloucester home, she was able to persuade her son to study, go to college and take a business management degree course.

'Once he had his degree, he applied for a job as an administrative assistant at a youth custody centre north of Cardiff. He was employed there from 1975, became head of the institution in 1982, and he and another employee, Gordon Mayfield, were arrested and sacked for sexually abusing young boys in 2001. They were both sentenced to seven years but were paroled after five.

'Two months prior to his release, his mother died and he inherited the house in Port Talbot, which is here on the records as his permanent home.'

Lambert braked sharply as the brake lights on the car in front showed it had reached the back end of a traffic hold-up. They were now reduced to a slow crawl along the two lanes as they neared the Llanelli turn-off.

'That was all very interesting,' Lambert said, 'but it doesn't tell us much about his relationship with his parents.'

DC Jones nodded thoughtfully. 'D'you think he was sexually abused as a child, by the father, maybe?'

'It's not always the case that sex offenders commit acts of indecency because they themselves were abused as children. But, reading between the lines, and thinking about the way his father made his living, by lying and cheating—'

'You mean because he was a psychic and a medium?' Jones interrupted.

'Absolutely. Those charlatans can commit fraud and not break any laws.'

Amused by her boss's scepticism, Jones shook her head and smiled. 'He might have been genuine.'

Lambert laughed. 'Come on, Debbie, you don't believe in that mumbo-jumbo, do you?'

'Well, I know you're going to find this hard to believe but I once attended a séance and the medium told me things he couldn't possibly have known, about my father who died of cancer six years ago.'

Lambert stared at the traffic ahead, concentrating and thinking. He liked DC Jones, liked her intelligence and found her attractive, but there was no way he was going to condone this nonsense.

'I'm a policeman, Debbie. I deal in facts. Nothing more, nothing less. End of story.' He thought that was a firm but gentle way of telling her he wouldn't subscribe to any superstitious drivel.

They were past the Llanelli junction now and the traffic was flowing quicker. DC Jones was silent for a moment while she thought about her boss's attitude to psychic phenomena and decided it was always the same with sceptics. They hadn't been there; they didn't know; how could they possibly understand?

She returned the details about Lubin Titmus to the folder and brought out the sheets concerning Gordon Mayfield.

'You want to hear about Mayfield?'

'Yes, I do. And then the second victim, Jarvis Thomas.'

The traffic moved more rapidly now they were only a few miles from the end of the motorway and Lambert was able to put his foot down and keep a steady pace in the outside lane. By the time they neared the end of the M4, DC Jones had finished reading the criminal records of the two other sex offenders.

Mayfield's childhood, they discovered, had been different from the first victim, inasmuch as social services had removed him from his alcoholic parents and he was taken into care at the age of ten. Sexually abused by both his mother and father, they had also subjected him to paedophile orgies in the front room of their shabby council house in Tregaron. He spent the next eight years in a succession of foster homes across South Wales, leaving at the age of sixteen to work in a coal mine. He bought himself a small house in Merthyr Tydfil in 1980 for only £5,000, putting down a fifty per cent deposit he had managed to save. In 1984, during the miners' strike, he joined the youth custody centre and in 2001 was arrested and charged for sexual abuse, along with his partner in crime, Lubin Titmus, and was released around the same time.

Jarvis Thomas's record was a real horror comic. He had a string of sex offences, starting in 1982 at the age of fourteen when he sexually assaulted a girl of ten, for which he received two years' probation. The son of an itinerant salesman, Thomas was brought up in Llanelli by an alcoholic mother, and it was believed she may on occasion have sexually abused him. During his second year of probation, aged sixteen, he molested a nine-year-old girl in a park, was caught and sentenced to two years in borstal. After his release, he worked in a small toy factory, where he stole some of the merchandise with which to ensnare young children. He lured a child of nine to his home when her mother was out and sexually attacked her. But her screams were reported to the police by neighbours, and he was apprehended, and this time he received a seven year jail sentence. Following his release, he was prosecuted for claiming benefits while working as a minicab driver, for which he received a fine and a two year suspended sentence. For the next five years he stayed out of trouble, indicating that he had changed his methods, because in 1997 he was convicted of having sex with a thirteen-year-old girl, having spent three months grooming her on an internet chatroom. Because of the seriousness of the previous convictions, the Crown Prosecution Service pushed for a maximum life sentence, but the defence discovered the girl had already had consensual sex with several adult men, and Thomas was given another seven-year sentence.

On his release, Thomas didn't return home to Llanelli and nothing has been heard of him for the last six years.

'Up until today,' Lambert commented at the end of the DC's reading. 'When the grim reaper came to call.'

Her throat a little raw, Jones swallowed several times before speaking. 'I can't help thinking, what goes around.'

'You mean he got what he deserved.'

'They both did.'

Lambert glanced at her out of the corner of his eye, seeing her expression grim and determined, staring at the road ahead. 'Maybe we ought to let whoever it is get on with it, and clobber the remaining four,' he said.

'I suppose we can think that. We can even wish it. But we can't let it happen.'

'Not after the chief super's little exit speech.'

DC Jones threw her boss a sidelong glance. She had often noticed how much the two men disliked each other, the way they desperately tried to keep it in check, yet there was always a bitter resentment bubbling beneath a transparent layer of civilized behaviour.

'Marden will want a speedy result on this case,' Lambert said. 'But I have doubts about this one.'

'Because there are so many victims out there with a reason for revenge?'

'Exactly. For a start, think how many abused youngsters there were at that youth custody centre.'

Jones shifted uncomfortably as she saw a road sign indicating one mile to the Pont Abraham Services. 'Would you mind if I made a request, sir?'

'Only if I can request that when we're on our own you call me Harry.'

'It's a deal, Harry. Would you mind pulling in at the services? I won't be long. I know I should have gone before I came out, but...'

Lambert was already indicating and pulling into the inside lane. 'I'm feeling a tad dehydrated,' he said. 'Perhaps you might like to get us a couple of takeaway coffees. I'll give you the money.'

He found a parking space near the services entrance. As Debbie was getting out of the car, he said, 'Let me give you some money.'

'It's okay. I think I can afford two coffees.'

'In a motorway services? I hope you've got a credit card.'

She smiled and asked how he wanted his coffee. He hesitated, wanting it black, but knew it would take a while to cool down, so asked for cappuccino instead. She slammed the door shut and he watched as she walked towards the entrance, admiring the smooth roundness of her backside and the alluring sway of her hips, but telling himself she was strictly a work colleague and out of bounds. Life was complicated enough without trying to make advances to one of his officers.

His thoughts drifted back to the job in hand. On the surface it seemed straightforward, a vigilante targeting paedophiles. There wouldn't be much public sympathy for the victims, that was for sure. But the worst thing about this case was the mirror in his mind, reflecting back from some deep and sickening bed of shame, a disgusting thought he had long denied. Had his father been like those men? Last year, at his funeral, when he protested to Helen that his father would never have laid a hand on their daughter, he could clearly hear the echoes of Helen's voice when she replied: 'No, but there was something about the way he used to look at her.'

And then there was Angela, his older sister, leaving home as soon as she could. She had confided to him her intention to emigrate to Australia, telling him it was an ambition, but somewhere in the back of his mind a dark voice told him she had a reason to distance herself from her family and make a clean start in life. She got the chance when she met a hardworking joiner, and they were soon married, with no family members invited to the wedding. Not even Harry himself, her only brother. That had hurt at the time. Then, soon after the wedding, they booked an assisted passage to Sydney, and had never once been back to visit their homeland.

He hadn't seen Angela for thirty-five years, since he was thirteen. Occasionally she'd remember to send a Christmas card, never a birthday card – he doubted she remembered the date – and when their father died, he sent her the news by email. She never replied.

Seven

Ellis turned the BBC radio news off as they turned into the one-way street. 'The main story,' he said. 'And I think it's going to get bigger, once the media know they can milk it for what it's worth; like they did in the Madeleine McCann case.'

'I wonder if McNeil will have heard it,' Wallace said.

'We'll soon find out.'

Wallace found a parking space right outside the shabby house with SCUM daubed on the front door, as if nobody wanted to park there for fear of being associated with the building or its occupant.

The young detective constable stared through his open window at the door. 'I can't say as I blame them, not wanting to live near one of those bastards.'

Ellis sighed resignedly. 'I know it must be hard living in close proximity to a convicted paedophile, but common sense tells us that if we know where they are we can keep an eye on them. Drive them underground and who knows what they're getting up to. Come on! Let's see how active a vigilante this McNeil is.'

As they approached McNeil's house, they saw the Renault Clio parked on the paved-over area where the garden had been, and exchanged glances. The front door of the building needed attention, the wood was exposed where the dirty green paint had flaked over the years, but the house number was carved on a smart slate plaque attached to the brick wall, probably a recent acquisition from a gift shop. There was no doorbell, so Ellis gave a hefty couple of knocks on the iron knocker.

After a moment they heard footsteps coming along the hall. The door opened to reveal a woman in her early fifties, short and slim in skin-tight denims and a bright orange T-shirt, and a wrinkled face with a tan that looked like it came from a bottle.

THE WRECKING BAR

Ellis showed her his warrant card as he announced, 'I'm Detective Sergeant Ellis and this is DC Wallace. Would you mind if we have a few words with your husband?'

Without batting an eyelid, the woman turned her head and yelled in a broad Valleys dialect, 'Norm! There's two coppers wanna talk to you.'

McNeil's muffled Glaswegian reply was hard to understand. His wife waited a moment before calling over her shoulder, 'Norm!'

The door of the front room opened and McNeil, purple in face and wheezing heavily, said, 'Am about to have ma tea, but you can come in for a wee while.'

The woman stood aside as they entered and they were shown into the living room by McNeil. The room was crowded with furniture, in a variety of styles, some of it old fashioned, some of it Swedish modern. A wide-screen television set dominated the room and was showing the regional news with the sound turned low.

Ellis and Wallace sat next to each other on a modern sofa upholstered in bright red with tubular steel arms, and McNeil sank into an old beige Parker Knoll easy chair opposite them, while his wife hovered near the door.

'Mr McNeil,' Ellis began, while Wallace took out a notebook and pen, 'you spoke with our detective inspector earlier on. Have you any idea why he was searching Titmus's house?'

McNeil glanced up at the ceiling before replying. 'I hadn't a clue. At first I thought he must be another one of those perverts, a friend of his. When he told me he was a detective, I just thought he must have been searching the house cos the bastard had been up to his filthy tricks again. I had no idea the bastard was dead.'

'So you heard it on the news.'

'It were on the telly.'

'And how did you feel about it?'

'I was just saying to Jackie—' McNeil turned to look at his wife. '—wasn't I? Shame we've got no champagne in the house. We coulda cracked open a bottle.'

She nodded vigorously and shouted, 'Good bloody riddance to him!' She seemed embarrassed by her outburst, so she leant across the back of her husband's chair, patting him reassuringly on the shoulder, and softened her voice. 'Would you two boys like a nice cuppa?'

'No thanks,' Ellis said, then turned his attention to the husband. 'You probably saw that he was murdered on his boat in the marina. Did you know he had a boat?'

'Of course not. Why would I know that?'

'Well, you might just have spotted him there. Do you ever visit the marina?'

'We go down to Sainsbury's for our shopping. Apart from that…' McNeil shrugged, indicating the marina was of no interest to him, apart from the supermarket trip.

Wallace laboriously wrote down McNeil's answers, his handwriting a scrawl which only he could decipher.

Ellis continued. 'The supermarket's only a short distance from where the victim's boat was moored. Is there any chance you might have seen him?'

'I'm telling you, I didn't know he had a boat at the marina. First I knew of it was on the telly fifteen minutes ago.'

'You're sure about that, Mr McNeil?'

'Of course I'm sure,' McNeil replied, a surge of anger darkening the purple hue of his complexion. 'What are you suggesting? That I killed him?'

Ellis smiled reassuringly. 'Sorry, Mr McNeil, I'm not suggesting any such thing. It's just that – I know I've done this myself – sometimes you see someone you think you recognize. Later on you might tell someone about it. "Guess who I saw", that sort of thing. A little bit of gossip can sometimes spread a long way and—'

McNeil interrupted belligerently. 'Look, I've already told you, I didn't see the bastard at the marina.'

'If you didn't see him at the marina, did you ever bump into him in this district?'

McNeil took his time answering and Ellis watched as he stuck a thumb in a nostril and rummaged around for a moment.

'We hadn't seen the bastard for ages, had we, Jackie?'

Mrs McNeil, posing supportively behind and to the side of her husband, like a Victorian photograph, put her fingers to her chin in an absurdly theatrical way. 'We hadn't seen him since we had our demonstration against him living here. But we knew he was coming back here from time to time.'

'If you didn't see him, how could you tell?'

McNeil, irritated by Ellis's question, scowled. 'You can always tell when someone's at home at night. Occasionally there was a light on. Or his car might be parked nearby.'

'What sort of car did he drive?'

'I'm not too sure.'

'But you said he parked it nearby. So you must have recognized it as his.'

'I think it was a Vauxhall. Something like a Cavalier or a Vectra.'

'What about your neighbours?'

The Wrecking Bar

'What about them?'

'How did they feel about having a man like that living in their street?'

'Same as we did. Angry. They wanted to get rid of him.'

Ellis smiled grimly. 'And someone has. Is there anyone round here you think might be capable of such an act?'

McNeil laughed. 'Nearly everyone round here would have liked to do it. Might have fantasized about it.'

'Norm's right,' Mrs McNeil broke in. 'I killed him loads of times in my mind.'

Ignoring her, McNeil continued. 'To actually do something like that takes guts. And the residents of this street might have been angry, but we had our own way of dealing with it.'

'How d'you mean?'

'We formed a committee and wrote to our MP. We even got banners made and got the press and TV down here.'

'How many of you are on this committee?'

'Most of the people in this street and the one that backs onto us.'

'So there'd be maybe fifty or sixty people, would you say?'

'Easily.'

Ellis felt a tightening in his stomach as he considered how many potential enemies these hated men had, and that was just the neighbours. There were probably as many child abuse victims, many from the youth custody centre, each with a motive. It meant a great deal of hard graft, starting with the process of eliminating all those who had an alibi that could be corroborated.

'Thank you for answering my questions, sir,' Ellis said, and looked up at the man's wife. 'And, Mrs McNeil, just one last question. Does your committee have a name, headed notepaper, that sort of thing?'

McNeil jerked a thumb at his wife. 'Missus does all the stationery and letters on the computer upstairs.'

'An' we've gorra name,' his wife added proudly. 'We have a – oh, what the bloody hell's it called?' She prodded her husband.

'Acronym.'

'Yeah,' she said. 'PASO. That stands for Parents Against Sex Offenders.'

Ellis frowned thoughtfully and tilted his head upwards. 'So I guess your children are quietly doing their homework.'

Mrs McNeil laughed. 'Don't be daft. Kids are all grown up. But my daughter's about to give birth. So we're almost grandparents.'

'Which is another reason,' McNeil growled, 'for not wanting that bastard in our street.'

Ellis stood up, followed by Wallace, who put his notebook away. The sergeant thanked the couple and apologized for taking up too much of their time. Now it was up to the young DC to ask the casual, conversational questions.

'This case is going to keep us busy,' Wallace began. 'It's an early start for us – and on a Saturday too. You got tomorrow off, sir?'

'I'm unemployed.'

'He's on incapacity benefit,' Mrs McNeil said. 'Bad back.'

'Oh, sorry to hear that, sir. What line of business were you in?'

'I used to work for my brother-in-law.'

'Doing what, if you don't mind my asking?'

'He had a small factory.'

As they walked out of the living room into the hallway, still keeping his voice light and casual, Wallace said, 'Not much light industry left these days. And difficult times economically. What did he manufacture?'

A slight pause before McNeil answered, 'Fertilizer.'

A small chuckle from Wallace, making a joke of it. 'Always plenty of demand from the farmers, I suppose. A sort of growth industry.'

McNeil stared at him unsmilingly.

'Right, well, thank you for your time.'

Watched by the couple from their doorway, the two detectives headed back to their car. As Wallace slid into the driver's seat, he saw McNeil waving his arms about, remonstrating with his wife.

'Looks like the start of a domestic,' he said.

Ellis chuckled. 'I hope that's not our fault.'

Then McNeil suddenly went off up the road, probably back to the pub, and his wife went inside and slammed the door.

Wallace turned to Ellis and raised two questioning eyebrows. 'Fertilizer, eh?'

'With sulphuric acid as an ingredient,' Ellis said. 'And the news gave details of the victim being bludgeoned to death with no mention of acid on the bollocks. So McNeil wouldn't have known that.'

'But did you notice the hesitation before he mentioned fertilizer?'

Ellis's gave his colleague a lopsided smile. 'Notice it? It was a thundering silence! And I'll tell you something else, Kevin.' He paused dramatically.

'What's that, Sergeant?'

Ellis looked at his watch. 'Ten minutes from now there's going to be another murder.'

Wallace grinned as he turned the ignition. 'You're going to show me how you can murder a pint. I've never heard that one before.'

Eight

Driving back to Swansea later that night, Debbie Jones stared at the distant hills, black and forbidding, small lights twinkling from lonely cottages, and she thought about the horrific crime scene she had witnessed. Lambert took his eyes off the road briefly and glanced in her direction.

'How're you bearing up under the strain of seeing your first gruesome?'

'Harry, I'm okay. I knew it wasn't going to be easy so I'd psyched myself up for it.'

Eyes back on the road, Lambert stared grimly at the carriageway ahead. 'I'll let you into a secret. The first time I saw something like we saw tonight, I threw up and I almost fainted. I still don't find it easy. So you acquitted yourself admirably. You must let me into *your* little secret.'

'It's called habituation.'

'So when did you get used to seeing blood and gore?'

'When I went to uni. I was going in for forensics; wanted to be a pathologist. So I've had some experience of cutting up cadavers.'

'What changed your mind about a different career?'

'I think it's because I was attracted to a job that would be different every day, and I thought with my degree I could fast-track to detective. I just think there are more opportunities for me in the police.'

Lambert chuckled. 'So you've set your sights on being the next female chief constable?'

She didn't reply, and he knew by her silence that he was right. She was ambitious, but for all the right reasons. Unlike his own motives: to university to study law simply to spite his working-class father, who hated students and further education. And later abandoning law to join the police, again to spite his father, whose loathing of the police was extreme, even though Lambert had never discovered a reason for this.

CHAPTER EIGHT

Changing the subject, DC Jones said, 'According to forensics' initial impression, Jarvis Thomas had been dead for well over a week.'

'Well into that disgusting state of decomposition. I think I could have worked that out. No wonder I fancy a nice long soak in the bath.'

'So if he was killed over a week ago,' Jones continued, 'that makes him the first victim.'

'Not necessarily,' Lambert replied. 'There may be others who have already been topped but not yet been discovered. Which means the stink of death will be even worse than that of Jarvis Thomas.'

When they had visited the crime scene, and were met by Sergeant Mark Sweet, who was based in Carmarthen, he had given them a quick briefing. Jarvis Thomas's corpse had been discovered in the mobile home he rented on a farm two miles outside the town. The farmer who owned the land had been pestering his tenant for rent arrears and called round to see if he could catch Thomas at home. After knocking and getting no reply, he tried the door and, finding it unlocked, entered. He said he was shocked but not surprised to find someone had murdered his tenant. He was open about knowing Thomas was a convicted paedophile, but said it was difficult to find tenants these days, and why should he be blamed for letting accommodation to someone who had done his time. After finding the body, he dashed back to his house and poured himself a large neat brandy, which he drank before making the 999 call.

Like Lubin Titmus, Jarvis Thomas had probably been knocked unconscious, had gaffer tape stretched across his mouth, was stripped and tied to a chair, and had had acid poured on to his genitals before being bludgeoned to death with a wrecking bar.

Lambert threw DC Jones a quick glance, admiring her attractive profile. She caught him looking, so he told her, 'I'd be interested in hearing your thoughts based on what you know so far, Debbie.'

'Well, I don't suppose we can be certain until we get the pathologist's findings, but my initial reaction is that both victims were alive when they were subjected to the acid torture. And that would indicate that the perpetrator has an abomination of sex offenders and wants them to suffer before death. But you know what's really odd about that?'

'Go on.'

'It looks as if the victims knew their attacker. So if the murderer is someone who was one of their abused victims, how come they invited that person in?'

'We can't be sure that they did.'

'Well, I wasn't present at the crime scene on the boat, but if it was similar to the one we've just been to…'

39

THE WRECKING BAR

'Almost identical,' Lambert said.

DC Jones continued. 'Well, there was no indication that Thomas put up a fight. It looked as if he was taken by surprise. Apart from the massive amount of blood spilled, and breakages from the bludgeoning with the metal bar, Thomas's home seemed to be reasonably clean and tidy; not what I expected at all. And it looked as if he was having a beer with his attacker. There were two cans of Special Brew among the wreckage.'

'It's the same as on the boat,' Lambert said. 'There was a broken bottle of Beck's beer and another one intact and unopened. What do you think that tells us?'

'That the killer didn't want to leave a DNA sample in his saliva. Which means we're dealing with someone fairly smart? And I'll bet there are no fingerprints on the unopened can or bottle.'

'Hmm,' Lambert reflected. 'Which would mean he'd be wearing gloves. Bit conspicuous considering we're in a bit of an Indian summer. Unless he had a reasonable explanation.'

'You're a convicted paedophile, and late one night you're visited by someone wearing gloves and carrying a heavy metal bar. What sort of explanation would you accept as reasonable?'

'My dermatitis is playing me up? I don't know. Until we talk to forensics, we won't know if he was wearing gloves or not.'

'Pound to a penny he was.'

'I don't think I'll take your bet.'

Smiling, DC Jones glanced at her boss. 'Coward!'

For a moment, Lambert thought she might be flirting with him. But flirting with one of his officers was stepping into inappropriate territory, so he chose to ignore it. Keeping his voice level and businesslike, he said, 'How about the victim's blood? The killer would have been splattered, quite liberally, I would have thought.'

'Suppose,' Debbie Jones began, slowly and thoughtfully, 'the killer has a holdall in which he keeps the wrecking bar and a change of clothes? He changes from one tracksuit, say, to another. At least if he's stopped on the way back, it won't show that he's been covered in blood. As soon as he gets home, he can shower and destroy both sets of clothes.'

'But under what pretence would he have visited his potential victims?' Lambert asked.

It suddenly became clear to the young detective that her boss had already reached these conclusions himself but was giving her the opportunity to prove herself.

40

'Perhaps he knows what these men are like, the way they groom their victims. So he turns the tables on them and becomes a groomer himself, grooming them for murder. Maybe he masquerades as a paedophile and calls on them with a promise to give or sell them child porn. Most of these men know they daren't use the internet for that sort of thing anymore, not since Operation Ore has managed to snare so many of them.'

Lambert nodded approvingly. 'Well done, Debbie. That's a reasonable theory. But the hard work begins tomorrow when one of our tasks will be to track down the abuse victims and eliminate which ones have watertight alibis and see who we're left with.'

'But you know one thing I can't fathom, if you go by the books: blunt instrument murders are usually frenzied, primitive killings. But this particular killer, maybe prior to the murders, tortured them in a cold-blooded way, watching as the acid ate into their more emotional parts.'

Lambert paused while he thought about this. 'Maybe, just maybe,' he began, 'this killer once went bananas and killed his abuser in a frenzied attack. Perhaps that one was more personal. But now he's on a mission, ridding the world of evil paedophiles.'

'That would make sense,' Debbie Jones agreed. 'We could log onto HOLMES and search for a similar crime – an unsolved – going back a few years.'

'It's worth a try,' Lambert told her as he clicked his indicator for the Swansea turn-off. 'Where can I drop you, Debbie?'

'Anywhere near the centre. I know it's nearly half ten but I need a bite to eat. I haven't eaten since breakfast.'

'Same here,' Lambert said. 'I know this pub where they do toasted sarnies up to closing time. I'm buying if you fancy it.'

'Thanks,' said the young DC. 'I could really fancy a toasted ham and cheese.'

'Pub it is then.'

Nine

At exactly eight on Saturday morning, Lambert stormed into the incident room brandishing a copy of the *Western Mail*. DCS Marden stood in the middle of the room facing the door and glanced pointedly at his watch, the gesture implying that the DI was cutting it fine. Debbie Jones was sitting at one of the desks, already busy on a computer, as was Sergeant Ellis, and DS Hazel was bent over a table, frowning in concentration as he wrote in the team's action book.

'I heard the news headlines on the car radio,' Lambert seethed, desperately trying to control his anger. 'So I stopped to get a copy of the *Western Mail*.'

He slammed the paper onto a vacant desk close to Marden. The headline read: 'TWO MURDERS AND TV MAN'S CHILD PORN.'

Lambert stared at Marden. 'Why weren't we told about this?'

Collectively, the room held its breath.

Marden's lips tightened. 'DI Ambrose was dealing with it, and it took up most of Thursday. You may remember I called you at home after the first body was discovered...'

'Do you think I could have a word in private, sir?' Lambert cut in.

Marden gave Lambert a frosty look. 'Permission denied, Inspector. No robust management here. We work as a team. Sing from the same hymn sheet. So if you've got something to say, let's hear it.'

Lambert glared at his boss for a moment. He had never liked Marden, and the feeling was mutual. He thought he was a creep, and once, at a police do, after one too many red wines, he had laid in to the coterie of fluent Welsh language speakers – of which Marden was one – and made a comment about them brown-nosing to get in with the Tafia. It wasn't Lambert's best career move.

Ignoring Marden, Lambert addressed the rest of the team. 'If none of you have had a chance to read the details of this sordid story let me give you a quick rundown. A television editor, man called Mark Yalding, was arrested yesterday for downloading child pornography images on the internet. He was traced through the FBI in the US, and they passed the information to South Wales Police.

'Yalding claims he was downloading the images as research for Green Valley Productions, the company who made the TV documentary. But his employer, Gavin Lloyd, had previously sacked his researcher, claiming the documentary was made more than nine months ago, and at that time he had warned Yalding about downloading pornography for research purposes.'

'What's happened to this Yalding bloke?' Ellis asked.

'He was bailed,' Lambert replied, and then shifted his focus to Marden. 'We should have been told about this Yalding's arrest on Thursday, sir. Who was dealing with the case?'

'Geoff Ambrose. Now listen, Inspector: yesterday, in the space of about four hours, you and your team had two murders to investigate. I think you had enough on your plate.'

'All the same, it looks as if this Yalding business is connected in some way.'

Marden looked like a poker player about to throw down a good hand. 'Exactly! Which is why we're having this meeting now and I'm leaving you to deal with it. This will be your investigation, for which I hope you get a quick result.'

Rather than being placated by being handed the controls, Lambert was immediately suspicious. 'What about Geoff Ambrose?' he asked.

'As we speak, Geoff's on a plane to Florida on his annual leave.'

'Presumably, after having arrested Yalding, he obtained a confession and thinks that's the end of the affair.'

'Hardly. I've got you the transcript of the interview and you'll see that Yalding totally denies downloading child porn – any sort of porn – off the internet.'

'But I'm assuming it was his home computer and he was caught in the usual way, by using a credit card.'

'We've got his computer. It was checked and confirmed that child porn was downloaded from his credit card. But he still denies all knowledge of it and claims he never used his credit card.'

'His denial sounds a bit flimsy.'

'It is,' Marden agreed. 'But after that actor gave research as a justification, and still got a custodial sentence, perhaps Yalding thought denying it a better option.'

'Even if unrealistic,' Lambert added.

THE WRECKING BAR

Marden glanced at his watch again. 'I'm trusting you to get a result on these murders, Harry. I've got my time cut out dealing with the press and a thousand and one other matters churned up by this mess. The media are hoping for longevity with this story, and there are all the political implications.'

'Should these people be set free in the community?' Lambert said. 'And is the killer doing us all a favour?'

'I take it they were rhetorical.'

Lambert nodded gravely.

'So the sooner you get a result, the better for all concerned.'

'I'll do my best, sir. Although I can see mega problems with this investigation.'

This wasn't what Marden wanted to hear. 'Oh?' he said, managing to give the exclamation a world of meaning.

'I'm thinking of just how hated these men were, sir. They've got a lot of enemies.'

'So you'd better start by eliminating those with cast-iron alibis.'

'Which is exactly what we're about to do.'

Marden stared guardedly at Lambert before he spun round and headed for the door. Lambert watched him, waiting for the exit speech. But he left without as much as a backward glance. Lambert smiled wryly. There had to be a first time for everything.

He turned towards the whiteboard where DC Jones now stood, holding a picture uncertainly. 'It's not necessary to display the corpses, Debbie. It's not going to forward our investigation in any way.'

Relieved, she inserted them back in the folder. The door burst open and Kevin Wallace entered breathlessly, his face a mixture of exasperation and stress.

'Well?' Lambert questioned.

Wallace shook his head. 'There's no CCTV of that part of the marina. Apparently, there was something technically wrong with the system, and everything's been inadvertently wiped.'

Lambert snorted loudly. 'Shit! Did the harbour master tell you what exactly was wrong with the CCTV?'

'The harbour master is on annual leave. I was dealing with a part-time relief, and he couldn't tell me what was wrong, except that no recordings exist for recent weeks.'

'So, in other words, he's seen news about the victim being a paedophile, and has decided to take the law into his own hands. Did you get this good citizen's name?'

Wallace tapped the breast pocket containing his notebook. 'Got it in here.'

'Later, we'll see if we can do anything about this.'

'A prosecution for obstructing a murder enquiry?' Ellis offered.

'If we can prove it,' Lambert said. 'Meanwhile, we'd better get on with it.'

He perched on the edge of a desk and said, 'Okay, let's all take a seat and do some brainstorming.'

As Wallace slid into a seat, he said, 'The killer's already done a fair bit of that.'

Lambert indulged him with a brief smile. He understood the need for a team to resort to gallows humour occasionally, which seemed to be a release valve. And he also understood the need to break the ice before embarking on the arduous and often tedious task ahead.

'Maybe that woman on the diversity training course was right,' he said, pausing for effect. 'She said it might not be politically correct to use the word brainstorming anymore.'

'I think that was because of stroke victims,' DC Jones offered.

Kevin said, 'So what we supposed to say instead?'

DS Hazel smiled, as if he already knew the answer.

A glint in his eye, Lambert replied, 'Thought showering.'

Wallace pulled a face, stuck two fingers in his mouth and mimed gagging.

Lambert chuckled and shook his head. Then, ice broken, it was down to business. 'Right! I'll keep it brief and leave you in Tony's charge. I've got to get over to Cardiff for the post mortem. And then I'll see Hughie at the forensics lab to see what they've uncovered. What they find or don't find, as the case may be, will be interesting, because I think we could be dealing with a killer who knows how to cover the traces.'

He went on to explain about the beer found at the crime scenes, and how in each case one of the beers hadn't been touched or opened. He also put forward the theory that he and DC Jones had discussed on their journey back from Carmarthen, about the killer knowing his victims. He said there was one thing of which he was certain, the way in which the perpetrator had tortured his victims prior to killing them, indicating a psychotic hatred of paedophiles and a lust for revenge. At the end of his short speech about the murders and the easy way the murderer had gained access to the victims' accommodations, he asked if anyone else on the team had anything to add.

Sergeant Ellis, lips pursed in concentration, said, 'We're assuming it's someone who was abused by these men or men of their kind. It could be a sex offender, someone who's done his fair share of abusing over the years, and now hates himself for it and has transferred the self-hatred and loathing to others of his kind.'

THE WRECKING BAR

'Someone who's got religion, the fire and brimstone sort,' Wallace added. 'Plenty of that in darkest Wales.'

'It's a possibility,' Lambert admitted, 'but let's have a look at all the options. For instance, Tony and Kevin, you interviewed McNeil. What did you make of him?'

'Definitely a vigilante,' Ellis said. 'He and the neighbourhood have formed a committee called PASO, Parents Against Sex Offenders. Although this organization seems to be going through the right channels to oust these men from their neighbourhoods, such as contacting the press and their MP, it seems more personal with McNeil.'

Lambert nodded agreement. 'And he's a heavy drinker with time on his hands.'

'He's got a Renault Clio,' Wallace said. 'And my nosy neighbour on the marina said it could have been a small saloon she saw.'

'And there's something else about McNeil that Kevin discovered,' Ellis said. 'He used to work at his brother-in-law's factory, manufacturing fertilizer.'

For a brief moment Lambert stared thoughtfully into the distance. 'Interesting. Don't fertilizers contain sulphuric acid? Although – correct me if I'm wrong – isn't sulphuric acid one of the world's most commonly used chemicals? But, taking everything else into account, it certainly puts him high on the list as a suspect. I mean, it's not as if he worked in a chocolate factory. But you say he no longer works at the fertilizer plant.'

Ellis shook his head. 'I don't think that means a great deal. His wife said he's got a bad back and he's on incapacity benefit. Maybe he's receiving state benefits and still working odd hours for his brother-in-law.'

'Could be,' Lambert agreed. 'I think what we need to do here is look for another motive. Check out McNeil thoroughly, see if there's anything on record that tells us he might have suffered as a victim of abuse, either from his parents or elsewhere.'

Debbie Jones, who had been making notes, got their attention by speaking quietly. 'I think this Mayfield's definitely suspicious. Why did he leave it for two hours until he called the police? Did he go back there to conceal a vital piece of evidence?'

'If he did,' Lambert said, 'why would he tell the truth about finding the body much earlier? He could have lied about phoning the police immediately after finding the body and no one would have known any difference.'

Wallace slammed a fist onto the desk. 'He's a devious bastard. He knows all those flats on the marina overlook the yacht basin. He knew he couldn't risk that particular lie.'

Lambert looked at the clock on the wall and made a decision. 'One of the most important jobs for this morning will be to try and trace the origin of the murder weapons. Debbie if you'd like to pin up the photos. But that's just one of our tasks. We also need to check with the youth custody centre where Titmus and Mayfield worked and see if we can get a list of their young offenders between 1975 and 2001.'

While Lambert was speaking, Debbie Jones took the photographs of the murder weapons from the file and stuck them on to the whiteboard.

'And, Debbie, you had an idea about checking the computer databases for similar unsolved murders from years ago.' He turned and addressed Ellis and Wallace. 'Debbie thinks a crime where the killer cold-bloodedly tortures his victims doesn't tally with a frenzied attack with a blunt instrument. So perhaps our murderer's an abused person who years ago carried out a frenzied attack, but now wants to rid the world of these evil men, first making them suffer, just like he suffered.'

Lambert got up off the desk and stood in front of the white board, pointing to one of the photographs.

'This one just says "Made in China", and there's no identifying serial marks or anything. But the other one – the one used to murder Jarvis Thomas – as you can see, says "US Patent", with quite a long serial number after it. It could well be that this is more expensive and comes from a reputable shop or chain store, so I think we could start with this one.'

From his pocket he took out the snapshot of Mayfield and the young boy and attached it to the board. 'This young boy, Tom Thorne, we need to check him out.'

'If that's his name,' Ellis said. 'Mayfield could have been lying again.'

'We still need to check if such a person exists. And we need to contact Mayfield again and see if we can get more information. We need to know when approximately this photograph was taken, how old the boy is now, and when he went to Spain. That's if any of what Mayfield told us is true. And see if there's anyone of that name on a young offenders' list.'

Lambert crossed hurriedly to the door and spoke to Ellis as he was about to pick up the phone. 'Tony, I've got to get over to Cardiff for the post mortems. Nothing for a year and now two in one day.'

'Must be your lucky day, Harry,' Ellis said.

Lambert rolled his eyes. 'On the way back I'll see Hughie at Bridgend. So I'll be gone for most of the day. I know it's Saturday but I'd like someone to get hold of the producer at Green Valley Productions, either at his home or office. I'd be very interested in seeing that documentary. If we meet back here

THE WRECKING BAR

later this afternoon to see what we've got, and then we can adjourn to our other incident room.'

Lambert swept out, and Debbie Jones raised her eyebrows questioningly at DS Hazel.

'I assume he meant the pub. Does that go in the action book?'

DS Hazel laughed. 'Actions go in the action book. The pub is for theorizing and – er – thought showering.'

***

Less than half an hour after Lambert's departure the team was startled by Wallace shouting 'Yes!' as he ended a telephone call. Ellis glanced at the clock and saw that it was just after ten and already it looked as if one of them had got a result.

'What is it, Kevin?'

Trying not to preen himself, and failing miserably, Wallace swaggered into the centre of the room and consulted his notebook.

'I've traced the murder weapon to a B & Q store in Llanelli. The same serial number as the murder weapon and it was sold on Saturday three weeks ago at 15.30 hours.'

Ellis tried not to raise his hopes too high. 'How was it paid for?'

'Cash.'

'Do they know the member of staff who sold it?'

Wallace nodded fervently. 'A Gareth Edwards. But I couldn't speak to him, he's not at work today.'

'On a Saturday?'

'Apparently he's already done six days on the trot.'

'Did you get his address and phone number?'

'They won't give it out over the phone.'

'We could email them in an official capacity. On the other hand, it might be more valuable if you get to Llanelli as fast as you can, get this Mr Edwards's address, and see if you can interview him. Let's hope he can remember selling this wrecking bar. They can't sell many of those items, can they?'

Pleased to be getting away from the office, Wallace grinned and said, 'Soon find out, won't I?'

Eyes narrowing, Ellis gave the young constable a knowing look. 'And as soon as you've spoken to this checkout bloke, straight back here please, Kevin.'

'Of course,' Wallace replied, making it sound as if there was no question of him doing anything to the contrary.

'Off you go then.'

Chapter Nine

DC Jones rose hurriedly from her work station and said to Ellis, 'Before Kevin goes, he might want to be a part of this information.'

Ellis waved a hand in Wallace's direction. 'Hang about, Kevin.' He looked up enquiringly at DC Jones. 'What've you got, Debbie?'

DS Hazel stopped working on his computer to listen.

'Mayfield didn't lie about Tom Thorne. He was a young offender at the youth custody centre. He was released aged fourteen in April 1991, went home to Cardiff where he lived on a council estate with his parents and younger brother, and he had to make probation visits weekly. After only two visits he stopped going. When his probation officer visited his home, she discovered he had left and no one knew of his whereabouts. He went on a missing persons register—'

Ellis interrupted to ask, 'And has he been missing ever since?'

DC Jones looked at the sergeant and nodded gravely. 'That's right.'

'Could he have been seeing Mayfield after he'd gone missing?'

'It's a distinct possibility. But there's no way he could have gone abroad. He's never applied for a passport.'

'So Mayfield told us another lie. But he was truthful when he told us his name.'

Leaning with one arm against the door, Wallace chuckled. 'I think our boss man may have frightened him into that one.'

DC Jones nodded agreement. 'Yes, he's now terrified for his life. And he needs the police to protect him, so he was forced into giving us half the truth.'

Ellis stared thoughtfully into the distance for a moment. 'I wonder what happened to this Tom Thorne?'

Jones shuddered. 'I'd hate to think.'

Freeing himself from troubled thoughts, Ellis told Wallace to get on his way.

Once he had left, Ellis told Debbie, 'I think we need to get Mayfield back here. Get on to the main desk and see if you can get the patrol car that's keeping an eye on him to bring him in.'

As soon as he finished speaking, his desk phone rang and he snatched it up. DC Jones was about to return to her desk but Ellis indicated with a raised hand for her to stay, listening intently to the received information from the call, making small exclamations to show the caller he was listening. He ended the call by saying, 'Thank you, Sergeant. I'll have a word with Chief Superintendent Marden and see if we can organize a helicopter search.'

Jones and Hazel were poised and tense, awaiting news of the sudden development.

Ellis said, 'After the change of shift with the patrol cars, the new shift was called to an incident in Singleton Street. When they eventually checked up on Mayfield's boat, it had gone. Our bird has flown. Or in this case sailed.'

Ten

As he drove to Llanelli, DC Kevin Wallace dreamt of his promotion following his contribution to this case. He was in great spirits when he arrived at the B & Q store, but his hopes were soon dashed when the store manager said:

'I'm sorry if you've had a wasted journey.'

After this jolt of disappointment, Kevin listened with growing impatience while the manager explained about the store policy of employing staff with special needs, and it was unlikely that Mr Edwards would remember who he sold the wrecking bar to. Yes, he had a great memory for every character and scene in every Harry Potter film, but as for remembering information such as Wallace wanted...

To his disappointment, this was confirmed when the young detective visited Gareth Edwards at his home. The young man could provide no information, had no clue what a wrecking bar looked like, and was only intent on barcode scanning and the operation of the sale itself.

As he headed back to Swansea, he cursed his luck.

***

After attending two post mortems, Lambert couldn't face lunch. It wasn't so much the dissection that was nauseating but the lingering smell that left an indelible stain on the memory. With a stomach that grumbled loudly, he drove quickly from Cardiff to Bridgend, parked outside the Science Support Building, which was all part of the same complex at Bridgend Police HQ, and phoned the incident room to see if there were any developments. He stopped himself from swearing when he received the news of Mayfield's escape, followed by a request from Marden to visit him in his office once he had met with forensics.

THE WRECKING BAR

'I'm not happy about this situation with Mayfield,' was Marden's opening line when at last Lambert entered his office.

Lambert shrugged and affected a mystified expression. 'Neither am I.'

'Then why did you let him go?'

'We had nothing to charge him with.'

Marden made a snorting sound in the back of his throat. 'He was a convicted paedophile, Harry, who lied to you when questioned. And now we have a helicopter search going on because his boat's gone.'

'Yes, that was bad luck… about the patrol car being called to another incident.'

Marden's face reddened. 'You're missing the point, Harry. If you hadn't let the bastard go, this might never have happened.'

'True.'

'Is that all you have to say?'

Lambert couldn't resist adding, 'Well, there's no point shutting the stable door, as they say.'

Marden's voice had an icy edge to it. 'I can't believe you let this man go before you heard what forensics and the pathologist had to say.'

'We had no reason to hold him, sir. With all due respect, what would you have charged him with?'

Marden gave Lambert an acid look and chose to ignore the question. 'I find it difficult to believe that someone of your experience and record let a suspect go. Were you distracted by the other murder in Carmarthen? Is that what it was? You took your eye off the ball?'

'Far from it, sir. The reason Mayfield lied to us was because of his past, and because he was scared. He knows he could become the killer's next victim. He had absolutely no motive for killing his friend Titmus or the man in Carmarthen. The reason Mayfield's scarpered is because he fears for his life. But that boat has to moor at some other port or seaside town. He won't have gone far in that thing.'

'Presumably this Mayfield knows a lot more than you got out of him during your questioning.'

Lambert hesitated. Should he tell him about Thorne being on a missing persons list since 1991? He decided against it, as that would only give the chief super fuel for his argument about hanging on to Mayfield. Lambert chose to change the subject instead and had just started telling him about McNeil and the vigilante group when the phone rang. Marden picked it up hurriedly, barked his surname, and then listened intently, his face a picture of troubled management. He sighed deeply and ended the call.

CHAPTER TEN

'That was the ACC. The chief constable wants a thorough briefing. This has become a major headache. The press are going berserk on this one, and it's thrown up all kinds of issues. It's fast becoming political.'

'I know,' Lambert said. 'It'll be a fight between freedom of the press and the civil liberties of our poor sex offenders.'

Ignoring the comment, Marden crossed to the door. 'Let me know, as soon as you can, what we need to tell the press.'

As he was being ushered out of the office, Lambert said, 'We know the store where one of the murder weapons came from. DC Wallace went over to interview the bloke on the checkout who sold it. And if he can't ID him, we may need to issue press details in case there's someone else in the queue who can.'

Marden, who was taller than Lambert, peered down at him like a headteacher staring at a troublesome boy. 'I hope for your sake, if you do get an ID, he doesn't bear any resemblance to this Mayfield.'

'I think someone with white wavy hair and a pitch-black moustache would be rather noticeable. No, it won't be him. I guarantee it.'

'We'll see,' Marden said, then turned and headed off down the corridor.

Lambert glanced at his watch. It was time to get back to the incident room at Cockett, and he wanted to view the TV documentary which Ellis had managed to get downloaded on to their system from the producer of Green Valley Productions.

As he walked along the corridor, in the opposite direction from the chief superintendent, he thought about the way Marden had trusted him with the case, even though he had found fault with his handling of the Mayfield interrogation. He knew Marden appreciated his unblemished police record, but their mutual dislike of each other boiled down to something deeper. Something personal.

But he didn't think Marden would let it get in the way of the investigation. At least the man was professional, he grudgingly admitted.

***

When he arrived back at the incident room, Lambert found DS Hazel alone, busy collating all the recently acquired information while he munched his way through a Mars Bar.

'There'll be a day of reckoning,' Lambert said.

'I'll cross that bridge when the time comes.'

'You might be crossing it sooner than you think, when you notice how tight your trousers feel.'

53

THE WRECKING BAR

Hazel grinned and patted his trim waist. 'I think you might be a bit jealous, Harry. How did the post mortems go?'

Not wanting to be reminded, Lambert muttered, 'Okay,' and changed the subject. 'How about this TV documentary?'

'Tony managed to track Gavin Lloyd, the MD of Green Valley Productions to his home. The guy couldn't do enough to assist us and drove into Cardiff where his office is based and loaded the film on to their website for us.'

'Did Tony say what this Gavin Lloyd thought about his researcher downloading child porn?'

'Yeah, he said the guy was disgusted, and appreciated that there might be a connection between Mark Yalding and the murdered paedophiles and agreed to do all he could to help.'

'Very public spirited.'

'Tony got the impression he was an "I" specialist. Liked the sound of his own voice.'

Hazel waved a hand towards one of the computers. 'It's ready and waiting for you. Let me know if it's better than last night's episode of *EastEnders*.'

'Thanks, Roger.'

Lambert sat at the computer that Hazel had indicated, expecting to view cutting-edge, sensational television journalism; instead, he found it was quite the opposite and was rather pedestrian. There was no presenter, a voice over provided the narrative, and it began with shots of the youth custody centre that Titmus had run, and spoke about society's responsibility to protect its young, asking questions about professional youth workers and social workers. The voiceover was distrustful, wondering how these evil men came to be in charge of such an institution. This was followed by street shots, ordinary two-up-two-down houses in one of the Valley towns, and an out-of-shot presenter asking residents how they felt about a released sex offender living in their neighbourhood. The response was predictable, so Lambert fast forwarded. As soon as he saw a shot of the marina he clicked the cursor back onto play. Here the presenter, again out of shot, talked to a man whose face was pixellated to disguise his identity, but Lambert could see the name of the boat and where it was moored, so he knew it was Titmus.

The presenter, somewhere behind and to left of camera, asked Titmus the questions that had been asked of Mayfield in the interview room. Why was he living on a boat and not at his home? Titmus's voice was authoritative, with just a trace of Welsh accent, sounding affronted as he replied, saying he had served his time and paid the price for his transgression.

54

Transgression. Not crime or offence or felony. But transgression. Clearly Titmus thought of his crimes as a mild form of misbehaviour.

Next, the presenter asked Titmus if he was in touch with any other convicted sex offenders, to which he replied, 'Of course not. I thought I had made it quite clear that I will commit no further misdemeanours.'

There it was again. The word playing down the enormity of the crime.

The rest of the footage showed three other paedophiles: the first, Jarvis Thomas, whose face was also hazed out, but Lambert was able to identify him from the interior of his mobile home; the second was a man in Birmingham, whose immediate neighbours knew he'd been in jail, but thought it was for theft; and finally a man who lived in a hostel in Cardiff who was selling *Big Issue* on the streets. There was nothing about Gordon Mayfield, who had either slipped under the TV researcher's radar or been excluded for editorial reasons.

The scaremongering conclusion of the programme was that in the programme makers' opinion these men would undoubtedly re-offend, but for legal reasons they could not be identified as it could never be proven that they might commit similar crimes at some time in the future.

But the *Sun* had no such qualms, for which Lambert felt grateful as he clicked onto their website. He could either get the article online or at least get them to email it to him so that he would know the identities and rough whereabouts of the other sex offenders.

Eleven

DC Jones drove carefully through one of the most depressing areas in Cardiff. Blocks of flats, the ground floors boarded up and desolate, and corner shops with wire mesh protecting the windows; rusting abandoned cars and litter-strewn streets. Sitting in the passenger seat, staring at the hostile environment, Ellis's mood began to sour.

'The recession must be another bloody great nail in the coffin for people round here,' he observed.

DC Jones swerved to avoid a football kicked into the road. 'I don't suppose,' she replied, 'they ever had high expectations, even before the economy took a nose-dive.'

'What about this Chislet? You think he might be a handful?'

Jones shook her head. 'Not if you think about the last five years. There's been no serious criminal activity.'

'You must admit, Debbie; of all the youngsters who passed through Titmus's institution, this one tops the list. His first crime was stoning a neighbour's cat to death at the age of ten. Then a spectacular list of juvenile crimes. A serious assault on another boy in an alternative curriculum programme, and then a three-year sentence at the youth custody centre. And, after his release, when he turned eighteen, some of his crimes were stomach churning.'

Jones laughed grimly. 'I can't wait to meet this little charmer.'

'You won't have long to wait.' Ellis pointed and tapped the windscreen. 'That must be him with the hotdog barrow.'

On a street corner, close to a shabby pub, a man stood by a hotdog stand, smoking and drinking from a can of Foster's. Although he was only in his early thirties, Chislet's thin, ravaged face and receding hair gave him the appearance of a much older man. Jones had seen his photograph and read his physical details but was still surprised by his small build.

'He's only a little geezer,' she said.

'They're the ones you have to be wary of. It's called over-compensating.'

She parked the car directly in front of Chislet's hotdog stand and they both got out. Chislet watched them calmly, not a muscle moving in his face. He flicked the stub of his cigarette into the road without taking his eyes off them.

Ellis showed Chislet his warrant card. 'I'm Detective Sergeant Ellis and this is Detective Constable Jones. We'd like a few words.'

'What about?'

'We'd like to know where you were on Thursday night.'

Chislet put his beer on top of the stand, next to the square cavity containing unappetizing-looking frankfurters, and lit another cigarette with a disposable lighter. Both detectives watched him carefully, aware of the delaying tactic. Once he had inhaled and let out a stream of smoke, he gave them a cold smile and jerked a thumb at the pub.

'What's that supposed to mean?' Ellis demanded.

'Means I was in the pub Thursday night. Go in and ask if you don't believe me.'

'I don't mean pub hours. I mean the middle of the night. Early Friday morning, say between one o'clock and 4 a.m.'

Chislet shrugged. 'I was in bed, fast asleep.'

'On your own?' Jones asked.

Chislet gave her a suggestive smile. 'Yeah. Too bad I never had no one to keep me company that night.'

'So you have no witnesses who can back you up?'

Chislet's eyes narrowed as he stared at Ellis. 'Why do I need a witness? If I say I was in bed, I was in fucking bed.'

'How's custom?' Jones asked, deliberately wrongfooting him.

'What?'

She nodded at the hotdog stand. 'You make much of a living at this?'

'I get by.'

'And do you offer your customers any other kind of stimulant?'

'What are you talking about?'

Ellis broke in sharply, 'She means are you using this as a front for dealing in drugs?'

Chislet laughed confidently and tapped his pockets. 'You're out of luck. You won't find anything on me.' He gestured towards the hotdog stand. 'And you won't find nothing in there neither. Go ahead and look if you wanna. Have a look under the sausages, if you don't mind paying for them.'

The Wrecking Bar

'That won't be necessary,' Ellis said. 'Because your customers come to you on the street corners and you take their orders. That's how you operate, isn't it? How is it you manage to pay the magistrates' fines selling hotdogs? Not exactly doing a roaring trade, are you?'

'At least, not in hotdogs,' Jones chimed in.

Chislet began to shift from one foot to the other, starting to look disturbed, and Ellis braced himself for an explosion. But just as the sergeant feared an imminent clash, Chislet's tension seemed to evaporate as he took another long drag on his cigarette.

'You got any proof of this?' he asked.

Ellis smiled. 'Let's forget the drugs for the moment. We're not drug squad. We'd like you to cast your mind back twenty years ago, when you were at the youth custody centre.'

Chislet stared into Ellis's eyes, clearly wondering where this was leading, and waited for him to continue.

'Running the institution was a man named Titmus, a convicted paedophile who abused many young boys in his care. He and another man, Gordon Mayfield, were sentenced to seven years and were paroled over two years ago.'

Chislet stared distantly at some dark memory and remained silent.

Ellis continued. 'We'd like to know if you had any dealings with Titmus or Mayfield.'

'Dealings?'

Ellis looked directly at Chislet and nodded.

'You want to know if those bastards abused me, is that it?'

'Like they abused loads of youngsters in their care.'

'Oh, they tried it on all right. Three of them there was. That bastard Titmus, Mayfield and another screw.'

'Screw?' Ellis questioned.

'Yeah, that's what we used to call them. I'd been locked up in this room as a punishment. It was where they kept some of the leisure equipment, table tennis table, an' that. But it was more like a cell, with a bed in one corner and no windows. Anyway, I'd been locked up for giving this older boy a good kicking. They kept me locked up all day, with nothing to eat or drink, just waiting. I knew they was coming for me and I was ready for them. There was no way they was gonna to touch me.'

DC Jones held her breath as she watched him relating his story, and she almost felt sorry for him.

'So what happened?' Ellis prompted.

'They came in and locked the door. I said to them, "You touch me and one of you's gonna lose an eye. I don't care which one of you it is, but after today one of you fuckers'll be blind in one eye." Chislet held up a thumb and mimed gouging out an eye, his lips clamped together as he imagined it. 'I showed them the thumb and told them how I was gonna enjoy seeing one of the fuckers squirm when he saw his eye in my hand. They left me alone after that.'

Ellis was certain that Chislet, even at the tender age of thirteen, was quite capable of committing such an act.

'Did they ever try again?' he asked.

'I told you: they left me alone. Picked on some other poor bastard.'

Although it was hot standing in the sun, Jones shivered as she imagined a more vulnerable child in that situation.

Chislet eyed them both shrewdly and said, 'So you think I killed that bastard Titmus.'

This took Ellis by surprise and he said rather lamely, 'We're just making enquiries.'

Chislet laughed confidently. 'Whoever killed those bastards should get a medal. And I don't have a fucking alibi. So what you gonna do about it? Eh? You gonna fit me up for this one? Well, I'll tell you something: if those fuckers had raped me, I'd have gone looking for them. But they didn't, so it's got nothing to do with me, has it?'

'And there's no one who can confirm that you were at home in the early hours of Friday? Neighbour? Someone who might have heard you?'

Chislet laughed again, enjoying the situation. 'I had my television on loud, watching some shit late-night film. My next-door neighbour might have heard it. But if I wanted an alibi, I could have left the TV on really loud, gone over to Swansea, killed Titmus, and that wouldn't really be much of an alibi, would it? But there's just one problem.'

Chislet, a triumphant glint in his eye, waited for one of the detectives to cue him.

'What's that?' Jones said.

'I can't fucking drive. I've never learnt. So how the fuck do I get over to Swansea in the middle of the night? Public transport?' He laughed loudly. 'If you'd checked with DVLA – and that's in Swansea – you could have saved yourselves a journey. Call yourselves fucking detectives.'

Ellis and Jones exchanged looks while Chislet's mocking laughter grew. Ellis gave Chislet a cursory nod before getting back in the car. As Jones drove away, she looked in the rear-view mirror and saw Chislet staring after their car, holding up his middle finger to her.

The Wrecking Bar

After a silent exit from the immediate neighbourhood, Jones muttered, 'We got that one wrong.'

Ellis shook his head. 'He still had to be checked out. And some of these tough guys may not be licensed to drive legally, but they still know what to do when they get behind a wheel.'

It sounded hollow, and he knew he was clutching at straws.

***

The Cockett Inn was situated conveniently close to the police station. Normally Lambert would have chosen to drink somewhere a bit further from where he was based, but it had been a long day for all concerned, and the rest of his team wanted to get away.

But not Lambert. Lousy flat. Fridge full of nothing. Nothing but crap on television. And nothing but the sound of his own thoughts for company. In other words, a big fat nothing.

The team, wanting to be reasonably private in their conversation, thought the pub might be heaving. But it was only just gone seven, and the heavy drinking brigade from the afternoon shift had staggered off home, leaving only a few stalwarts at the bar, the kamikaze drinkers who would be talking nonsense by closing time, if not sooner. And the Saturday night shift was yet to arrive, so they were able to find a table that was relatively secluded.

After they'd bagged their seats, Lambert gave Wallace a £20 note to get a round in.

'I'll give him a hand,' Jones offered, and joined Wallace at the bar.

'Shame Roger couldn't make it,' Ellis said as they sat.

Lambert gave a throaty chuckle. 'He told me how much his wife was looking forward to the show at the Grand tonight. If I'd insisted on his presence, I might be the next murder victim.'

Ellis laughed politely and surreptitiously glanced at his watch. It had been an eventful two days, and he wanted to get home to see Sharon, who had nearly gone the full term in her pregnancy. But he felt this was part of his job, the way Lambert wanted to work it, knowing that a more relaxed discussion away from the incident room could produce ideas.

Lambert saw him glancing at his watch and said, 'I know you want to get home, Tony...'

'No, that's okay,' Ellis jumped in, keen to show his commitment to the investigation. 'Baby's due very soon but I think I can spare another half hour.'

Once Wallace and Jones arrived with the drinks, and they were all huddled around a table, Lambert kicked off the discussion.

'This investigation,' he began, 'might not be as straightforward as it seems.'

Frowning, Debbie Jones said, 'Something to do with motive, d'you mean?'

'No, the fact that whoever committed this crime wanted his victims to suffer seems to be a clear indication of some sort of revenge, either perpetrated by someone who was abused, or by someone who's on some sort of ruthless crusade.'

'Someone like that Norman McNeil.' Wallace suggested.

'Whoever it is has been scrupulous in not leaving any traces, fingerprints or DNA. Both murder weapons were clean, suggesting that gloves were worn. The only prints that were found on the boat belonged to the victim and Mayfield. Mayfield's were on the handrail leading down to the cabin, where you'd expect them to be.'

DC Jones leant forward on the table, claiming her boss's attention. 'Okay, there were no traces on or around the boat. But it seems hard to believe they didn't find anything outside Jarvis's mobile home. Tyre marks or footprints. I seem to recall that was rough ground around there.'

'All forensics found,' Lambert said, 'were his landlord's more recent footprints. Between the time of Jarvis's death and him finding the body, there had been two days of heavy rain. Any traces may have been washed clean.'

Ellis said, 'Either that or the killer's clever enough not to leave any traces. Nothing too unusual in that, is there? These days—'

'But,' Jones interjected, 'if he'd been wearing something like latex gloves, or any kind of gloves, that would have looked pretty suspicious to the victims.'

Lambert smiled. 'Earlier on I joked to Debbie about the killer saying something like his dermatitis was playing him up, but there could be an element of truth in that.'

'Then he's offered a beer,' Wallace added. 'And he doesn't open it because he knows enough about DNA in saliva. Or it was simply because he doesn't want it to look like the victim had a visitor who knew him.'

Almost as if he was talking to himself, Lambert spoke softly. 'The killer arrives at his intended victim's place, presumably by car, and he's probably masquerading as another sex offender. He has a bag with him, inside of which is concealed the weapon, but his victims think he has something for them. Maybe youngsters' addresses from the internet. He's offered a beer, which he doesn't open. Presumably he entices them to open and look in the bag which he has placed on the floor. While they bend over to look inside, he knocks them unconscious. When they come round, they discover they've been stripped and trussed up, and then he tortures them by pouring sulphuric acid on their genitals. Incidentally, the post mortem result on Titmus revealed

THE WRECKING BAR

that he died from a heart attack, probably brought about by the excessive burning pain from the sulphuric acid.'

'So why the head injuries if the victim's already dead?' Wallace asked.

'Presumably,' Lambert answered, 'that's his MO, which Debbie suggested earlier might have something to do with a frenzied crime following an abuse. Possibly an unsolved from years ago.'

'Debbie's already checked with HOLMES,' Ellis said, 'and there's no match.'

Debbie Jones gestured by turning her hands palms up as she looked at Lambert. 'So what about this case not being straightforward?'

'Yeah,' Wallace agreed. 'A revenge motive with dozens of suspects. Maybe hundreds. Seems pretty straightforward so far.'

Lambert took a long swig of beer before speaking. 'Titmus and Mayfield were paroled at roughly the same time, just over two years ago. And Jarvis Thomas had been at large for a lot longer. So whoever had committed these crimes waited a long time to get their revenge.'

'And all this kicked off with the *Sun* revelations,' Ellis said.

'It goes back further than that, Tony.'

'The TV documentary?'

Lambert nodded. 'And now this TV researcher who worked on the documentary has been charged with downloading child porn. Even the newspapers have picked up on the connection. So I think tomorrow I'll have a word with him and see where it takes us.'

Ellis's mouth twisted into a lopsided smile. 'He'll have the gentlemen of the press camped out on his doorstep.'

'That happened on Thursday. Hopefully they'll have got their story and photos by now. And I think first thing Monday I need to appeal via the media for anyone who might identify the purchaser of the wrecking bar bought at Llanelli B & Q.'

Wallace put on a glum expression. 'Yeah, that was a bloody bind. The guy who sold it him turns out to be a retard.'

Jones glared at him. 'Kevin!'

'What?'

'You can't use words like that these days to describe someone with a disability.'

Lambert smiled thinly and shook his head. Wallace still had a hell of a lot to learn. He pushed his empty pint glass towards him.

'Your round I believe, Kevin.'

Twelve

He moved the curtain a fraction and peered through the crack. Earlier on there had been two photographers hanging around. These were the ones hoping for something a little bit extra. The others got what they came for two nights ago: photos of him running from the car, hands hiding his face, scrambling to get the key in the door, the whirr, click and flash of a whole barrage of paparazzi as he slammed the front door closed.

Now the street was quiet outside and there didn't appear to be any photographers or reporters lurking about. The sky was black with just a faint glimmer of pink from where the sun had disappeared as night descended rapidly.

Even though the last remaining photographer had gone, he was still a prisoner in his own home. The neighbours would have heard all about it. How the hell was he going to get out? He'd eventually run out of food. And drink. He needed a drink now. Christ, did he need it!

What the hell could he do? He could try sending her a text from his mobile. He couldn't risk phoning, it was out of the question. But in all the time since he'd been released and allowed to come home, surely she could have found time to ring him. So why hadn't she rung or even sent him a message? Perhaps she believed all of it was true and was cutting him loose.

After he'd sent her a brief text, asking her to call him urgently, he went into the kitchen and poured himself a large single malt whisky, adding plenty of ice. He went back into the living room, sank heavily on to an easy chair and swallowed a large amount of cleansing alcohol.

He surveyed his living room with sadness. He'd been happy here, and enjoyed seeing the house gradually taking shape. He remembered the first time he saw the cottage just over two years ago, how it became love at first sight. It was on the small side, and should have been part of a terrace of similar cottages, but was separated from the terrace by a wide lane and right of way to a public footpath at the back, and was detached. Seeing it for the first time from the outside, he knew at once he was going to make an offer on it, as long as the inside was in reasonable shape.

And the cottage was more than just a residence. It had become their love nest, with afternoons or evenings full of passion, followed by such contentment, never thinking it would end, and often making plans for the future, when she would eventually be his.

Now all that had vanished, leaving him with nothing but empty, negative emotions. His self-pity grew as he sipped his drink and thought about the pleasures of the past. He finished the whisky, returned to the kitchen and poured himself another. Back in the living room, he peered through a gap in the curtains. Everything was quiet and peaceful outside; exactly as it was before the press pack descended. Having got their sensational pictures, the paparazzi had vanished into the night, and the Sunday newspapers had already gone to bed with tomorrow's scandal.

Even though the nights were quite chilly now, he loved going out to the garden for as long as he could stand the cold. And, as it was dark, he thought he might sit out there undisturbed and drink himself into oblivion without bothering about the temperature.

He never locked the side gate; there was no need in this district. And the reporters and photographers hadn't attempted to enter the back garden, probably because of the privacy laws, even though the story was considered to be in the public interest.

But for now he could venture outside, perhaps for the last time. Daytime was out of the question, as the public right of way at the back overlooked the garden. Now he was imprisoned, suffering a shameful banishment from society, and would eventually have to move from the district.

The back door was through the kitchen and he picked up the whisky bottle on his way through. He opened the door and stepped outside, breathing the sweet smell of damp grass.

A dark shadow caught his eye, and he was aware of a swift rustling sound and a swish as something painful screeched through his brain, and the bottle of whisky fell from his grasp with a crash.

***

An intense pain beat in his head as he came round. He wanted to take a deep gulp of air through his mouth but found it difficult to breathe. His mouth was obstructed by something sticky and the plastic smell was nauseating. As he forced open his eyes, with no memory of what had happened, he found he was staring into the face of his captor.

At first he was puzzled. Why was this happening to him? And then he realized he was tied to one of his upright chairs and he was stark naked. Why had he been stripped? He couldn't understand what was going on. Suddenly, the cold understanding of his predicament stirred the fear inside him and his body began to shake uncontrollably. He tried to speak, but the gag was too tight, and all that he could hear were his own muffled cries of terror.

He saw his captor had a holdall bag at his feet, out of which he took a large metal bar which he placed on the floor. Jesus Christ! He remembered the murders of those men on the news. Beaten to death with a metal bar. And this man thought he was one of them. Jesus! No! If only he could speak. Tell him!

This is a mistake!

Why are you doing this?

The man wore surgical gloves, and his movements were precise, like a surgeon preparing for an operation. Bending over, taking a bottle out of the bag and unscrewing the top.

What the hell was that? Some sort of liquid.

And then he realized what was about to happen, and why he was naked.

Dear God! No!

If only he'd give him the chance to speak, he could tell him. Tell him he was wrong. So wrong. But all he could hear were his own cries of fear, muffled and useless as he tried to signal with his eyes that it was all a mistake.

Moving closer now. Tilting the bottle. Getting ready to pour.

Please, dear God! Please! No!

Thirteen

The banal chatter of a radio presenter dragged Lambert from an alcohol-heavy sleep. He blinked and stared at the radio alarm. Seven o'clock, on the dot. His brain was fuzzy as he struggled to recall recent events. So much had happened in such a short space of time. And he couldn't even remember setting the alarm the previous night. Following the discussion at the Cockett Inn, he had returned to his own local in the Mumbles area and continued boozing until closing time, which he now regretted, especially as he needed to continue the investigation, Sunday or not.

He groaned as he swung himself out of bed, and then slipped into his dressing gown before going into the bathroom and turning on the bath taps. While it was running he made himself strong fresh coffee, returned to the bathroom to turn off the taps, and went into the living room.

For days now he hadn't checked the emails on his laptop, which lay sleek and anachronistic on top of the late-1940s heavy oak dining table in a flat furnished by a landlord with a taste for post-war austerity.

While he switched on the laptop and waited for it to boot up, he sipped his coffee and tried to focus his thoughts on the investigation, hoping that, as sometimes happened, a troubled sleep and a bombardment of ideas would pay dividends. But all he felt this morning was a muddled, washed-out feeling, and he almost wished he'd never chosen policing as a career.

He clicked on to Internet Explorer and saw there were ten emails waiting to be read. He opened them up and there was one which immediately caught his eye. It was from his sister's husband in Australia. The message had been sent five hours ago, about lunchtime that side of the world. There was an attachment, but first he clicked open the message and read:

Chapter Thirteen

Dear Harry

I'm sorry if this comes as a shock. I don't know if Angela had told you of her illness, but for the past six months she was having chemotherapy for cancer, which worked for a while. Then the cancer spread to her liver, and she went rapidly downhill after that. I'm sorry to have to tell you that Angela died yesterday.

I know you two haven't been close over the years, other than exchanging the occasional card, but I'm sure you would want to know.

If it's any consolation, she died peacefully here in her home, surrounded by her friends.

Of course, other than you, she had no family, but her friends were very loyal, and I think of myself as her closest friend as well as her loyal husband and the only true family she could relate to, and I shall miss her terribly. Sadly, we were never blessed with children.

The funeral is on Tuesday. If you want to telegraph flowers and a message, I've attached the address details to this email.

Once again, sorry to be the bearer of bad news, and I wish you luck for the future.

Gary.

Lambert stared at the screen, his mind numb and unmoved by the message, which was about a woman he had never known; a total stranger. His thoughts were clouded by something so nebulous that he could feel nothing but a distant sadness for the brother-in-law he had never met.

After closing down his laptop, he took his mug of coffee with him to finish in the bath. As he lay trying to soak off the dirty, unwashed feeling from a restless night and investigating mind-blowing crimes, he thought about Angela, knowing the truth about his sister would forever elude him. It pained him to think about it and he screwed his eyes closed. The warmth of the bath water brought him little comfort as he thought about her, wondering if she might have confided to her husband about the past and her relationship with their father. But he knew he would never get in touch. All he and Gary had in common was his sister. And now she was gone. There would be no point in contacting him. Ever.

***

As soon as he arrived at the road in Cowbridge in which Mark Yalding lived, Lambert took great care to park a little way away from his house. The houses in the street were only on one side, and where Lambert was parked on the opposite side was a wire fence bordering allotments. On the far side of the allotment, Lambert could see a man in khaki shorts and a blue vest digging with a fork.

He didn't get out of the car immediately, but sat watching and waiting, just in case there were reporters still keeping an eye on the place. But all seemed to be quiet.

He switched off the engine and watched the house for a moment. About ten or fifteen yards in front of him was a parked Honda Civic, and in front of that was a Land Rover Freelander, parked diagonally opposite Yalding's house. The road sloped, giving Lambert's Mercedes more height, so that he could observe the Land Rover over the height of the Honda; but he couldn't make out if anyone was inside it, mainly because of the height of the four-by-four and its spare tyre on the back. But something, maybe it was a gut feeling, told him to sit tight and wait.

It was another cloudless day, and now that he'd switched the engine off along with the air conditioning, the sun's rays burnt through the glass and the temperature began to rise rapidly. He clicked the ignition key forward and let the window down.

His thoughts on the drive over to Cowbridge had been mainly about Angela and his father, so he had given little consideration as to how he intended to interview Yalding. Now he thought about it, he realized that if the TV researcher had all along protested his innocence, however far fetched and unlikely his story was, he would in all probability be open to talking about his dilemma.

Still no sign of life from the Land Rover. Perhaps it belonged to someone from one of the other cottages. Lambert moved to open the door.

He froze, hoping whoever was getting out of the Land Rover didn't look back and see him. And then she emerged, walking hesitantly towards Yalding's cottage.

She was blonde, and he guessed she could have been in her late forties or early fifties maybe. She was what Lambert would describe as petite, with beautifully slim legs in tight blue jeans that looked brand new, and she wore a light blue T-shirt with some sort of design on the front, but she was too far away for him to see the motif clearly. He couldn't see the colour of her eyes, but her bright red lipstick seemed to accentuate a pale skin. Even from a distance, Lambert could see she was attractive.

She stopped at Yalding's gate and looked around tentatively before deciding to approach his front door along the short, narrow path. With more determination now, she raised the brass knocker and knocked twice.

Chapter Thirteen

Lambert heard the clacking sound and watched as she stepped back away from the door and looked expectantly at the windows, also craning her neck back to look at the upstairs windows.

After waiting for less than a minute, she knocked twice again, but still no one answered. He saw her delve into her jeans pocket and bring out a mobile phone, and watched her scrolling for a number. She put the phone to her ear and listened for a minute. He watched carefully to see if her lips moved, but she abandoned the call without leaving a message and tucked the mobile back into her pocket.

Taking one last, and clearly hopeful, look back at the cottage, she crossed the road and got back into her Land Rover. Then she did a three-point turn and drove back past Lambert's Mercedes. He ducked out of sight.

As soon as she had driven away, Lambert got out of the car and hurried towards Yalding's cottage. There didn't seem much point in knocking on the door the same as Yalding's visitor had, so he went straight to the side gate and tried it. It wasn't locked, and he swung it open quickly and hurried around the back.

He stopped at the back door, wondering whether or not he should try entering. He thought he could smell alcohol, and his attention was drawn to some broken glass that looked like a broken whisky bottle that had been dropped near the door.

A tremor of shallow breath rippled in his chest as excitement and fear surged through his body. He thought about entering but stood frozen to the spot, staring at the back door, almost as if he expected it to open of its own accord. His mouth felt dry and he was fearful of what he almost certainly knew he would find, although a slightly more optimistic voice in his head told him he could be wrong.

But first he went back to his car and fetched a pair of latex gloves which he kept in the glove compartment. When he returned to the rear of the cottage he didn't hesitate. After putting on the gloves, he turned the doorknob on the back door and pushed. It wasn't locked. He eased it open and entered the kitchen.

He took a deep breath, hoping to overcome his fear, which was uncoiling in his stomach like a spring. He crossed the kitchen, his eyes quickly scanning the work surface with its clutter of utensils, but not really taking it in as he stared at the open door leading to the living room, dreading the horror of what he knew he was about to face. As he walked cautiously towards the open door, he could almost imagine he was being beckoned by a malignant force, and his leg movements felt unreal, as if they belonged to someone else. But this time he felt no nausea; no waves of panic. In spite of the bloody mess on the carpet, and the naked body trussed up in the chair, genitals mutilated, and brains spilling out from the battered head, he felt he could cope this time.

He knew he'd have to call headquarters soon and get the crime scene people out here. But first he needed to get details of that last telephone call before someone else rang. He avoided looking directly at the corpse, and his eyes darted around the room, focusing on a cordless phone, fitted to its cradle, on a mahogany occasional table under the window.

It was a small room, and the phone was within easy reach. Avoiding the pool of blood on the carpet, he walked over, grabbed the phone and dialled 1-4-7-1. Right away the automatic female voice told him the last call was made the previous evening at 17.00 hours and the caller had withheld the number. Either someone had called via a company switchboard or the number had been deliberately withheld. Perhaps it was the former, another reporter trying to contact Yalding from a newspaper office.

Lambert replaced the phone in its cradle and thought about the woman who had visited a few minutes ago. She must either have been calling someone or else ringing him on his mobile.

Then the image suddenly struck him. His brain must have automatically registered it when he entered, and he dashed back into the kitchen. There was the victim's mobile phone, lying on the surface near the inbuilt hob, surrounded by a corkscrew, half-empty bottle of red wine, a tray of melted ice cubes and the screw-top from the whisky bottle.

He picked the phone up, pressed the main menu button, went to the log and missed calls section and clicked the button. The last call was from someone called Rhi, timed at less than ten minutes ago.

He took out his pen and a small notebook from his breast pocket and copied the name and number. Then he clicked off the mobile and left it where he'd found it.

Breathing deeply to calm himself, he went out into the garden for some fresh air, and called headquarters with details of the crime. Pretty soon this quiet area would be swarming with police, and not long after it would be the focus of the entire UK.

Lambert thought back to Friday lunchtime, when he received Marden's call, followed by three brutal murder scenes in less than forty-eight hours. It had to be some sort of record.

Fourteen

While Lambert waited for SOCO to arrive, he thought about Yalding's recent visitor.

Rhi!

It was a strange name, sounding more like a nickname or pet name. Or maybe it was short for something. Rhiannon, perhaps? A traditional Welsh name, and one that might have inspired the song by Fleetwood Mac.

He punched in her number on his mobile. It rang for some time, and he realized she was probably driving her vehicle, unless she lived close by. He didn't think leaving a message on her voice mail was a good idea and was about to hang up when he heard the phone click, the sound of a car engine and her voice, urgent and high-pitched.

'Hello! Who is it?'

'Is that Rhiannon?'

'Yes, yes! Who is that?'

He'd guessed right about the name.

'This is Detective Inspector Harry Lambert of South Wales Police.'

'What?' she yelled.

'I want to talk to you about Mark Yalding.'

There was a slight pause before she said, 'Just a minute. I'm going to pull over.'

Lambert smiled to himself, wondering whether to admonish her for using a mobile while driving, then thought better of it. After all, in the great scheme of things, what did a crime like talking on a phone while driving matter when weighed against brutal serial killings?

When she came back on the phone, she said, 'What's this about?'

'I was hoping you could tell me?'

'I don't know what you're talking about.'

THE WRECKING BAR

Lambert cleared his throat softly. 'I want to talk to you about your friend, Mark Yalding.'

There was another pause before she said, 'He's not really a friend as such. I do know him, of course.'

Lambert decided to cut to the chase. 'You were round at his place about fifteen minutes ago. I saw you there, and you also tried to ring him.' She was silent at the other end. 'Hello? Are you still there?'

'Yes, I'm still here. But what's this all about?'

'I need to talk to you urgently. Give me your address and I'll come over.'

'You can't come to my place.' There was a tremor of panic in her voice. 'You really can't. Look, I'll make some excuse later today and meet you somewhere. A café or a pub.'

'Do you know the Wheelwright's Arms, about halfway between Cowbridge and Bridgend?'

'I'll find it.'

'Can you meet me there at, say, two o'clock?'

'I'll try.'

'I think you need to do more than try. Unless you want me to pay you a visit.'

Her voice suddenly became strident. 'Look… all right… I'll be there. But how will I recognize you?'

'Don't worry about it. I'll recognize you.'

A distant wail of sirens alerted him to the approach of police cars screaming towards the crime scene. He closed the phone hurriedly, before she heard them. Obviously she didn't know her friend was dead, and Lambert wanted to be the one to confront her with the news, judge her reaction and find out what her relationship was with the victim.

And, of course, discover her identity.

***

'More of the same,' was Hughie's comment. 'The third in less than two days. Although, strictly speaking, the one in Carmarthen had been dead for a week. How come you found this one?'

Hughie studied Lambert carefully as he answered.

'I came out here to interview him in relation to the investigation. There was no reply from the front door, so I came round the back and found the broken whisky bottle. It seemed suspicious, so I stuck on a pair of gloves, tried the door and found it was unlocked.'

'And that's when you hit on yet another dead paedophile.'

CHAPTER FOURTEEN

Lambert shook his head. 'There's no evidence the victim was a paedophile. He's got no record of any sex offences. In fact, he's got no police record of any sort.'

'What about his arrest for downloading child pornography on the internet?'

Lambert shifted out of the way of one of the SOCO team, and there was another flash from the police photographer as the corpse was photographed from another angle.

'It seems odd,' Lambert said, and left it at that. 'Mind if I take a look upstairs?'

'Be my guest.'

Lambert started to leave the room, and then turned back as he thought of something else.

'Hughie, you searched through the victim's trouser pockets yet?'

'Nothing in them. Empty.'

Lambert nodded thoughtfully, went out into the small hallway and climbed the narrow stairs. On the wall were framed photographs of various television productions, some of which showed the victim with his arms about an actor or a crew member, smiling and confident.

Lambert stopped and studied the victim's face. Yalding was in his late thirties, he guessed, had slightly receding, pepper and salt hair, and a pleasant, boyish face. He looked too wholesome to be a man taking initial steps towards child abuse, but then Lambert knew child abusers didn't always come from the same mould.

He carried on up the stairs. At the top, to the left and back of the cottage, was a reasonable size bathroom. There were two more rooms, and the first was a small bedroom being used as an office. The computer workstation had a flat-screen monitor on it, and an all-in-one scanner, printer and copier, but the tower computer was missing, having been confiscated by the police.

Lambert looked through the first workstation drawer but found it contained mostly spare ink cartridges and items of stationery, and very little else of interest. But the contents of the next drawer down was more interesting as it contained scraps of paper and notepads with names, phone numbers, websites and email addresses. Hopefully, there might be some revealing information here, and because all this private paperwork wasn't too near the body, Lambert didn't think it needed bagging by forensics. He could get Tony and Kevin to sift through this lot, to see what they could find. But what he was looking for right now was something far more personal, and he thought he might find it in the main bedroom.

As he entered Yalding's bedroom, Lambert smelled stale sweat locked in the airless room. The window was closed tight and clothes lay strewn across the floor, but the rest of the room appeared to be reasonably neat, perhaps indicating that Yalding's recently distraught state had made him careless in his hygiene. But what Lambert was most interested in checking were the bedside tables either side of the double bed, one of which – the one furthest from the door – was empty. On the other table lay some loose change, a bunch of keys and a packet of chewing gum. But there was no wallet. Not in the trousers the victim was wearing, nor on the bedside table with the rest of the contents of his pocket.

Lambert moved to the built-in wardrobe with a single sliding door that had been left open and rummaged among the victim's jackets, searching for his wallet, although he doubted he'd find anything.

Having been through the victim's entire wardrobe and finding nothing, Lambert returned to the living room, and found Dave, the crime scene manager, talking to Hughie about the press pack that had already begun to arrive in the street outside.

'With the other two murders,' Lambert interrupted, 'we found wallets and we were able to identify the victims immediately. But we've found no wallet on the victim this time. And I've searched most of the house and found nothing.'

Dave raised a finger to make a point. 'Not all blokes carry wallets. Some just keep their folding stuff in a pocket.'

'So where is the folding stuff belonging to the victim? He's emptied the contents of his trouser pockets upstairs by the bed, and there was only some loose change. There's no paper money, and there are no credit or debit cards.'

Hughie scratched his cheek thoughtfully with his gloved hand, making a rubbery sound. 'Are you suggesting the perpetrator stole the wallet this time?'

'Yes, although I don't think the motive was robbery. I think the killer knew there was something in the wallet he didn't want us to find.'

Lambert's mobile rang and he stepped out into the kitchen to answer it. It was DCS Marden.

'So you just happen to discover another body, Inspector.'

Lambert smiled to himself. It was typical of Marden to get straight to the point.

'That's right,' Lambert agreed. Not much else he could add to that. He imagined Marden's irritation sweeping across the airwaves.

'Would you care to elaborate?'

Lambert gave him the same story as he'd told Hughie, but added the details about the woman visitor and how he had phoned her.

'So what made you decide to interview this Mark Yalding?'

Chapter Fourteen

'Because I think he's deeply connected to this case. And my finding his body confirms that.'

There was a slight pause before Marden grudgingly agreed. 'Yes, well, good work, Harry.' He cleared his throat before continuing. 'I'm on my way over as soon as. I'm going to deal with the press on this.'

Lambert knew Marden pretended to find this a chore but suspected he rather enjoyed the attention. He imagined the chief super probably had video and DVD copies of his television appearances. Or was he being unnecessarily harsh?

'Could I make a suggestion, sir?'

'Yes, what is it?'

'The murder weapon that was purchased at B & Q, Llanelli—'

Marden interrupted. 'I'd already planned an appeal for witnesses to identify the purchaser, since you mentioned it yesterday.'

'But I was going to suggest that you get someone to buy a copy of the weapon from a DIY store to show it on TV. It might help to jog a few memories.'

'That's a good idea. And I hope to get to the crime scene within the next half hour. Meanwhile, if you can help it, avoid talking to the press.'

Lambert had no intention of doing so; it was something he always tried to avoid.

'And before I speak to them,' Marden continued, 'you can give me everything you know so far.'

'Will do. And then I'll need to get over to that pub for two o'clock, meet with this woman, find out who she is and her connection to Yalding.'

Marden sounded surprised. 'You arranged to interview her in a pub? Why didn't you get her address?'

'She was reluctant to give it.'

Marden's voice rose indignantly. 'Sod that for a game of soldiers.'

'I suspect she might be married and doesn't want her husband knowing about her and Yalding. Sounds like they might have been lovers.'

'And she'll know he's dead before long.'

'That's why I want to tell her myself, to see her reaction, before she sees it on the news. I'd like to take DC Debbie Jones with me.'

'Woman to woman, and all that?'

'Exactly.'

'What about Sergeant Ellis?'

'I was just about to ring him and Kevin Wallace. The victim's got a lot of private correspondence in his study which I'd like them to go through with a fine-tooth comb.'

THE WRECKING BAR

'Okay. I'd better get moving. I'll see you in a little while.'

Lambert ended the call and returned to the living room.

'Hughie,' he said, 'if a wallet turns up when you've given the house a thorough going over, would you let me know?'

'If you haven't found it having looked in all the usual places, what makes you think—'

'I'm not expecting it to turn up,' Lambert interrupted. 'I think it's been taken for a reason.'

Hughie, holding tweezers and picking a tiny thread from the thigh of the corpse, said, 'I might posit the opinion that the killer on this occasion has the same revenge motive, but being a bit broke decides to rob his victim.'

'Then why didn't he take Titmus's wallet? That had over a hundred quid in it. No, I think there was something in Yalding's wallet the killer didn't want us to find.'

Hughie had stopped listening; he was too busy bagging minute items of evidence, his tongue poking from his mouth like a child. Sick of looking towards the mutilated corpse, and starting to feel nauseous, Lambert turned away.

Hughie noticed and said, 'Do this often enough and you get used to it. I can guarantee that by the time justice catches up with the other sex offenders, you won't give it another thought.'

Lambert knew Hughie had a point, but it didn't seem to work that way. However many violent crimes he had witnessed, it didn't seem to get any better. The inevitable reaction was depression, loss of appetite, sleepless nights and too much alcohol. All of which compounded the problem.

And now Hughie had reminded him that possibly there was more to come.

There were still three more sex offenders out there who were targets. And where were they? Could they be found before the killer struck again?

'There are two ways of looking at this,' Hughie said, interrupting his thoughts.

Lambert braced himself for one of the forensic man's sick observations.

'These homicides play murder – no pun intended – with your social life, but they do offer a fair bit of overtime.'

Fifteen

DCS Marden arrived at the scene as he said he would, exactly half an hour after speaking with Lambert on the phone. In the back garden, Lambert gave him the details and latest developments and thoughts on the case, and then left hurriedly by the side entrance. Beyond the police barricade, crowds of photographers, journalists and a few television reporters and cameramen surged forward, jostling each other and shouting questions.

'What's happening in there?

'How was Yalding killed?'

'Have you any comments to make about how the case is developing?'

'Is there a serial killer on the loose?'

'Was the victim another paedophile?'

Ignoring the questions as he pushed his way through the press, Lambert stopped briefly and gave them a strained smile before he spoke.

'Detective Chief Superintendent Marden will be with you in just a moment, and he'll be pleased to give you the details and answer your questions. Now if you'll excuse me, I have to dash.'

He barged his way ill-temperedly through the throng and headed for his car. A local reporter who recognized him called, 'Inspector Lambert! Where are you off to right now?'

None of your business, he thought, as he got into his car.

He turned the car round and headed for Swansea, putting his foot down as it was now almost noon and there were some things he needed to do back at Cockett. But it was Sunday, and the Sunday drivers seemed to be out in force. He crawled along behind an elderly man until he found an opportunity to overtake.

When he eventually arrived at Cockett Police Station, he immediately requested the arrest and interview tape of Mark Yalding. Although Marden

THE WRECKING BAR

had given him a transcript of the interview, he wanted to hear the interview itself. The transcript wouldn't give pauses, hesitations and the sometimes dry voice and tremor of the suspect. From hearing Yalding talking, he would get a better impression of what the man was like.

He went into the incident room, and while he waited for one of the uniforms to bring him the tape, he boiled the kettle, switched on one of the computers, made himself an instant coffee and sat by the desk with the opened-up computer. He'd just accessed his Inbox when a uniformed officer knocked and entered, hurried over to Lambert's desk and gave him the tape. Lambert signed for it, giving the young constable a cursory, 'Thanks, son,' then clicked the tape into the machine and sat back to listen.

Conducting the interview was DI Geoff Ambrose and DS Mary Leigh. Also present was Yalding's solicitor Graham Chapman-Smith. The interview was conducted at 13.30 on the previous Thursday.

DI Ambrose got straight to the point.

Ambrose:	Mr Yalding, have you heard of Operation Ore?
Yalding:	Of course I have.
Ambrose:	You seem clear on that, yet there are many people who wouldn't know anything about it.
Yalding:	As you probably know, I work in television, and part of our remit is making documentaries, so we are very involved in current affairs.
Ambrose:	So it won't surprise you to learn that the FBI has traced a download of child pornography to your computer, paid for with your credit card. How do you explain that?
Yalding:	I can't. I know it sounds ridiculous, but it wasn't me.
Ambrose:	Are you telling us it was someone else using your computer?
Yalding:	No. I mean… I don't know.
Ambrose:	Do you live alone?
Yalding:	Yes… yes, I live by myself.
Ambrose:	You seem a bit uncertain about that.
Yalding:	No, no, of course I do. I definitely live on my own.
Ambrose:	And so you have no way of explaining how those images came to be on your computer.
Yalding:	Absolutely none.
Ambrose:	You made a documentary about a paedophile ring in South Wales a while back. Was downloading child pornography anything to do with your work?

Yalding:	No. That documentary was in the planning stages at least nine months ago – maybe longer – and we shot it back in February.
Ambrose:	So you had no legitimate reason to download that pornography.
Yalding:	Look, Inspector, no one has a legitimate reason *ever* to download child pornography. But I have no idea how this has happened. Someone must have set me up?
Ambrose:	Set you up, sir? How is that possible?
Yalding:	I don't know. Maybe... maybe someone hacked into my computer. These computer geeks, they can do all kinds of things.
Ambrose:	Well, I'm not an expert myself, sir, but these images are on your hard drive. I don't think I've ever heard of a hacker sending website images to someone else's computer hard drive.
Yalding:	Well, these... these things are changing daily. As soon as a virus is eliminated another one takes its place.
Ambrose:	But we're not talking about viruses. These are images downloaded from a website and paid for with your credit card.
Yalding:	That's just not possible. I've only used my credit cards in restaurants in the past month.
Ambrose:	You're sure about that?
Yalding:	Yes. No. I did fly to Paris three weeks ago and I used a credit card for that.
Ambrose:	How many credit cards do you have?
Yalding:	Well, I think... um... I think I've got four of them.
Ambrose:	You don't seem that certain.
Yalding:	Only because I paid one off and cancelled it, and did a balance transfer on another.
Ambrose:	Have you used any of your credit cards for online purchases?
Yalding:	Well, yes, I have... in the past.
Ambrose:	And for what sort of services?
Yalding:	Not services. Goods. Products.
Ambrose:	Such as?
Yalding:	Um... a few DVDs and CDs. That sort of thing.
Ambrose:	What types of credit cards do you have? Visa or Mastercard?
Yalding:	I have, I think, one Visa card now, and three Mastercards. Or is it the other way round? No, no, I'm certain I've got more Mastercards than Visa. Not the other way round.

THE WRECKING BAR

Ambrose:	The child pornography was paid for by a Mastercard in your name. How do you explain that?
Yalding:	Oh God! This is a nightmare. I swear to you I haven't done this. It must be someone else… someone else who's responsible.
Ambrose:	Any idea who that might be, sir?
Yalding:	No, I don't. But it must be someone… someone who got into my house.
Ambrose:	Do you mean someone who might break in?
Yalding:	Well, yes, maybe. While I wasn't there.
Ambrose:	OK, let's just suppose someone did use your computer when you weren't there. They would also have had to use one of your credit cards. Do you carry them around in your wallet or do you leave them lying around at home?
Yalding:	Well, I keep them in my wallet. But maybe I'd left one by the phone.
Ambrose:	And why would you do that?
Yalding:	Well, maybe to make a payment that was due.
Ambrose:	But you can't remember for certain if you did or not?
Yalding:	Well, I think I must have done. What other explanation can there be?
Ambrose:	I have to have a password or a security name for my credit cards. Usually it's your mother's maiden name. Have you any idea how someone would know yours, Mr Yalding?
Yalding:	They wouldn't need to know it. You only need your mother's maiden name or a secure number when you contact the credit card company to make a transfer or get account information. If you make online purchases you don't need any of that. Just the card number and the three letter code on the strip on the back. If anyone had my card, they could make an online purchase.
Ambrose:	That's assuming someone had your card. And also assuming they had access to your home and computer. Does anyone have a key to your home?
Yalding:	I… No, of course not.
Ambrose:	I just thought a girlfriend perhaps.
Yalding:	No. No one has a key to my place.
Ambrose:	You live alone, but do you have a girlfriend, Mr Yalding?
Yalding:	I… no, I don't have a girlfriend at the moment. But I'm not…
Ambrose:	Not what, sir?

Yalding:	I'm not... I mean, I've got normal... I'm a straight bloke.
Ambrose:	Do you mean straight as in the opposite of gay?
Yalding:	Yes, I'm just a normal bloke.
Ambrose:	But not in any relationship of any sort?
Yalding:	Not right now. No.
Ambrose:	How long?
Yalding:	Sorry?
Ambrose:	How long is it since you were in a relationship?
Yalding:	I broke up with my girlfriend two years ago.
Ambrose:	Was there a reason for the break-up?
Yalding:	These things happen.
Ambrose:	And apart from someone breaking and entering your home and happening to find a credit card conveniently waiting for them, you have no other explanation as to how these horrendous child pornography images came to be on your computer?
Yalding:	Look, I've told you, I can't explain how they got there. But I haven't done anything. I promise. It's all a mistake. And I wish there was a way out of this nightmare.
Ambrose:	Mr Yalding, I am terminating this interview, as I believe we have enough evidence for a prosecution.
Yalding:	No, you can't. Oh Christ! This is a nightmare...

Lambert clicked the tape off. Knowing Yalding's arrest and interview had happened on the Thursday, prior to the discovery of the two murders, Lambert could see that Ambrose obviously thought he had all the evidence he needed and, coupled with the suspect's lame excuses about some mysterious intruder in his home, felt he had enough to put forward a case for the CPS. A clear-cut case, one which he could put behind him as he and his family set off on their Florida holiday.

While he waited for DC Jones, he thought about Yalding's interview. It was clear-headed and coherent in most parts. Not that this meant a great deal. Many sex offenders were intelligent, and most were cunning and manipulative. But Yalding, when almost handed a lifeline by Ambrose asking him if downloading child porn might have had anything to do with research, had actually refuted this, and even admitted that downloading child porn was inexcusable whatever the reason.

Then there were the slight hesitations. Like when he was asked if he lived alone. Ambrose had picked him up on that, commenting on him not

THE WRECKING BAR

sounding certain. And that's when Yalding emphatically denied it, almost as if he was protecting someone.

Could it be the woman Lambert saw that morning at Yalding's cottage?

Then there was the business about the credit card, for which Yalding had no credible explanation. But still he emphatically denied using a credit card. Was this because he'd been caught in the act and thought it better to play dumb? Or was it because he was genuinely confused?

The final hesitation in the interview, and a slightly more telling pause, came when Ambrose asked him if he had a girlfriend. Obviously he knew where the DI was going with this, so he protested his staunch heterosexuality.

From what he'd heard, Lambert was convinced that Yalding had lied to protect this Rhiannon woman.

He glanced at his watch. It was almost 12.30. DC Jones was due to arrive at any moment. He sipped his coffee and winced. Instant just didn't do it for him. The computer screen stared accusingly at him, reminding him that he needed to continue what he'd started, even though he knew he was going through the motions and doing what was expected of him. He opened up his brother-in-law's email, clicked on the attachment and got the address of the Sydney crematorium. Then he found an international florist on the internet and sent a wreath costing over £60. A lot of money for a pointless gesture. But the hardest part was writing the message of condolence. He made several attempts and eventually settled on a simple message:

'In memory of my dear sister, Angela, from her brother, Harry.'

As he completed the transaction, paying for it with his Virgin credit card, he reflected on how easy it was to buy goods or services online – all one needed was the card details, name and address. How easy was that?

'The traffic's bloody murder,' said a breathless DC Jones as she burst through the door.

Lambert looked up and smiled. 'Tell me about it. On the way here I got stuck behind a man who thought he was driving a bath chair to Lourdes.'

Jones laughed. 'That must be the same bloke I got stuck behind in the outside lane of the M4.' She spotted the florist's website before Lambert pressed Exit. 'Who's the lucky girl who's getting flowers?'

Lambert didn't think it was any of her concern and said rather brusquely, 'In this instance, not so lucky. My sister died yesterday and that was a wreath for the funeral.'

There was sudden stillness and coldness in the incident room. DC Jones's vulnerability was like an adolescent's as her face flushed and she stammered, 'I – I'm sorry.'

CHAPTER FIFTEEN

Feeling guilty for deliberately causing her embarrassment, Lambert cut in, 'You weren't to know, Debbie. I'm just going through the motions and doing what's expected of me. My sister left to live in Australia when I was thirteen-years-old and never came back.'

'Not even to visit?'

Lambert got up, shaking his head. 'A person I didn't know. A stranger that's just cost me sixty quid in flowers.'

Like a dog shaking off the wet, he gave her a sudden grin, which she interpreted as her boss's way of saying 'life goes on'.

'Come on, Debbie, we need to get on the road back to Cowbridge.'

'We're going to the crime scene?'

'No. There's someone we need to meet.'

'Where are we going?'

'To a pub. Life's not all work and no play, you know.'

***

During the drive to the Wheelwright's Arms, Lambert told Debbie about Yalding's female visitor and the conversation he had with her on the phone. After he'd finished, he asked, 'What does the name Rhiannon mean to you?'

'Well, I guess it's a good Welsh name. Apart from that...' She pouted and shrugged.

Lambert chuckled. 'Too young to remember Fleetwood Mac?'

'Oh, I think I've heard of them.'

'Philistine!'

She could have sworn he was flirting with her and wasn't sure if this was a good idea or not. One half of her liked the attention, and there was also the chance of job advancement from being favoured by the boss. On the other hand, it could be dangerous. If it went too far and she turned him down, that could lead to all kinds of complications. Far better to keep it on a professional level.

'What has this woman got to do with Fleetwood Mac?'

'Probably nothing. They had a bit of a hit with "Rhiannon" in the mid seventies. This woman would probably have been born in the early sixties. I'm only guessing, but I would put her age as late forties maybe.'

'So her parents chose the name because it was a traditional Welsh name, not because it was a song from a favourite band. Is that relevant in any way?'

'It might tell us something about her background. Her parents were probably quite well-to-do. Intellectuals. Cultured. A bit posh, maybe.'

'Because they chose a traditional Welsh name?'

'The name comes from *The Mabinogion*, an old Welsh book dating back centuries, and I think Rhiannon was a princess.'

'Have you ever read it?'

'I started it but didn't get very far. It's all that sword and sorcery nonsense, which I can't stand, literature or not. But my point is this: if this Rhiannon's parents had lived in a council house in the Valleys, she might have been called Sharon or Tracey. Names are sometimes great indicators of a person's background.'

'Is that why Jordan went back to being Katie Price?'

'Probably. Now she realizes all the chavs have adopted the name. I know that sounds like a generalisation – and it probably is when it comes to names like yours and mine. But a pound to a penny says that a pre-Fleetwood Mac Rhiannon comes from a very good family. And what about you, Debbie?'

The abrupt change confused her. 'What about me?'

'I've never asked you before: you're half Welsh and half Asian, yes?'

She wondered where this was heading.

'My father's Welsh. And my mother's father was Welsh, but her mother was Indian. My grandmother came from Bombay, now known as Mumbai.'

'So your mother's maiden name would have been Welsh rather than Indian?'

'Not unless you think Sinclair is Welsh.'

Lambert chuckled to himself.

'What's so funny?'

'I was just thinking how easy it is to find out a person's maiden name without them attaching any significance to it.'

'I'm not sure if I follow what you mean.'

'Hang on, Debbie, I think this is the turn-off.'

He started to brake before a turning on the right, with a signpost indicating that it was two miles to the next village, and a huge square board in the corner of a field, showing the Wheelwright's Arms was 100 yards from the main road.

The large pub was set back off the B road, up on a hill, with a car park at the front. It looked as if it had been converted into a pub rather than purpose built and might once have been the property of a rich landowner in the early part of the twentieth century. The beer garden at the side was fairly crowded, not only with families, as there was a play area for children, but also with serious drinkers who were able to smoke outside and sit beneath large mushroom-shaped gas heaters.

Lambert managed to find a space in the car park, letting Jones get out before he squeezed his Mercedes into a narrow gap between an enormous Toyota four-by-four and a Renault Espace.

As they walked towards the pub's entrance, Lambert said, 'Let's find a place to sit inside, shall we? And I think we've got time for a bite to eat. We've got forty-five minutes before she gets here.'

'That's *if* she turns up.'

'I think she will. She doesn't want us at her place for obvious reasons.'

'But we don't know where she lives.'

'We've got her first name and mobile number. It won't take much to find out.'

It seemed gloomy inside the pub, but that was probably because of the stark contrast between sunshine and a dark interior. The place was doing a roaring trade, and most of the customers being served at the bar were loading their drinks on to trays to take outside. Lambert found a corner table that was free and picked up a menu.

'I'll buy lunch,' he told Jones, glancing hurriedly at the menu. 'Ham, egg and chips'll do me.' He handed her the menu. 'What about you?'

'I'll have the same.'

'And what would you like to drink?'

'I'll have a soft drink. J2O or something similar.'

While Lambert ordered at the bar, Jones sat and thought about the murder of Yalding. She wondered how this Rhiannon would take the news. If Yalding was her lover, badly she guessed. Was this why Lambert wanted her along, as the more compassionate one of the two detectives, offering comfort and sympathy to the grieving lover?

As Lambert carried the drinks over, he saw the heavy frown on the young DC's face and guessed what she was thinking.

'I'm sorry, Debbie, but I need you to do the woman-to-woman bit and give her a shoulder to cry on. It's not going to be fun in such a public place. But as we can't go to her home, there's little we can do about that.'

She noticed how weary her boss seemed, the strain of too much death showing in the tiredness about his eyes and the pale, waxy texture of his skin.

She raised her glass. 'Cheers!'

'Yeah, cheers!'

She watched him knock back a good half of his pint of bitter, and was amazed to see the sudden recovery, as if the drink had pumped fresh life into him, and a bit of colour flooded back into his cheeks.

'So when are you going to tell her about the murder?' she said.

'After I've got enough information about Yalding and her relationship with him.'

The Wrecking Bar

***

While Tony Ellis thoroughly examined the contents of Yalding's desk upstairs in the cottage, Kevin Wallace went house-to-house knocking on doors, as did a uniformed constable in the opposite direction.

The first two cottages Wallace called at there was no reply. He made a note of the numbers so that he wouldn't overlook calling back, when hopefully there might be someone in. When he knocked at the third cottage, a dog began barking furiously. There was a long pause while he heard doors opening and closing and a voice reassuring the dog that all was well. And then the front door was opened by a short, elderly man, probably no taller than Ronnie Corbett and not dissimilar in looks. He smiled as he looked up at Wallace and the detective thought he saw a triumphant glint in his eyes.

'Ah! I wondered when you'd get around to it.'

'Sorry?'

'To ask the neighbours if they'd seen anything unusual; anything suspicious.'

'And have you?'

'I might have. Which begs the question: why didn't I approach you with what I know? Why have I waited for you to call on me?'

Wallace gritted his teeth impatiently. He was in no mood to play games.

'I really don't know, sir. But I'd be grateful if you could tell me if you've seen anything suspicious.'

'I lived in Cardiff most of my life. Remember that knife murder in Roath Park early one morning, when a young nurse was on her way to work an early shift?'

'No, I don't think I remember that one.'

'It must have been before your time. Back in 1978. I was a park keeper there. And although I wasn't working that early, I saw a suspicious-looking bloke hanging around at other times. So when I approached the police to tell them about it, know what they said?'

Even though he felt like throttling the little squirt, Wallace kept deadpan and shook his head.

'They said: "It's all right, sir. We've got everything in hand." They didn't want to know what I'd seen. They weren't interested. Consequently, they got the wrong bloke. A miscarriage of justice it was. He was let out in 1990 and probably got a huge compensation.'

Wallace let his breath out slowly, telling himself to keep calm.

'I think you'll find that police methods have changed for the better in recent years, sir.'

CHAPTER FIFTEEN

'Huh!' the man exclaimed with a laugh.

'So if you did see anything suspicious last night,' Wallace said, 'I'd be grateful if you could let me have the details.'

'I took Benjie – that's my dog – out for his constitutional a bit later than usual last night. Must have been about half-eleven. When I got back I noticed this white van parked almost opposite his house.'

Wallace felt a ripple of excitement in the pit of his stomach. 'And why was this unusual?'

'Because I know all the neighbours' cars, and nobody's got a small white van like that. Kerry up at number sixteen's got a large blue van, cos he's a mechanic, but no one else has got a van.'

'What time did you start out to walk the dog?'

'Just before half-eleven. I'd been watching a film on TV, otherwise I'd have taken Benjie earlier.'

'And was the van there when you started out?'

'No, it was there when I got back. That's why I noticed it. I thought it was strange arriving that late, seeing as it didn't belong to anyone in our road. And I thought there was someone sitting inside the van.'

'You saw someone?'

'I felt there was someone there. Then when I came indoors, I didn't put the light on and I went and peeked through the front window. That's when I saw him getting out of the van.'

Wallace felt the excitement rising in his chest.

'You saw someone? Where did he go?'

'I think he went to that Mark Yalding's cottage. He was going in that direction. I couldn't be certain from the angle I was looking.'

'This man: what did he look like?'

'Hard to tell. It was dark.'

'How tall d'you think he was?'

'I haven't a clue.'

'What about his hair colour?'

'He might have had dark hair. But all I could see was this man in the shadows, just a dark figure crossing the road. I only saw him for a few seconds, like. And he was carrying something.'

'A bag of some sort?'

'Yeah. It might have been one of those – um – sports bags.'

Wallace knew this had to be the killer. Trying not to show the excitement building inside him, he asked the man for his name.

'It's Williams. Ian Williams.'

'Thank you, Mr Williams, that's been a great help. We might require you to make a statement later on.'

Williams nodded and a smile played at the corners of his mouth. 'That was the killer, wasn't it?'

'It's possible,' Wallace replied.

'Go on. It has to be him. The white van man.' Williams chuckled to himself.

'What did you do,' Wallace asked, 'after you'd seen this man going towards Yalding's cottage?'

'Do? I just went to bed.'

'And thought no more about it?'

'Well, I never thought it was a murderer, did I? Otherwise I'd have been on to the police. Don't talk daft.'

'So who did you think this man might have been?'

'How the bloody hell should I know? It could have been a friend of Mr Yalding, coming to stay with him. That's why he had a bag.'

'Okay, Mr Williams, you've been a great help. We might be in touch later.'

As he walked away from the cottage, Wallace heard the smugness in Williams's voice as he called after him:

'Good job you come looking for me then, wasn't it?'

As Wallace hurried back, ducking under the police tape surrounding Yalding's cottage, reporters and photographers surged forward, and he 'no commented' them with a wave of a hand.

But one of the reporters, a shrewd operator who had observed Wallace talking for quite some time to one of the victim's neighbours, thought he'd wait until the rest of the pack were distracted by the statement from Detective Chief Superintendent Marden before making his move.

***

They had only just finished their meal when Lambert spotted her entering. She hovered nervously near the entrance, eyes scanning the tables, clearly hoping someone would approach her soon.

Lambert rose and moved towards her. 'Rhiannon?'

She nodded, and Lambert thought he detected fear in her eyes, a foreboding of bad news.

'I'm sorry,' she said. 'You told me your name on the phone but...'

'It's Detective Inspector Lambert, South Wales CID.' He gestured for her to move towards their table. 'And this is Detective Constable Jones.'

She gave Debbie Jones a brief nod before sitting.

'Can I get you a drink?' Lambert offered.

'I wouldn't mind a dry white wine.'

DC Jones stood up quickly. 'I'll get it.'

While she went to get the drink, Lambert sat back in his chair and gave the woman an understanding smile, intimating he was a man of the world and her infidelity was of little consequence.

When he had watched her outside Yalding's cottage, he had noticed how attractive she was, but now that he was close to her he was overwhelmed by her classical beauty. Her pale complexion, high cheekbones and swan-like neck gave her an artistic elegance, as if she had stepped out of a Pre-Raphaelite painting, and her light auburn hair, which had looked blonde in the distance, added sensuality to her attractiveness. She wore a light beige lipstick and lightly applied emerald eye shadow, which highlighted her green eyes.

Lambert observed her change of clothing. She had gone home and changed into white trousers and a green, sleeveless shirt. Her engagement ring sparkled extravagantly, and her platinum wedding ring was discreetly thin. And the thin wrist watch she wore looked as if it might be expensive.

She glanced apprehensively around the bar before speaking. 'Do you mind telling me what this is all about?'

Her dialect, he noticed, was what he would describe as 'posh Welsh', a hybrid practiced by Dylan Thomas and Richard Burton, speaking with a sing-song lilt of the Valleys but adopting the high-class vowels of Oxford.

'I want to talk to you about Mark Yalding. Is he a close friend of yours?'

'Is this to do with that nonsense about the internet pornography?'

'What makes you think it's nonsense?'

'I just know Mark isn't like that.'

'How can you be so sure?'

'I just know.'

'So would you be prepared to stand up in court in his defence and swear to his innocence?'

She paused, staring down at the table. 'It shouldn't even go to court.'

'Nevertheless, the pornography was downloaded from his computer and paid for with his credit card.'

She frowned hard, concentrating on a single thought, until something seemed to click in her brain. 'If he's been charged and scheduled to appear in court, what were you doing watching his place? And why do you need to speak to me?'

Lambert suddenly found himself on the receiving end of the awkward questions. Fortunately, DC Jones arrived with the white wine.

THE WRECKING BAR

The woman thanked her in Welsh. '*Diolch yn fawr.*'

'You're welcome,' DC Jones said as she sat, exchanging a brief look with her boss.

'You seem utterly convinced Mark Yalding is innocent of the child pornography charge,' Lambert said. 'So how well do you know him?'

'Can you accept that I know him well and leave it at that?'

'How long have you known him?'

She hesitated. 'I – I've known him for about two years.'

'That's not long, is it, to be so certain about what goes on in someone's private life?' Lambert sighed impatiently. 'You're obviously married, and you don't want your husband to know about this meeting. Is there a reason for that?'

Again, the hesitation. 'He – he's a very jealous man.'

'And has he got a reason to be jealous?'

Instead of replying, she held her glass to the light, sniffed it as though she was an expert wine taster, and took a small sip. The two detectives watched her, waiting for an answer.

Staring into her wine glass to avoid eye contact with them, she said, 'Mark and I are lovers, which is why I find that business about child pornography hard to believe.'

DC Jones prompted her gently. 'Because you both have a good sex life?'

She nodded.

Lambert decided it was time to change tactics.

'What does your husband do?'

She hadn't been expecting this question and was thrown by it.

'Do?'

'Yes. What does he do for a living?'

'He has his own business.'

'What line of business?'

'What has this got to do with Mark?'

'I don't know until you answer the question.'

She took another sip of wine before answering. 'My husband's a management consultant.'

DC Jones said, 'Rhiannon's a lovely name.'

'Thank you.'

'We can't really call you Rhiannon, though.'

'Why not?'

'It's partly to do with our training. It's either sir or ma'am or a surname. What's your surname?'

'Williams.'

90

CHAPTER FIFTEEN

Lambert noticed how much less hesitation it took to answer this question, almost as if she was prepared for it.

'And that's your married name, not your maiden name?' Jones asked, and a sudden thought sped like lightning through her brain. Why had Lambert made such a thing about her own maiden name and its significance?

'Yes, that's my married name. I'm Mrs Williams.'

Lambert leant forward on the table. 'Mrs Williams, did your husband know or have grounds for suspicion about your affair with Mr Yalding?'

She shook her head. 'No, I don't think so.'

'But you're not certain.'

'No, I don't think he did. I'm almost certain.' She laughed nervously. 'Almost certain! Isn't that what they call an oxymoron?'

'Mr Yalding,' Lambert continued, 'is adamant that he's been set-up in some way. Is there anyone else you can think of, apart from your husband, who might want to incriminate your boyfriend?'

'No, there's no one. Mark's a lovely man; he gets on well with everyone. He's well liked and popular.'

'Do you have a key to his cottage?'

Another slight hesitation before she answered. 'Well, yes, I do but—'

Lambert cut in, 'So when I saw you call at his cottage this morning, and there was no reply, why didn't you let yourself in?'

'I didn't have it with me. I'd misplaced it. We have a drawer in our kitchen full of odds and ends, and I rummaged through and couldn't find it.'

'You think it might have gone missing?'

'Of course not. If you saw the state of this drawer, you'd realize how hard it is to find anything.'

Lambert nodded slowly, deep in thought. In the background he could hear music playing, just about audible over the sound of pub banter and laughter. He identified the number as one he liked: Marc Almond singing 'Say Hello, Wave Goodbye'. As he took a deep breath, preparing himself for the worst, a delicious smell of garlic swamped his senses.

'Mrs Williams, I have some bad news. After you left the cottage this morning, I went round to the back door. It was open so I let myself in.'

She seemed to shrink into herself as she stared at him, her eyes desperate and pleading, fearing one of the worst things she knew she would hear.

'I'm sorry to have to tell you: I'm afraid Mr Yalding is dead.'

At first she looked as if she had been turned to stone. Then, like a volcano erupting, her body shook as she choked and sobbed, unable to control her grief.

The Wrecking Bar

Several people standing at the bar stared at the scene, embarrassed but curious. Jones slid an arm across her shoulder and muttered soothingly:

'I'm sorry. It's a tragic loss. I'm so sorry. He must have meant a great deal to you.'

'I knew,' she sobbed, 'when I went to the cottage this morning, and there was no reply… Oh, God! I just knew something dreadful must have happened. Can we go outside, please?'

She began to rise shakily, hanging on to the table for support. Jones gave her an arm to lean on and helped her towards the door. Lambert picked up a spare serviette and followed them. A cursory glance at the bar told him they were the focus of everyone's attention. DC Jones managed to steer her away from the pub entrance and found a quiet area far from the beer garden, close to the pub's trade entrance and a wooden boundary fence, which Rhiannon Williams leant against for support.

She sniffed noisily and Lambert pressed the serviette into her hand. 'Oh, God!' she moaned. 'Oh, God! I must pull myself together. I must. I must.'

'Because of your husband?' Jones asked.

Rhiannon Williams nodded tearfully, wiped her eyes and blew her nose on the serviette. 'Though how I'm going to do that, Christ only knows. But I must.' Like a cornered animal, her expression became suddenly fierce as she stared accusingly at Lambert. 'Why did you wait to tell me? Asking me all those questions, and all along you knew he was dead.'

'I'm sorry. There were things we needed to know.'

'Yes but what's the bloody point? If Mark killed himself because he felt so ashamed, you asking me all those questions—'

'You don't understand,' Lambert interrupted. 'He didn't kill himself. He was murdered.'

'Murdered? Who would want to murder…' It took her a moment to comprehend, but when the realization hit her, she opened her mouth in alarm but seemed unable to speak.

'He was beaten to death just like the two recent murders of the sex offenders,' Lambert said.

'But Mark was no sex offender.'

'We know he had no convictions and no police record of any sort. But because of the child pornography charge, the killer probably thought differently.'

Her eyes fired up with rage. 'If the police hadn't arrested him, and if it hadn't got into the papers, he'd still be alive. Mark would still be alive.'

'We have no way of knowing that.'

CHAPTER FIFTEEN

'Don't lie to me. Those other men who were killed… it was after it was reported in the papers.'

'The police had no choice but to arrest him, following an FBI report of the child pornography download from his computer. If you want someone to blame, go for the press and paparazzi.'

Her anger subsided and huge tears bubbled in her eyes. 'Mark would never have done such a thing. I know he wouldn't. And now he's gone, and he'll never be able to prove his innocence.'

She dabbed her eyes and wiped her nose with the sodden serviette. DC Jones moved a little closer to her and spoke softly.

'If it's any consolation, we'll find the killer and bring him to justice.'

'It won't bring Mark back.'

'But is there anything we can do to help in the short term? You might find it tricky going back to your husband in this state. Obviously he'll start asking questions.'

'I'll go and visit my mother and stay with her for a few days.'

'Where does she live?'

Rhiannon Williams stared at Jones, trying to decide whether she could trust her with information about her private life. After a brief pause, in which she sighed and shuddered, she mumbled, 'She lives on her own in a house in Porthkerry. It's much too big for one person, and she should really be in a home – for her own good. Her short-term memory's gone and she lives almost entirely in the past. She remembers me from years ago, and when I go round she won't remember that I called to see her two days ago.'

Lambert took out his wallet and offered her his business card. 'If you think of anything and you need to contact me, it's got my number on it.'

She stared at the card with an uncomprehending, dazed expression. 'I don't see what I could possibly…'

'You never know. However trivial it might seem, it could help us with our enquiries.'

She nodded, and looked off into the distant hills, her eyes searching for some meaning to the way her life had suddenly been devastated.

'Are you all right to drive?' DC Jones asked.

Without answering, she turned decisively and walked towards her Land Rover, which she had parked on the grass verge at the roadside.

They watched her drive off, and Jones asked, 'I presume you got the licence number when she was parked outside the house?'

'Of course. And I intend checking it.'

'You think she lied about her husband's occupation?'

Lambert nodded. 'And I've got a feeling she lied about her surname as well. I don't think she wants us to know who she is.'

'Because of the affair she was having?'

'Yes, and she has even more of a reason to keep it from her husband now that her lover's dead.'

Frowning, Jones stared searchingly into her boss's eyes. 'That's a very cynical outlook you have, Detective Inspector.'

'It goes with the territory.'

Sixteen

Sunshine, no school for a whole week, and a shipwreck! Mickey and Steven couldn't believe their luck in finding the launch. An exciting discovery, and something told them it was about to become an adventure.

It lay half submerged at the water's edge, where the beach dipped from shallow to deep water suddenly; a good beach for swimming when it was calm but slightly intimidating in choppier seas.

They wondered how the boat came to be shipwrecked, and then they saw the battered hull and gaping hole on the uppermost side, probably the reason for its destruction. Even though they lived near the sea, they had only ever heard or read about shipwrecks, but this was 'wicked', as Mickey commented, and promised to up their standing in the young community.

'Bet you're glad you listened to me now,' Steven boasted.

They had been camping out in a small tent in Mickey's back garden and had woken at five in the morning. Steven suggested a bike ride before breakfast, and Mickey had reluctantly agreed after a brief argument. Now he had to admit his friend was right. This shipwreck adventure was worth the risk of his mother's wrath on finding the tent empty and their bikes gone.

'Awesome!' Mickey exclaimed, staring open-mouthed at the boat. 'I wonder what we ought to do.'

'We could explore it.'

'What, you mean inside the boat?'

'Yeah, you never know what we might find. Something valuable, maybe.'

Mickey frowned, his eyes filled with doubt. 'It might be a bit scary going in there. And it means getting wet.'

Steven shrugged. 'So what? Our shorts'll soon dry.'

'And it's a bit scary.'

'Can't be any more scary than last September.'

THE WRECKING BAR

Mickey's frown deepened. 'What happened last September?'

Steven giggled, teasing his friend. 'You was the one who was worried about our first year at secondary school.'

'I wasn't.'

His friend laughed loud and mockingly. 'You was shitting your pants. And now you're scared of exploring an old shipwreck.'

'No, I'm not.'

'Prove it then.'

Mickey stood at the water's edge, hesitating, feeling the salt breeze blowing against his cheeks and the early-morning sun warming the back of his neck. He stared at the tilted deck, which was only submerged in about two feet of water, and the entrance into the cabin was way above the level of the water. He could get inside there with no difficulty and it would provide him with an opportunity to dispel the suggestion of cowardice. 'Okay,' he said. 'I'll do it.'

Not to be outdone, Steven said, 'I'll come with you.'

But now that Mickey had overcome his fear, he didn't want to lose any of the glory.

'Yeah, but I'll go first.'

They waded into the water and Mickey raised himself onto the tilted deck by clutching and pulling at the rail above. Because the boat was tilted at such an unnatural angle, he worried about twisting his ankle or getting it caught in something.

Steven followed him and copied the way he slid along towards the cabin entrance by grabbing the rail. The boat creaked and strained in the lapping waves as the children panted and grunted with the effort of clinging on.

As Mickey reached the cabin entrance, he said, 'As I'm first in the cabin, I get the first pick of anything valuable.'

He lay sideways on the stairs leading into the cabin and started to slide cautiously inside, eyes peering into the gloom. A beam of sunlight cut through one of the portholes like a blade and a patch of light filtered through the shattered hull.

'Go on,' Steven urged. 'What can you see?'

Mickey froze as he saw the corpse, twisted into a foetal position under one of the fitted seats. A cold hand gripped his throat and squeezed.

'Quick! Get out of here!' he screamed, panicking and banging his head on a metal rail.

His friend knew he had seen something horrific and hurled himself backwards off the boat and into the sea. Mickey joined him seconds later and both of them scrambled up the beach and away from the boat.

CHAPTER SIXTEEN

***

He couldn't remember a worse case than this one. All the years Lambert had spent in CID and this had to be the record breaker for so much death in such a short time.

They had convened in the incident room last night to discuss and regroup. Another Sunday evening up the spout, but Tony Ellis would be hit hardest as his Sharon was expecting any time soon.

And now that he'd spent another restless night, the death toll was beginning to show in Lambert's face. His brain had been chewing over the case most of the night, and then his own ghosts took over and provoked and nagged him until the early hours. He had just drifted off to sleep when the alarm shattered his hopes of getting a decent rest.

And the last thing he felt like was this meeting with Marden, under scrutiny like a lab specimen by the man's avenging angel stare. As Lambert began explaining that it wasn't suspects they lacked, but that they had rather too many, Marden sniffed disparagingly and peeled a newspaper off the top of a pile that lay before him on the desk.

'When I gave the press briefing outside victim number three's home in Cowbridge, I think it went well, and they've printed most of what I said, including details of the murder weapon. However, you can always rely on the gutter press to cock things up for the police.'

Marden pushed the tabloid towards Lambert. The headline screamed at him:

'WHITE VAN MAN KILLER.'

Lambert scanned the first paragraph quickly and saw that it was the neighbour Kevin Wallace had interviewed who had given the details to a reporter.

Lambert sighed heavily. 'Oh, that's just great. Compromises our investigation and alerts the killer. If he or they are targeting the other sex offenders, it's good to know the gentlemen of the press have given them advance warning that their vehicle's been identified.'

'You said "they". Any reason you think there might be two of them?'

Lambert shook his head. 'Just keeping an open mind.'

'And you've never considered the killer could be female?'

'I think it's highly unlikely.'

'Yes, you're probably right. I think one of your priorities should be to find the whereabouts of these other sex offenders before the killer gets to them. We can't afford to lose our credibility with yet another murder.'

Lambert tapped the newspaper in front of him. 'Especially now the cat's out of the bag and they know about the sulphuric acid. I wonder how they got that story.'

An uncomfortable beat before Marden spoke. 'I told them at the press conference.'

Lambert feigned open-mouthed surprise.

Marden stared at Lambert with undisguised irritation. 'We need someone to come forward who can give us information about acid going missing or being purchased. I would have thought that was obvious. Exactly like the murder weapon from the Llanelli store.'

'Yes, I suppose you're right,' Lambert mumbled grudgingly.

He knew Marden had had a difficult decision to make when he gave this story to the press and he didn't envy him the job. And on reflection he thought the chief super was probably right about the acid, and it might help them to draw in some valuable information. But it was the public knowing about the killer's white van that was a problem and could result in many false leads. White vans were hardly rare.

Clive Marden leant forward on his desk, his hands clasped together as if in prayer. He fixed Lambert with a steely gaze. 'I have a problem with you telling me we have too many suspects. That's of no great help in this case. And I hope that sort of defeatist attitude doesn't rub off on the rest of your team.'

'I'm just being realistic.'

Marden clicked his tongue impatiently. 'Move quickly to eliminate as many of the suspects as you can. Then give me some evidence. I know you can do it. You've done it before, Harry.'

Lambert stopped himself from smiling as he realized this was as close as Marden would get to making a motivational speech. But it must have shown on his face, because the chief super began finger waving.

'One of your prime suspects got away, Harry.'

'Who? Gordon Mayfield?' Lambert exaggerated a tone of incredulity. 'He was never a prime suspect.'

'But have you asked yourself where he might be this very minute? He could have sailed east along the coast. Supposing he moored somewhere like St Donat's? It's only six or seven miles from there to Cowbridge. Christ! You can practically walk it.'

'Why would he walk all that way? We know the perpetrator drove a white van, sir.'

The colour in Marden's face deepened as if he was about to explode, but then his phone rang and he grabbed it.

CHAPTER SIXTEEN

'Yes?'

He listened intently to the caller, his eyes flitting to Lambert and away again. He scribbled something on a notepad and asked, 'You're sure about this?' He nodded. 'Okay, as soon as they've made a positive identification, perhaps you could ask them to let us know. I'm well aware it's almost bound to be him, but we have to be one hundred per cent certain. Get on to it right away, will you? Thank you.'

He hung up and stared into space for a moment. Lambert could have sworn he saw a beaten look in his eyes, but it only lasted a moment. He soon recovered and leant forward across the desk again to confront Lambert with the news.

'North Devon CID has made contact with us. They found the wreck of a boat called *The Amethyst* washed ashore along the coast near Bideford.'

Lambert felt cheered by this news but remained deadpan. 'Do they know what happened?'

'Two youngsters found the wreck, went on board and discovered a body.'

Although Lambert could guess the identity of the body, he said, 'Have they any idea who it is?'

'They haven't formally identified it yet, but they think it could be Mayfield.'

'How did he die?'

'They think the boat was scuttled, probably by the owner himself – perhaps by deliberately hitting some rocks. Or maybe it was an accident. They can't be certain at this stage.'

'I presume he drowned?'

Marden nodded.

'So I guess,' Lambert said with a tight smile, 'he had a perfect alibi during the time of Yalding's murder. Unless that little craft of his was a power boat in disguise.'

Ignoring Lambert's sarcasm, Marden glanced at his watch. 'I think that's all for now. I suggest you get your team to find these other sex offenders and keep them under surveillance.'

'Do we have the resources for that?'

'I hope so. Needs must and all that. I'm seeing the assistant chief constable in…' He made a show of checking his watch again… 'Precisely three minutes' time.'

Lambert's cue to leave. He stood up and walked to the door. Marden surprised him by saying, 'If Mayfield killed himself, was that from guilt, fear or both, do you suppose?'

Lambert shrugged. 'We may never know. But the end result is the same.'

Marden sniffed and said, 'Yes, that's precisely the sort of existential response I would have expected from you, Harry.'

***

As Lambert left police headquarters and walked across the car park, he thought about Mayfield and the young boy from the photograph. He seriously doubted they would ever find out what had happened to the youngster, and he knew the knowledge was lost, drowned with Mayfield in his watery grave. Another unsolved. Another missing child. He hoped Mayfield had suffered in those last moments as he fought for breath.

As he got behind the wheel of his car, his mobile, which he'd switched to 'vibrate' for his meeting with Marden, alerted him to a call. It was DC Jones, getting straight to the point in a voice that told him she had got a result.

'Harry! I thought you'd like to know that Rhiannon Williams lied about her surname. I checked with DVLA, and her Land Rover is registered to Rhiannon Lloyd. And guess who her husband is.'

'I have no idea.'

'His name's Gavin Lloyd, the producer who runs Green Valley Productions, the company who made the documentary about the sex offenders.'

'So he was Mark Yalding's employer.'

'Yes, and I wonder if he knows Yalding was having an affair with his wife.'

'I think I need to have a word with this Gavin Lloyd.'

'I thought you might. Would you like his office phone number and address? Green Valley Productions is based in central Cardiff.'

'Yes. Hang on a second while I grab pen and paper.'

After he had scribbled the address on to his notepad, Debbie asked him if he'd like her to accompany him there.

'Sorry, Debbie, but I'd like you to help Tony with his enquiries and the chief super wants the other remaining sex offenders traced.'

'Fair enough,' she said. 'You planning on ringing this Gavin Lloyd's office before you shoot over there, just in case he's out?'

As he turned the ignition key, he replied, 'If he employs other staff, I wouldn't mind a word with them. And if he is there, far better to arrive without due warning.'

Seventeen

Searching for the fertilizer factory on the small industrial estate on the outskirts of Carmarthen, Tony Ellis drove past the entrance and came to a dead end in the road, realizing he'd missed the small lane leading to Hallam Biofeed.

He turned the car round in a three-point turn, intending to drive up the lane to the small factory, but had to brake sharply as a vehicle hurtled out of the lane as if it was being driven by a reckless boy racer. But it wasn't that which had caused Ellis to slam on the brakes so violently.

The vehicle was a small unmarked white van.

And it was being driven by Norman McNeil, the self-appointed vigilante.

***

Entering the reception area of Green Valley Productions, Lambert quickly noted the subdued ambience of media sophistication: the expensive brown leather L-shaped sofa; the silver-framed original watercolours and industry awards certificates; the large pot plant in an exquisite ceramic tub that dominated the water cooler, as it was clearly intended to.

The receptionist, a brunette in her early thirties, looked up and caught Lambert's eye as soon as he entered, offering him a warm smile from straight gleaming teeth that looked cosmetically enhanced. She had a slightly masculine face, but softened by skilfully applied make-up, and her sequin studded T-shirt would have looked more suitable on a club dancefloor. She spoke in what Lambert recognized as a toned-down Cardiff dialect.

'Good morning. Can I help you?'

'I'd like to see Gavin Lloyd.'

She raised her eyebrows in surprise and glanced at her desk diary. 'Do you have an appointment?'

The Wrecking Bar

Lambert held his warrant card in front of her. 'Detective Inspector Lambert, CID. I'd like to speak with Mr Lloyd as soon as possible.'

Lambert noticed the curiosity in her eyes as she digested this information, and he might have been wrong but he thought he detected a slight gloating, evident in her private smile. That, and the way she eagerly grabbed the phone.

'Hold on a minute, will you?'

She lifted the receiver and pressed the internal button. Lambert watched her, wondering how much she knew about what went on in the company.

'Gavin,' she said as soon as she was connected, 'I have a Detective Inspector Lambert to see you. He hasn't got an appointment but says it's important.' She paused, listening, and made eye contact with Lambert. 'Yes, I'll tell him.'

As soon as she replaced the receiver, she said, 'Please take a seat. Gavin's just got one quick phone call to make and he'll be right with you. He won't keep you long. Can I get you anything? Tea or coffee?'

'No thanks.'

He turned away, sank into the leather sofa, and caught the receptionist studying him.

'How long have you worked here?' he asked her.

She tilted her head up, remembering. 'Let's see, it must be a good four years last March.'

'Have you been involved with many television dramas?'

'I have, funnily enough. I don't just do reception work. I've always wanted to go into the production side of things. We're a small company, so I guess I'm like a sort of Girl Friday.'

'What's your name, if you don't mind me asking?'

'Of course not. It's Jackie Dearlove.'

Lambert smiled. 'Nice name. And what are you working on at the moment, Jackie?'

A slight hesitation before she pulled a wry face and said, 'It's been deathly quiet for months now. Gavin's got a few things he's pitching but nothing definite in the pipeline.'

Lambert studied the framed BAFTA certificates, showing Green Valley's nominations for various categories, all of them more than ten years old.

'Must be a hard old business to work in. One minute you're flavour of the month, and the next...' He gave her a palms-up gesture, letting the incomplete sentence do its work, hoping she would open up about the state of Green Valley Productions.

Lowering her voice, she started to say, 'The last two drama productions...', but was interrupted by the buzz of the phone.

Lambert glanced at his watch. It was just gone 11.30. Hopefully he'd be able to question Gavin Lloyd for a good half-hour. He fully expected the producer to be open to answering all his questions, seeing as Tony Ellis got the impression that he had an enormous ego and liked nothing better than to talk about himself.

Jackie, receptionist and Girl Friday, hung up the phone and pointed to a door marked *Private* to the side of the reception desk. 'If you'd like to go through there, Gavin will be pleased to see you. Sorry to keep you.'

Lambert got up, nodded and smiled his thanks, gave a tap on the door and entered. Just as he knew the producer might not be shy and retiring, he wasn't prepared for such a demonstrative greeting.

Gavin Lloyd leapt up from the seat behind his desk, bounded forward, offered Lambert his hand, and spoke as if they might have been old and cherished acquaintances. 'Good to meet you, Inspector Lambert. I hope you found my documentary interesting.'

Lambert shook his hand. 'Yes, thank you for your co-operation. It was very useful.'

'Good, good,' Lloyd replied, gesturing for Lambert to take a seat. As soon as he was seated behind his desk, he surveyed the detective with a confident stare that bordered on rudeness.

If Lambert were to hazard a guess, he would put Lloyd's age at forty-nine or fifty, roughly the same age as his wife Rhiannon. He was of average height, with undulating waves of floppy brown hair, almost too uniform in colour, showing no signs of middle-aged grey. His face, although round, was not fat, and his complexion was ruddy, cheerful and healthy-looking, and pale blue bedroom eyes peered out from under half-shut lids and long lashes. He wore an expensive-looking pale blue shirt and yellow silk tie and had removed his suit jacket, which was draped over the back of his swivel chair.

'And *now* how can I be of assistance, Inspector?'

'I'm investigating the murder of one of your employees – Mark Yalding.'

Lloyd looked down at his desktop, his face a mask of seriousness. 'A terrible tragedy. I saw it on last night's news. I still haven't taken it in. Mark may have compromised himself with that sleazy business of the child porn, but the punishment didn't fit the crime. What an awful thing to do to anyone.'

'He was no longer an employee of yours, I believe. How long ago did he leave your employ?'

'Let me see. Roughly speaking, I think he finished about two months ago.'

'And what was the reason for his leaving?'

THE WRECKING BAR

'I sacked him.'

'I see. Did he have a contract of employment?'

'He did, yes.'

'So why did you sack him?'

'Over the downloading of child pornography.'

Lambert rubbed his chin thoughtfully, play-acting uncertainty. 'Now let me get this straight: it was reported in some of the papers that you sacked Mr Yalding after his arrest, saying that you had warned him about the internet pornography. But now you're telling me you sacked him almost two months prior to his arrest.'

Lloyd raised his hands in surrender. 'If I gave that impression, I have to take the blame. But have you ever known reporters to get their facts right? Let's face it, half the time they make it up.'

'Forgive me, Mr Lloyd, but you just told me you sacked him because he was downloading child pornography, yet this wasn't revealed by the press until Saturday, only two days ago.'

Lloyd sighed impatiently, as if he was dealing with someone who couldn't grasp an obvious concept. 'Two months ago he told me he was going to follow up the documentary by writing a book on the subject and was planning his research, part of which involved downloading child pornography. We had an argument about it. I said it was morally wrong. If there was no market for child pornography, then there might be less child abuse. But he wouldn't listen, and I told him he was sacked. When he threatened me with an industrial tribunal, I retaliated by threatening him with public exposure about the child pornography.'

'But he had only *spoken* to you about downloading porn at that stage,' Lambert said. 'Hardly a strong enough reason for dismissal as far as a tribunal was concerned. He might have changed his mind.'

'You must understand, Inspector, this goes back a long way. This child abuse had become an obsession with him. It was his idea in the first place to make that documentary. And during the making of it he wanted to download child porn, for research purposes, he said. I managed to persuade him against it at the time.'

Lambert decided it was time to go for his wrongfooting tactic.

'Who do you think was responsible for leaking your documentary sex offenders' details to the *Sun*?'

Gavin Lloyd's face was expressionless, stilled by Lambert's question. After a brief hiatus, he shrugged and said, 'I have no idea. They could have got the names of the sex offenders from some other source.'

'It seems too much of a coincidence that each one who appeared anonymously in your film was named by the paper. And I tend not to believe in coincidences. How many staff do you employ?'

'Well, up until fairly recently there was Mark Yalding and Jackie – who you met in reception and has been with me some time. And I can't see Jackie doing something like that. But although we're a small company, we employ a heck of a lot of freelancers. The film crews for a start. There could have been at least a half-dozen people on the making of that documentary who might have leaked those names to the press.'

'And would they have known the names of the sex offenders?'

Lloyd smirked. 'I doubt if it would have been any big secret as far as the crew were concerned. And film crews are the biggest gossip merchants going. Maybe Mark told some of the crew who those men were, especially if it was that one with the unusual name.' He clicked his fingers several times. 'What was it?'

'Lubin Titmus.'

'That's the one,' Lloyd laughed.

'During the making of that film, did you still get on with Mark Yalding?'

'Yes, of course.'

'So, up until the time you had this disagreement about child porn, were there any other problems in your relationship with him?'

'None at all.'

'Can you think of any reason why someone would want to murder him in such a brutal fashion?'

Lloyd shrugged and pouted. 'Not really. Unless the killer thought he was a potential paedophile. Which clearly he was.'

'How long had you known Mr Yalding?'

Lloyd gazed at the ceiling for a moment. 'Let's see now, I think it must be all of twelve years. He started working for me back in 1998 when there was more going on in the way of drama. Nowadays everything's reality TV shit. No one has enough money for drama, it seems, especially as one episode of a drama might cost over a million quid. Costume drama – forget it!'

Lambert had been searching for an opening to his next question and Gavin Lloyd had just provided it. Using the same conversational gambit he had used on the producer's receptionist, he said, 'It must be a precarious business.'

Lloyd smiled confidently. 'I get by.'

'One minute champagne and strawberries, the next—'

'Beans on toast!' the producer interrupted with a laugh. 'But things are not that bad.'

'Even so,' Lambert said, doggedly pursuing the theme to get to the question. 'I'd hate to own a luxury car one minute and then have to downsize to something below average. I recently treated myself to a Mercedes but that's after years of hard graft. I hope you still manage to drive something suitably exclusive.'

Lloyd smiled thinly. 'As a matter of fact, I don't. I still own a BMW, but I don't drive. Never have done.'

'You don't drive! But you own a car?'

The producer chuckled, obviously enjoying the way the detective's probing question had been shot down in flames.

'I have a chap – Jack – and I pay him to do my driving.'

'A chauffeur?'

'Well, yes, I suppose you could call him a chauffeur,' Lloyd laughed. 'But I don't make him wear a hat.'

'It's very unusual these days not to be able to drive. Did you never attempt to learn?'

'I was always too busy with other things. I did think about it, and then I went to university. Oxford.'

'Which part of Wales are you from?'

'I was born and bred in Y Drenewydd.' Seeing the blank expression on the detective's face, Lloyd added, 'That's Newtown in Powys. I take it you're not a Welsh speaker, Inspector.'

'I never found the time to learn. I didn't find it necessary.'

Lloyd sniggered. 'Well, I thought it necessary. My wife's a fluent Welsh speaker, and some of the circles she moves in, they refuse to speak English. So I tried to learn, just to keep up. But, apart from a few words, I failed miserably.'

'What about Mark Yalding? Was he fluent?'

Lloyd seemed genuinely surprised. 'Mark wasn't Welsh. He was from the north of England. What made you think he spoke Welsh?'

Thinking of the murdered man's relationship with Lloyd's wife, Lambert said, 'I just wondered, perhaps he might have thought it advantageous to learn.'

'Are you suggesting Mark wanted to ingratiate himself with the educated class of Welsh speakers they disparagingly refer to as the Tafia?'

'Possibly.' Lambert patted his forehead as if he'd overlooked something. 'But then of course you've just told me he hadn't learnt any Welsh, so he probably wasn't looking to recruit to the Tafia.'

Lloyd's eyes narrowed as he surveyed Lambert. 'You know, it's funny,' he began, waiting for Lambert to pick up on it.

CHAPTER SEVENTEEN

'What is?' Lambert obliged.

'You've asked me a few questions about Mark, but mainly we've talked about cars, speaking Welsh and which part of Wales I come from. What's that got to do with Mark's murder?'

Lambert smiled disarmingly and shrugged. 'I think I got sidetracked. But back to Mr Yalding's murder. Did he ever mention any threats against him?'

'None that I know of.'

'Notice anything unusual or peculiar about his behaviour?'

'I think I might describe his behaviour as a bit furtive.'

'How d'you mean?'

'Nothing I could put my finger on. He seemed quieter than normal. A bit secretive. Maybe it was something to do with the child porn.'

'Over the years, you must have got to know him quite well. Would you describe him as a friend or colleague or employee?'

Lloyd shifted awkwardly in his chair. 'Um – I guess it would have to be all three.'

'What about his background? Did he talk about his parents?'

Lloyd sighed deeply. 'I suppose I should have got to know Mark better, but we were always talking about work. There seemed to be little time for other things.'

'So is there anything else you can think of that might help? Any mysterious phone calls he might have received in the office?'

'No, there was nothing unusual.'

'And those sex offenders he filmed for your documentary, did he see any of them again after the filming had been completed?'

'Well, if he did, he never mentioned it to me.'

Lambert glanced at his watch and stood up. 'Thank you for your time, Mr Lloyd. If you think of anything, however unimportant it might seem, perhaps you wouldn't mind giving me a call.'

He handed the producer one of his cards.

'Glad to help in any way I can.'

'And if I get the slightest indication of your old friend's innocence regarding the child pornography, I'll let you know.'

As Lambert exited to the reception area, he caught the deep expression of doubt eclipsing Lloyd's bombastic self-confidence. The door closed behind him, not slammed exactly, but it was a robust end to their meeting.

Lambert knew he should have delved a little deeper into what had gone on in the Lloyd household and found out whether or not Gavin Lloyd knew about his wife's affair with Mark Yalding. Had he known, it gave him a motive for killing his employee. But Lambert was reminded of his own shortcomings and the way he had cheated on Helen, and how last year he had attempted in vain to rekindle their marriage. At the time there was no way he would have wanted outside interference, some well-wisher reminding Helen about his affair with a psychiatric nurse. And that's how he felt about Gavin Lloyd. Even though it was a murder investigation, why disclose Rhiannon Lloyd's infidelity knowing that he could be responsible for destroying a marriage that might still survive?

Now Lambert felt cheated by his own sense of fairness.

The receptionist was busy talking on the phone as he left. She flashed him a smile and he gave her a wave before stepping out into the glare of the noon sunshine.

Gavin Lloyd's office was diagonally opposite the New Theatre, so Lambert crossed the road, went into the theatre foyer, and hung around, pretending to show an interest in the leaflets advertising forthcoming productions.

It was just before midday, and he hoped he wouldn't have long to wait.

***

Tony Ellis sat in the factory manager's office and stared at him expressionlessly across the desk. His name was Alan Hughes and he was Norman McNeil's brother-in-law. The desk was cluttered, and the desktop computer monitor was grey with age. The office reminded Ellis of his motor mechanic's office, untidy, unclean, harbouring years of grease and grime, and randomly scattered were long-forgotten invoices and yellowing papers curling at the edges. The room was stuffy, the window was shut tight, and it looked as if the rusty metal frame was jammed.

With a studied appearance of machismo ruggedness, Hughes matched his office. He was in his mid to late forties, and wore a V-neck mauve T-shirt with a row of buttons in the V. Although he had the jowly face of an overweight man, he seemed to be attempting a Bruce Willis *Die Hard* image, the way he was dressed and the way his hair had been closely shaved, with a hint of stubble on his ample chin. His bulbous eyes with dark brown pupils showed the ravages of drink, and it was difficult to distinguish the motifs of the faded tattoos on his hairy arms, which were smudged like Rorschach inkblot tests.

'What's this about?' he asked.

'We're enquiring into some recent murders. Perhaps you've seen the news. On Friday a man was murdered on his boat on the marina. And another man's body was discovered in a mobile home not far from here—'

CHAPTER SEVENTEEN

Interrupting the sergeant, Hughes made a gesture by turning his palms over on top of the desk and said, 'Whoa! What the hell's this got to do with me?'

'That's what I'm here to find out.'

Hughes stared at him, mouth slightly open, still expressing bewilderment.

'Your brother-in-law, Norman McNeil, works for you.'

Hughes glared with hostility at Ellis before answering. 'Wrong. He used to work for me.'

'But I thought...' Ellis began.

'Not any more. He left over a year ago. Had back trouble.'

'Well now, that is peculiar, because I just saw him leaving your factory in one of your vehicles. Was he making a delivery for you?'

Hughes pursed his lips as if he couldn't care less. 'So what if he was?'

'I believe Mr McNeil's on incapacity benefit. If he's claiming benefits illegally while still working—'

Hughes raised a hand. 'Whoa! Hold on! I never said he was working for me.'

'But he was making a delivery for you.'

'No, he wasn't.'

'But I saw him driving one of your vans.'

'Yeah, but he weren't making no delivery. He was collecting for us.'

'Please, Mr Hughes – don't split hairs. You know very well what I mean. I'm suggesting he works for you occasionally, while collecting state benefits.'

'We're short staffed at the moment and Norm offered to help. He ain't getting paid. I just buy him a few drinks now and then; buy him the odd bottle of whisky and that. Payment in kind, you see. Strictly legal.'

Pleased with himself, Hughes leaned back in his creaking chair. He smiled, though there was little warmth in it.

'Are you by any chance a member of PASO?'

There was a sudden stillness in the room. They both heard a fly buzzing and hurling itself against a window pane behind Hughes's back. After a long pause, Hughes must have decided that Ellis could check up, so he nodded slowly.

'Yeah, I am. What of it?'

'It's a group of vigilantes, I believe.'

Hughes leaned forward across the desk and stared defiantly at Ellis. 'We gorra right to protect our children. I've got two little girls, eleven and nine, and we don't want those bastards living within fifty miles of us. If I had my way...'

He stopped, realizing he had said too much.

'Yes, what would you do, Mr Hughes?'

Hughes controlled himself and leaned back in his chair. 'I'd pass a law to bring back capital punishment for crimes against children. And if that didn't work I'd lock them up for life. And I mean *life!*'

'And if the laws are not adequate, what then?'

'If the law can't deal with them, we want them to bugger off and live somewhere else. And that's why PASO was formed, so that we can get rid of them legitimately. That doesn't make us murderers.'

'Let's get back to the work your brother-in-law does for you.'

'I've already told you, he's just helping out on a voluntary basis.'

'Delivering and collecting?'

'That's right.'

'And when I saw him leaving your factory less than half an hour ago, he was driving a white van. Is that your van?'

'It belongs to Hallam Biofeeds. It's not mine personally.'

'Do you drive it occasionally?'

Hughes shook his head emphatically. 'I don't do deliveries. In case you hadn't noticed, I'm the manager here.'

'I wasn't suggesting you did the deliveries yourself, Mr Hughes. I wanted to know if you ever drive the van home.'

Jerking a thumb at the grubby window behind him, Hughes laughed and said, 'That's my Mitsubishi gas guzzler in the car park.' He saw Ellis was about to ask another question and anticipated it. 'And that's Norman's Renault next to it. We only use the vans for work purposes.'

'Where are they kept at night?'

'Here on the premises, of course. Let me ask you something, Sergeant.'

'Go on.'

'How many white vans d'you think there are in South Wales?'

'Hundreds, I should think.'

Hughes feigned an expression of incredulity, patting his chest theatrically. 'And you suspect me of murdering those blokes because I happen to have access to a white van? Bit of a coincidence, don't you think?'

Ellis stared deep into Hughes's eyes, seeing if he could shake the man's confidence as he said, 'One coincidence I can accept. But when you add another two to the mix... like your brother-in-law living a few doors from one of the murdered men. And thirdly...'

Ellis hadn't heard the vehicle pull up outside. He stopped speaking as Norman McNeil entered the office. He saw Hughes trying to silence his brother-in-law with a look as he started to speak.

'I got that consignment of—'

He looked as if he'd been punched in the stomach as Ellis turned to face him.

Calmly, Ellis addressed Hughes. 'I was saying – oh, yes – and thirdly, the other coincidence. The consignment your brother-in-law's talking about: would that happen to be sulphuric acid, by any chance? That chemical must be running in short supply here lately.'

***

Lambert had been waiting in the foyer for twenty minutes when he spotted Jackie Dearlove leaving her office and walking towards the shopping precinct. He left the theatre and followed her past the Park Thistle Hotel and saw her entering a sandwich shop. He waited, standing to one side of the door.

As soon as she came out, he said, 'Miss Dearlove!'

She stopped, a puzzled frown screwing up her face as she squinted through the sunshine at him.

'I wonder if I could take up ten minutes of your time. Just a few questions about Green Valley Productions. I'd be happy to buy you a coffee.'

She laughed, suddenly finding his presence amusing. 'Have you been following me, Inspector?'

'I needed to speak with you outside of your work environment.'

She hesitated. 'Well, I promised Gavin I'd only be a few minutes today. Hence the sarnie.'

He looked her straight in the eye, impressing on her the importance of his request. 'Every employee's allowed a proper lunch break. And ten minutes is not too much to ask. You could say there was an extra long queue.'

Her face broke into a smile. 'Go on then. It's not as if it matters anymore. There's a Starbucks over there.'

'Thank you, Miss Dearlove.'

'Please! Call me Jackie.'

Inside Starbucks she spotted a corner table and he told her to grab it while he got their coffees, a standard cappuccino for her and a large espresso for himself.

Once he was seated opposite her, he smiled reassuringly. 'When you agreed to have this meeting with me, Jackie, you said it's not as if it matters anymore. What did you mean by that?'

She glanced round, as if someone might be listening, and lowered her voice. 'I've got a new job with another company. And I haven't told Gavin yet.'

'Any reason for your move?'

THE WRECKING BAR

'It's a sinking ship. I don't know how Gavin manages to keep it afloat. Well, I do, but that's another story. He's pitched loads of ideas to the BBC and ITV networks, but none of them have been taken up. And his last drama series for the BBC wasn't recommissioned.' Seeing the frown on his face, she explained, 'Because it slumped in the ratings, they didn't go for a second series.'

'Tell me about this other story,' Lambert said.

'Sorry?'

'You said you had an idea how he manages to keep his company afloat.'

'His wife's loaded. Old money. Have you heard of the Crachach?'

'I hadn't until William Hague married that Ffion Jenkins and it was in all the papers.'

'Well, Rhiannon Lloyd comes from that artistic and well-to-do class of Welsh people. The Crachach.'

'And what about her husband?'

Jackie Dearlove pursed her lips and shrugged. 'I get the impression – and it's just an impression mind – that Gavin's not really top drawer. I think he'd like to be thought of as Crachach, but I think he's from more humble origins.'

'And how did you form that impression?'

'I don't know. It's just the way he tries too hard to be one of them. If you are, you don't have to try, if you see what I mean.'

'So you think Rhiannon Lloyd is footing the bill for his company.'

'I know she is. I heard them arguing about it in his office one day, about three weeks ago. And he hates her coming into the office or having anything to do with the company.'

'Have you any idea what their argument was about?'

'I think it could have been something to do with the London flat, which Rhiannon considered unnecessary.'

'This London flat, is it for the family to use?'

'No way. It's purely for Green Valley Productions. Gavin often goes to London for business meetings and to pitch ideas to various networks, and he stays at the flat.'

'What's the address of this flat, d'you know?'

He waited while she took a dainty sip of coffee before replying.

'Ten Asquith Mansions, Coach Road, Hammersmith.'

'And was this flat for Gavin Lloyd's exclusive use, or did anyone else in the company use it?'

'Well, when I first came to work for the company, about four years ago, there was more staff. We had Bill Knight who was a producer and partner. I

112

think he saw the writing on the wall and got out while the going was good. He got a job at the BBC. I think he used the flat a few times.'

'And what about Mark Yalding? Did he ever use the flat?'

She looked down into her coffee and frowned. When she looked up again, he noticed her eyes were moist.

'I cried buckets after I saw it on the news last night. What a terrible thing to have happened. I liked Mark, although when I found out he'd been downloading child porn on the internet…'

She sighed deeply and shook her head as if she couldn't quite believe it.

'Whose idea was it to make a documentary about the sex offenders?' Lambert asked.

'That was Gavin's idea.'

'Not Mark Yalding's?'

'No, I don't think Mark was very enthusiastic about it. But when it got the green light from Channel 4, he had no option but to go along with it.'

'So when Gavin Lloyd sacked Yalding—'

'I don't think he was really sacked,' Dearlove interrupted. 'I think they probably had words and it was mutually agreed that he would go. At the time Mark wanted to pursue a writing career and was going to take a year out to do that.'

'So why d'you think Gavin Lloyd told the newspapers about warning Mark Yalding about downloading porn?'

'I've no idea. I didn't know everything that went on between them.'

'So did Mark Yalding ever use the London flat?'

'I think he did a couple of times.'

Lambert paused, sipped his coffee, savouring its rejuvenating sharpness. He watched as she knocked back her cappuccino and then looked expectantly in his direction, thinking the interview was ended. But there was one more thing he needed to know.

'Did you know Mark Yalding was having an affair with Rhiannon Lloyd?'

It was as if he'd slapped her in the face. Her jaw fell open, like someone parodying shock.

'Mark and Rhiannon! No! Are you sure?'

'I'm one hundred per cent positive.'

'How can you be so sure?'

'We have it straight from the horse's mouth.'

'Rhiannon told you! I can't quite believe she would do such a thing.'

'Put it this way: she had very little choice.' He saw her intense expression shifting into curiosity. 'Clearly you had no idea about the affair,' he said before

THE WRECKING BAR

she could press him for details. 'What about her husband? D'you think he might have known?'

She thought about this for a moment. 'Well… I… I really don't know. If he did, he never let it show.'

'Is it likely he could have kept that sort of thing to himself?'

She shrugged. 'I haven't a clue. But then he's always been difficult to read. He's one of those people you could know for years and never really get to know.'

'What about family? Have they any children?'

'They've got two, a boy and a girl. Angharad and Rhys. Angharad's the youngest. She's on a gap year, travelling in Italy before she starts university at Aberystwyth in September.'

'What about the boy?'

'I don't know much about him. I think he's a bit of a drifter. Goes home when he's flat broke.'

She stared pointedly at her watch. 'I really must get back….'

'One last thing,' Lambert said hurriedly. 'Gavin Lloyd told me he can't drive.'

'That's right.'

'A bit unusual, isn't it?'

'Apparently he's never learnt. Jack, that's his driver, takes him everywhere.'

'What's he like?'

'Jack? He's very shy and withdrawn. He lives with them, you know.'

Lambert raised his eyebrows and waited for her to elaborate.

'They've got a very palatial house, and quite a few acres of land – her inheritance, I believe. And Jack's got the granny annex, so he's always on hand to drive his master to wherever he wants to go.'

Lambert heard the sarcasm in her tone and smiled. 'Your employer obviously thinks of himself as a high flyer.'

'Yes, I feel sorry for poor old Jack sometimes. Gavin's got this business meeting in Edinburgh tomorrow, and rather than fly up there, Jack's driving him all the way there.'

Seeing her about to rise from the table, he said, 'Finally, before you dash back to work, I'd be very grateful if you didn't let on to your employer about his wife's affair.'

'Why would I do that?'

'I'm not suggesting you would but…'

Dearlove stood up hurriedly. 'Please! Give me some credit for intelligence.'

'Yes, I'm sorry. That was a bit patronizing of me. Good luck with the new job.'

'Thank you.'

She gave him a rather lukewarm smile before leaving. Lambert was about to follow her out when his mobile rang. He flipped it open and the display revealed it was Tony Ellis. He clicked answer and listened intently while Ellis filled him in on what had happened at the fertilizer factory.

After hearing the sergeant's account, he said, 'Tony, I want those two brought in on suspicion of murder. I'll be over right away.'

Eighteen

While Tony Ellis and Kevin Wallace interrogated McNeil in one interview room, Lambert conducted the questioning of Alan Hughes with Debbie Jones in another. Prior to their interviews, both men were routinely offered the services of a solicitor but both declined, as if this in itself proved their innocence. They both seemed so self-assured that Lambert suspected their confidence came from having pretty strong alibis. And as soon as he asked Hughes the appropriate question, he knew he was right.

'Can you remember where you were late Saturday night?'

Hughes made a show of trying to remember. 'Yes, missus and I went into Swansea and had a meal at an Italian restaurant.'

'What time did you get back?'

'We left the restaurant about eleven or just after, and must have got back to Carmarthen about half past.'

'And did you go anywhere else after that?'

'Yes, I gave our babysitter a lift home. She stayed and had a cup of tea and I took her home about half twelve.'

'And can you tell me where you were last Thursday night around two or three in the morning? Presumably you were at work on Friday, so you must have been tucked up in bed.'

Lambert thought he detected a pinprick glint of triumph in Hughes's eyes before he answered.

'No, I was out, along with Norm.'

Lambert breathed evenly, keeping his voice level. 'Where did you go?'

'We went over to Llanelli. We were playing poker with some mates. About six of us.'

'You were playing poker?'

Hughes smirked. 'Not illegal, is it? We weren't breaking any laws, were we?'

Lambert stared at him, aware of how convenient it was on both occasions to have a watertight alibi. That's if the alibis were watertight, and he suspected they were. But they would still have to be checked.

As though amused by his own private joke, Hughes chuckled. 'So you think I murdered those nonces just because our factory happens to have a white van. And how common is sulphuric acid as a chemical? Have you tried all the adhesive manufacturers, or paints, car batteries, water and effluent treatment plants, leather tanning—'

'Thank you, Mr Hughes!' Lambert snapped. 'I get the picture. Now perhaps you can tell me where you were a week ago – last Monday to be precise, between the hours of 9 p.m. and 1 a.m. on the Tuesday morning.'

Lambert could see that Hughes was smart enough not to reel his alibi off right away. He stared at his fingernails and frowned thoughtfully.

'I'm trying to remember. Maybe I was at home with the missus. Sunday I was in my local boozer – always go there Sunday night. But Monday…' He looked up and clicked his fingers. 'Oh yeah. I went with Norman to Cardiff, and we went out on the piss with some mates.'

'What time did you get back?'

'I didn't. I stayed the night in Port Talbot, with Norman and my sister. Cos we was having more than a few sherbets, we went over on the train, and caught the last train back. Gets in to Swansea at around 2.15. We got a cab from Swansea to Norm's house. You can check up on all this.'

'We will, don't worry.'

Lambert stared thoughtfully at Hughes, taking his time while he considered his next move. The fact that Hughes had an alibi for the night of every single murder struck him as odd. Having an alibi for one of those nights he could accept as a coincidence, but Hughes remembered exactly what he was doing on all three nights, and he wasn't at home with his wife watching television but was in the company of other people. No wonder he looked confident and relaxed.

It was time to rattle that composure.

'What were you doing the following night? That would be… last Tuesday?'

Hughes was surprised by the question. His mouth opened and closed, and he seemed momentarily lost.

'Well, Mr Hughes, that's a perfectly straightforward question. What were you doing last Tuesday?'

'But I thought…' Hughes began.

Lambert could see the skidding brakes in the man's mind as he stopped himself from continuing.

'You thought what, Mr Hughes?'

'Nothing.'

'Were you going to say you thought Jarvis Thomas was murdered on Monday night?'

'Of course not.'

'So what *were* you going to say?'

'Just that I thought you wanted to know what I was doing on the Monday night. Why would you be asking me about Monday if that was not the night the bloke was murdered? You can't be that interested in my social life.'

Thinking he'd found a good explanation to justify his blunder, Hughes's self assurance began to return.

'So if you want to know what I was doing on the Tuesday,' he continued, 'I was feeling a bit fragile having been on the sauce the night before. I just sat in front of the telly with the missus.'

Ignoring him, Lambert turned to DC Jones. 'Get the names and addresses of all the people who can confirm what Mr Hughes was doing on those three nights.'

As Lambert rose prior to leaving the room, Hughes said, 'After you've checked with these people and see I'm telling the truth, what happens then?'

'We have to continue with our investigations.'

'What's that supposed to mean?'

Lambert turned away without replying. DC Jones announced for the tape that he was leaving the room. As soon as he'd gone, she said to Hughes, 'Now let's start with the name and address of your babysitter.'

***

Hughes and McNeil, in their separate interview rooms, were given tea and sandwiches and were each guarded by a uniformed policeman, giving the four detectives time to sit in the canteen and compare notes. Their alibis had been checked and they were, as Lambert guessed, watertight.

'They may not have committed the crimes themselves, but they're bloody covering for someone,' Lambert stated. 'I know they are.'

The next step was to look at CCTV footage, to see if the white van from the fertilizer company was anywhere near the marina late on Thursday night, or if it was driven through Carmarthen late Monday night.

'We got exactly the same story from McNeil,' Tony Ellis said.

Lambert nodded. 'I've no doubt they were where they said they were on those nights.' He looked at Jones with a knowing smile. 'But did you notice his reaction when I suggested the murder took place the following night?'

Chapter Eighteen

'Yes, he practically wet himself. He didn't have a strong alibi for Tuesday, and he seemed confused about the murder happening on the Tuesday.'

'You mean,' said Ellis, 'he might have known in advance that the murder was supposed to happen on the Monday?'

'It looks that way,' Lambert replied.

'You think it could be another vigilante, sir?' Jones suggested. 'One of these PASO members, using the van from the fertilizer company?'

'And their sulphuric acid,' Wallace added.

'We need to get the names of all the PASO members,' Lambert said. 'And they'll need to be thoroughly checked.'

His mobile rang. Flipping open the screen he saw an unidentified number.

'DI Lambert,' he said.

'It's Rhiannon… Williams.'

Lambert noticed the briefest of pauses before she gave her surname. 'I must see you some time tonight, Inspector. I need to talk to you. This is important. I can't go into details on the phone.' She sounded distressed, as if she'd been crying and was trying to recover.

'Can you give me some idea of what it's about?'

'It's about Mark Yalding. He was innocent of that pornography business.'

'How can you be so sure?'

She spoke rapidly. 'Please… can I meet you? I'll explain then. It's difficult to talk right now.'

'Very well, Mrs Lloyd.'

He waited for it to register. And then, after a pause, she said, 'I'm sorry I lied, Inspector, but I didn't want Gavin to find out.'

'I understand. I could meet you in, say, half an hour?'

'No, my husband is leaving for Edinburgh at four. Supposing he's delayed with business at the office. Can we make it later? Could we meet at half seven?'

'Yes, that's fine. Shall I come to your place?'

'No, I'll come over to Bridgend. Perhaps I could meet you at the M4 services there.'

'As good a place as any, I suppose.'

'I've got to go. See you at half seven.'

She cut the call.

Ellis, Jones and Wallace were frozen with anticipation, listening and waiting for an explanation of the phone call.

'That was Rhiannon Lloyd, who has some concerns and information concerning the death of Mark Yalding. She sounded a bit distraught to say the least.'

119

THE WRECKING BAR

'This Gavin Lloyd character,' Ellis began slowly and thoughtfully,' are you certain he doesn't know about his wife's affair?'

'No, I'm not. But his receptionist has worked for him for at least four years, and she seemed genuinely shocked and surprised when I told her.'

'But if he does know about the affair, it would make him a suspect in Yalding's murder,' Ellis said.

DC Jones rubbed her forehead in frustration. 'But Yalding's killer used the same MO as the killer of the two sex offenders. Why would Lloyd kill the other two if his motive was revenge for his wife's infidelity?'

Wallace, who felt it was time to input an opinion, said, 'Maybe he killed Yalding in the same way to make it look like a copycat killing.'

Lambert stared at Wallace. 'But the sulphuric acid details were released to the papers *after* Yalding's murder.'

'True. So that rules out a deliberate copycat kill.'

'You interviewed that witness who spotted the white van. In your opinion, how reliable was that witness?'

'I think he definitely spotted the killer's van.'

'And Gavin Lloyd has never learnt to drive,' Lambert said. 'I checked up and he's never even held a provisional licence.'

Jones sighed heavily. 'So it's unlikely he's our white van driver. I wonder what his wife's phone call was all about.'

'We'll find out in just over three hours' time.' Lambert said, glancing at the clock before giving DC Jones an encouraging smile. 'And I think it might be useful if you accompany me, Debbie – same as before.'

'Woman to woman. Shoulder to cry on?'

'Exactly.'

***

They got to the M4 services a little before 7.30. Lambert bought the coffees in the coffee shop area, from where they could keep an eye on the main entrance.

DC Jones watched her boss absently stirring his espresso, even though he didn't take sugar. She knew he'd recently had a long meeting with DCS Marden, and suspected it hadn't gone well, especially knowing how much they disliked one another.

'What's happening about McNeil and Hughes?' she asked him.

'Because of the lack of evidence, and the way both their interviews went, the chief super doesn't think we've got enough to hold them. He knows the CPS would want more evidence, and he's probably right. It took all my powers of persuasion to let me hold them until all the CCTV footage has been seen.'

Chapter Eighteen

'That shouldn't take long, should it? I mean, we know the approximate time of death, especially in the marina murder.'

Lambert's mobile rang and he answered it hurriedly. 'Yes, Tony.' He listened intently then said, 'It could have been a false number plate. If it is, it's probably going to be difficult to trace. The vehicle it came from may have ended up in a breaker's yard. Well, all you can do is try. Yeah, I'll speak to you later, after I've met Rhiannon Lloyd.'

After he hung up, Jones said, 'I presume the CCTV showed a white van with different number plates to the ones on Hughes's van.'

'Spot on, Debbie. Same type of van but different number plates. This will please Marden. We've haven't got a shred of evidence with which to hold and charge McNeil or Hughes. Nothing but coincidence.'

'And that's a great deal of coincidence, if you ask me, Harry.'

Jones glanced at her watch. 'Where is she? It's a quarter to eight.'

Lambert slammed his cup on to its saucer with a clatter. 'This stinks to high heaven! She phones me up in a distressed state saying she has some vital information but she can't be that desperate to meet me if she turns up late.'

The young DC gave her boss a knowing look over the rim of her cup. 'That's if she turns up at all.'

Lambert grabbed his mobile from the table and began to scroll. 'I've saved her number. I'll give her a call.'

Jones watched him listening to the empty ringing, and saw the frustration and impatience building to a sense of urgency as his frown deepened and his eyes danced with troubled thoughts. Eventually, he gave up and clicked off the phone.

'No reply.'

'Maybe she's driving.'

'It didn't stop her answering before.'

Lambert spent a moment deliberating, then pocketed his mobile and stood up. 'Come on! We're going!'

He hurried from the coffee shop area and Jones followed, rushing to keep pace with him.

'Where are we going?' she asked, mainly as confirmation, because she could guess the answer.

'We're going to pay a visit to the Lloyds' marital home. I'd be interested to see how the Crachach live.'

'Who?'

'I'll explain on the way over.'

THE WRECKING BAR

***

Between Barry and Penarth, Lambert swung round a sharp bend, knowing the house was somewhere nearby, less than half a mile past a church. They found it difficult to see the houses that stood back from the road as it was now dark and there were no street lights.

'There's the church,' Jones said, as the giant shadow of a building loomed into view. 'Can't be far now. What's the name of the house?'

'Glyndŵr.'

'Slow down. There's an entrance just ahead with a house name on the gate.'

Lambert braked gently and let the car glide towards the entrance to a wide driveway. He spotted the sign the same time as Jones.

'We're here,' she said.

He turned into the drive, his headlights picking out the bushes on either side, which could have been rhododendron but it was too dark to see clearly. The house was a long way back from the road and the drive led to a semi-circular car park at the front, in which Rhiannon Lloyd's Land Rover stood. The house was dark, there was not a light to be seen anywhere.

Lambert parked a little distance from the Land Rover and the house. They got out of the car and had walked only a couple of paces forward when two halogen security lights lit up the area. Shielding his eyes from the glare of the lamps, Lambert scanned the house, getting a vague impression of discreet affluence, with its high windows, impressive stone steps leading up to an enormous front door, and a castle- like turret on one of the corners of the house above the second floor. Just below one of the second-floor windows was a burglar alarm.

'Her four-by-four's here but the place is in darkness,' Jones observed.

The shapes of their shadows were long and angular and crept up the stone steps as they approached the front door. Lambert pressed the doorbell, and they heard a chime echoing through the house.

They waited, listening for the sound of footsteps, but no one came to answer the door.

'I wonder where she's gone.' Jones whispered. 'Any point in ringing it again?'

'None at all,' Lambert said. 'Come on – I've got a torch in the glove compartment. Let's take a look round the back.'

Once he'd got his torch, Lambert switched it on and shined it to the left of the house and then the right. 'What it is to have money, eh? As the house stands in its own grounds, I don't think it matters which side we go round.'

'Let's go left,' Jones suggested.

'Any particular reason?'

'I just like to make a decision.'

Their feet crunching on the gravel, they walked to the left of the house as the beam from Lambert's torch danced along the side walls and path in front. It was cold now that night had descended and Jones shivered. A rustling sound from the undergrowth caused them to halt, until they realized it was either a fox or some other nocturnal creature foraging for food. They continued around the back until they came to a large patio with steps leading down to lawns and gardens. There were French windows at the top of the terrace, leading to what was probably a living room. Lambert tried the handle but it was locked.

He shone his torch to the other side of the house, and there appeared to be another building, which seemed to be an extension to the main house. Then Lambert remembered Lloyd's receptionist telling him they had a granny annex as the driver's living quarters.

They walked across the patio, knowing there had to be another back entrance, either leading to a utility room or kitchen. They hadn't gone very far before the beam of Lambert's torch focused on an open door. The top half of the door was glass and this had been smashed.

'I think,' Lambert whispered, 'she's had unwelcome intruders. But I don't think they're still here. Let's go in and take a look.'

Feeling a tension in his chest, he eased open the door and entered, his feet crunching on shards of glass. He shone his torch up and down the wall beside the door, found the light switch and clicked it on. The enormous kitchen was suddenly washed in light, revealing a room that was used for socializing as much as cooking, with a refectory table in the centre. There were two doors, one was closed, perhaps leading to a utility room, and the other was wide open and led to the hall.

Lambert nodded at a glass panel beside the kitchen door. 'Alarm couldn't have been switched on,' he whispered.

As they crept out of the kitchen and into the hall, they passed an open door leading into what was perhaps the living room. Lambert reached in and switched on the light.

Wall lights and expensive art deco standard lamps illuminated the spacious room, which was tastefully furnished but a mess. An antique bureau in an alcove had had its drawers pulled right out and the contents were scattered across the thick pile carpet. There was a discoloured empty square above a marble fireplace, indicating that a picture had hung over it.

'This place has been ransacked,' Lambert said. 'Let's go and see what else we can find.'

At the end of the hallway, near the front door, Lambert saw the light switches for the hall and upstairs landing and switched them on. The front hallway was lit by a chandelier and they both stood still for a moment, surveying the grand, carved oak staircase.

'Usually,' Jones said, tilting her head to indicate the staircase, 'anything of value is in the master bedroom.'

Lambert nodded his agreement and led the way up the stairs. As they rounded the first landing, they saw the remnants of a broken vase on the floor, which had presumably stood on the window sill by the leaded windows looking out on to the back garden.

They started up the next flight to the first-floor landing and stopped. The cream-coloured carpet was splattered with blood, spread out across an area of staircase like an explosion of red paint.

Jones's mouth suddenly felt parched and her stomach quaked. She stared at her boss, whose expression was fixed, as if he was carved from stone.

'Tread carefully,' he said quietly.

Leading the way again, he climbed the rest of the stairs, avoiding the smears of blood, and reached the landing.

'My God!' Jones said as she joined him, and saw the dark trail of blood leading to the bedroom.

Lambert now strode purposefully towards the bedroom, just in case whoever had shed the blood was still alive and needed attention.

As soon as they entered they saw her body, lying near the double bed, as if she had tried to escape her killer by crawling underneath. As they stared at the crumpled, bloody figure, they knew there was no way she could still be alive.

It looked as if Rhiannon Lloyd had been shot twice; through the shoulder and then in the back of the head.

Nineteen

Gavin Lloyd and his driver signed in at their hotel. The receptionist, an attractive young Hungarian woman, smiled warmly and brushed a stray wisp of hair away from her cheek.

'Thank you, sir. Mr Lloyd, you are in Room 342, and Mr Collier, it is Room 356, both on third floor.'

They took their plastic keys and Lloyd said, 'We'll just put our bags upstairs and then perhaps you would be so kind as to tell us where the restaurant is.'

'For breakfast?'

Lloyd looked as if she had asked him to clean the kitchens. 'No, I don't mean for breakfast. I mean for now! For dinner!'

'I am sorry. The restaurant is shut. The last dinner was at nine o'clock.'

'Well, I'm sure they can rustle us up something. Just show us where it is.'

She began to look concerned, knowing she had an awkward customer standing in front of her desk.

'Sorry. It is shut.'

'Look, am I talking gibberish or what? All I asked you for was directions to the restaurant. My driver and I have driven all the way from Cardiff, and it's taken us over six hours. So the least we expect from a four-star hotel is a meal on our arrival.'

'There is room service for snacks and sandwiches, or you can enjoy them in the bar.'

Lloyd stared at his driver and raised his voice. 'Obviously I'm not making myself clear.'

'Can I help you, gentlemen?'

The man suddenly appeared from behind them. He was dark-haired and spoke with a trace of an Italian accent. 'I'm the manager here,' he added.

THE WRECKING BAR

As if speaking to an imbecile, Lloyd slowed and emphasized his words. 'We have driven from Cardiff – more than six hours. My driver and I are very tired and hungry. Is it too much to ask you to get a hot meal?'

The manager shrugged. 'There is only one person in the kitchen, doing sandwiches and room service. The chefs have gone home.'

'I don't believe this! A sodding four-star hotel!'

'If you don't mind my saying, sir, this is Edinburgh. Just step outside the door and you have many restaurants of all kinds. Whatever you like to eat...'

With a dismissive wave of the hand, Lloyd interrupted him. 'Oh, forget it! We're too tired to go walkabout. We'll have one of your bloody sandwiches.'

Lloyd stormed off to the bar, with Collier following a few paces behind. The manager watched them go, fantasizing about this being his last day at work and how he had told that objectionable customer exactly what he thought of him.

***

While SOCO were busy gathering evidence at the immediate crime scene and the rest of the house, Lambert and Jones, both wearing latex gloves, sifted through the scattered contents of the bureau in the living room.

'Can you translate Welsh into English?' Jones asked as she picked up a slim, burgundy-coloured book.

'Not a chance,' Lambert replied, looking over her shoulder at the book. 'On the other hand, the numerals should give us a clue. To hazard a guess, I would think *dyddlyfr* is Welsh for diary.'

She opened the diary and flicked through to January. 'It can't be his diary; it must be hers because the entries are written in Welsh.'

'Translation won't be a problem: Dave and several of the SOCO team speak Welsh.'

She turned the diary pages until she came to October. 'She has an appointment to see someone in Abertawe tomorrow.'

'That's Welsh for Swansea.'

'Yes, thank you – I do know that much. I can read the road signs, you know.'

'Does it say who she was supposed to meet?'

'Someone called Morgan Jones.'

'Any relation of yours?'

'We're quite a big family, but not that big. There's a phone number by his name.'

126

CHAPTER NINETEEN

Lambert produced his mobile and said, 'Call out the numbers for me.'

He dialled the numbers as she read them out. After it made the connection it switched to voicemail. He listened to the message and hung up. Jones looked at him expectantly.

'They'll be there from 9 a.m. tomorrow.'

'They?'

'Someone called Francis, Jones and Prosser.'

'Sounds like a firm of solicitors.'

'I'll call them first thing in the morning. Is there an address section in the back of the diary?'

'There is, but it's empty. Most people keep their phone numbers in their mobiles now.'

Lambert snapped his fingers. 'That's a point: I haven't seen her mobile phone anywhere, have you?'

She shook her head. 'Now you come to mention it...'

'This what you're looking for?'

They turned towards the door as Jason, one of the younger members of the SOCO team, entered, holding a mobile.

'Where d'you find it?'

'It was just under the bed, near to where she was shot in the head. She managed to dial the emergency number but it hadn't been sent. Presumably the fatal shot got her before she could press "send". Hughie asked me to let you have it post haste. He said he thought you might want to access her address book right away.'

He handed the phone to Lambert.

'That's very useful. Thanks, Jason.'

'*Dim* problem,' Jason said as he exited.

Lambert smiled at Jones. 'Strange sort of language that uses both Welsh and English in a two-word sentence.'

He found Rhiannon Lloyd's address book on the mobile and scrolled down to the letter G. 'Here we are. There's two numbers for her husband: his office and mobile.'

'I don't envy you this call.'

'Giving a relative the bad news is something I would normally loathe and detest. But in this instance...'

'You don't like him, do you?'

'I wouldn't go so far as to say that. I've only met him once. And he seemed like he could be really charming. But if I shook hands with the man, I'd count my fingers afterwards.'

THE WRECKING BAR

***

Gavin Lloyd and Jack Collier sat at a table in the centre of the bar, Collier drinking lime and soda, and his boss had a half of bitter with a large whisky chaser. They had both just finished eating roast beef sandwiches, with a small salad garnish, and had barely spoken two words to one another since entering the bar. Their small-wheeled suitcases stood beside the table, and Lloyd's mobile sat on the table next to his sandwich plate. He stifled a yawn and cast his eyes around the bar. It seemed to be fairly quiet, but that was understandable, it being a Monday night. A married couple sat in an alcove, their eyes focused on some distant longing, each separated by years of habitual silence. They didn't appear to be hotel residents, because the man had an anorak draped across the seat next to him, and his wife was wearing a long woollen coat and chiffon scarf. At the bar a company of businessmen stood laughing and talking loudly about banking and poor investments and were clearly residents because all their drinks went on their room tabs.

The barman, seeing the empty plates on Lloyd and Collier's table, hurried over to collect them. Lloyd nodded to him and spoke to Collier.

'I know you're the driver, Jack, but after six hours in the car I feel really knackered.'

He knocked back his whisky and was about to chase this down with a draught of beer when his mobile rang.

Collier stared at his boss, observing the theatrical way he took the call, leaning back in his chair, smiling confidently, his head tilted upwards slightly and projecting his voice.

'Gavin Lloyd! Inspector Lambert! What can I do for you? I didn't expect to hear from you so soon. It was only this morning you came to see me in Cardiff. I'm up in Edinburgh right now.'

Collier watched Lloyd intently and their eyes met briefly. And then his boss's face suddenly crumpled and his eyes filled with tears.

'No! No! This can't be happening. Please tell me it's not true. Oh, Jesus Christ! Please! Not Rhiannon!'

The businessmen at the bar stopped speaking as they witnessed this tragic scene unfolding a few feet away.

Lloyd bent over the table, weeping and holding his head in his free hand.

'I can't believe this is happening. Oh God, no! Not my Rhiannon. Yes, yes. Please! Just give me a minute. Of course, I'll come home right away. No, I don't think there'll be a direct flight from here to Cardiff at this time of night.

Oh Jesus Christ! This can't be happening. Yes, yes. We'll come straight back. Hang on a second, Inspector, I need to talk to Jack.'

He held the phone away from his ear and stared tearfully at Collier. 'It's Rhiannon. She's been killed.'

Collier's normally inscrutable face contorted into an expression of empathic grief. 'I'm sorry,' he muttered. 'How did it happen?'

Ignoring the question, Lloyd said, 'We have to go back right away. D'you think you'll be all right to drive?'

Collier nodded. Lloyd sniffed and wiped his eyes. 'Jack thinks he's okay to drive. It's another six-hour journey. If we have to, I'll book into a motel halfway and he can get his head down for a couple of hours. We should be back early morning. Oh God! This is a nightmare.'

Lloyd hung up and leant over the table, holding his head in his hands.

Collier stood, reached out awkwardly and touched Lloyd's arm. 'It's a long drive,' he said. 'I think we'd better leave.'

Twenty

Sitting next to Gavin Lloyd, Mark Powell, his solicitor, shot a frosty look at Lambert, but the slight lisp in his voice tended to kill any attempt at authority.

'Inspector Lambert, my client has been up all night, and it has been a most distressing and stressful time for him, I don't think it unreasonable to expect an explanation for—'

Lambert interrupted. 'Well, how's this for an explanation? We have concrete evidence that your client had a motive for killing his wife.'

'That's bloody absurd, and you know it is,' Lloyd shouted. 'My house was burgled… robbed… and you think I had something to do with it? You must be mad.'

Lambert was about to reply but Lloyd's solicitor jumped in first.

'My client has already told you he was in Edinburgh, and he can prove he was there with his driver at the time of this terrible homicide.'

Lambert threw a sideways glance at DC Jones, a heard-it-all-before expression. When he turned back to confront the solicitor, he made a point of wiping the cynical smile from his face.

'Mr Powell, I would appreciate it if I could continue to question Mr Lloyd, and then the sooner we can get all this cleared up, the sooner your client can go home and get some sleep.' He focused his attention on Lloyd. 'Assuming, of course, you are able to sleep following these terrible events.'

The solicitor sighed pointedly before reluctantly accepting Lambert's demands. 'Very well. Let's get it over with.'

'Mr Lloyd,' Lambert began as he consulted his notes and then looked up again, 'have you heard of a firm called Francis, Jones and Prosser?'

Lloyd tilted his head sideways, as if trying to recall. 'Yes, my wife's solicitors I believe.'

Chapter Twenty

Lambert exaggerated an expression of surprise. 'You believe? Most families retain the same firm of solicitors. Unless there's a conflict of interest. Do you and your wife use separate law firms because you don't see eye to eye about something?'

'Of course not. My wife used the same solicitors as her parents did. As you yourself said, most families retain the same firm.'

'Would it surprise you to learn that your wife had an appointment today to see her solicitor?'

Lloyd hesitated. 'Well, yes, that's news to me.'

'I've already spoken to a Mr Morgan Jones at the firm. When I explained the gravity of the situation, and that it was a murder enquiry into the death of his client, he was quite open about why she was going to see him. It was in order to obtain a divorce from you.'

'What?'

Lambert and Jones studied Lloyd's reaction, whose glassy stare of incomprehension seemed genuine.

'I really had no idea. None at all. This has come as a complete shock. Did he say why she was seeking a divorce?'

'You mean you don't know?'

The solicitor butted in. 'My client has already told you he didn't know, Inspector.'

Ignoring him, Lambert continued. 'Did you know your wife was having an affair with another man?'

Lloyd's mouth opened slowly as he was forced to confront the truth. His eyes misted over and he looked like a helpless forlorn youth. It was impossible to know if he had genuinely not known of his wife's affair or was giving an Oscar-winning performance.

'I can't believe Rhiannon was having an affair.' Lloyd looked straight into Lambert's eyes. 'Was she leaving me for another man?'

'No, she wasn't, Mr Lloyd.'

'But I don't understand.'

'The man with whom she was having an affair died last Saturday night. Mark Yalding, your ex-employee.'

Not a muscle moved in Lloyd's face.

'It was a serious affair that had gone on for quite some time. No doubt she was planning to leave you for Mr Yalding. But someone got to him first. Did you really not know how close she was to Yalding?'

'No, I had no idea.'

'And did your wife never do anything to arouse your suspicion?'

THE WRECKING BAR

'Well… no…'

'Why did you hesitate over that answer, Mr Lloyd?'

'I didn't think anything was wrong with our relationship. I suppose I just thought our marriage had gone the way of most marriages after twenty-five years. Now that you've told me about the affair she was having, I can see… yes… with the benefit of hindsight, she had been acting a little strange in recent months. Nothing I could put my finger on. It was mainly her moods.'

'And how is Green Valley Productions doing?'

The abrupt change of subject seemed to catch Lloyd out for a moment. He turned towards his solicitor as if hoping for support. But Powell sat stony-faced, avoiding eye contact with his client. Lloyd clearly expected his solicitor to intervene, to perhaps challenge the relevance of the question. But, unlike his client, the solicitor couldn't see where Lambert's questions were heading now.

'It's a simple enough question, Mr Lloyd. How is your production company doing financially?'

Lloyd shifted uncomfortably in his chair and fiddled with his wristwatch.

'Well, just lately we've had one or two setbacks.'

'Such as?'

'We pitched some projects and none of them were taken up.'

'It must be difficult to keep your company afloat when you have no income. Did your wife agree to bail your company out of financial difficulties the same as her father did twenty years ago?'

Alarm flickered in Lloyd's eyes briefly. 'My father-in-law didn't bail me out of difficulties, as you put it; he offered to finance the company when I first set it up.'

'So was this a long-term loan?'

Lloyd murmured something incomprehensible.

'I'm sorry,' Lambert said, 'I didn't catch that.'

'Yes, I think it was a loan.'

'And was this ever paid back?'

'I'm afraid he died before the production company was in a position to pay back the loan.'

'So, as his beneficiary, your wife would be owed the loan from your company. And, according to her solicitor, the amount involved meant that if she divorced you, and the proceeds of the properties were divided, once the loan was paid back you would receive nothing. Did you ever argue about finances?'

'Occasionally. What married couple doesn't?'

132

'Mr Lloyd, you have two motives for killing your wife—'

Panic in his eyes, Lloyd interrupted. 'But I swear to you I didn't know about my wife and Mark Yalding! And I wouldn't have done anything to harm Rhiannon. I loved her. You're not suggesting I'd kill her for money, for Christ's sake....'

A single tear trickled from a corner of an eye, and he gave a low animal moan as his head dropped forward into his hands. A momentary silence followed as they watched him sobbing, and then his solicitor jumped in. 'I think that's quite enough, Mr Lambert.'

Lambert nodded at Jones. 'I think we'll take a break and resume the interview in half an hour.'

***

When he first set eyes on Jack Collier, Ellis had searched his mind for an elusive word in his vocabulary to describe Gavin Lloyd's driver. Now, as he was about to ask Collier the first question of the interrogation, the word flashed into his mind like a neon sign.

Cipher. That was it. A cipher.

Collier was a nonentity. Which was strange, really, because Ellis could see that the driver was better-looking than his boss. He had an almost conventionally handsome face with features that were perfect: full lips, a perfectly proportioned nose, high cheekbones which were not overly prominent, and steel-blue eyes with the sort of long dark lashes that most women covet. But there was not a single hair on his head, which was white and smooth as a cue ball. He might have been considered striking, but there was something seriously lacking. Perhaps it was all to do with personality. Ellis felt the man was insipid and dull, and probably had very little to offer socially.

Sitting beside Collier was his solicitor, provided by his employer from the same firm of solicitors as his own. This solicitor, as Wallace had dropped in an aside to his sergeant prior to entering the interview room, made young coppers look like pensioners. He was fresh-faced, wore frameless, slightly tinted glasses, and looked like he had just left the sixth form.

'Mr Collier,' Ellis began, 'if, as I believe, Mr Lloyd doesn't drive, and you take him everywhere, you must have got to know him quite well? How long have you worked for him?'

Sitting beside Ellis, DC Wallace studied Collier's reaction, or rather the lack of reaction in his inscrutable face. What leapt into Wallace's mind was the expression: *the lights are on but there's no one home.*

THE WRECKING BAR

After several beats, Collier answered, 'Twenty-five years.'

'And how old are you now?'

'Forty-eight.'

Ellis suspected he was going to get monosyllabic answers from this man and wondered how he could draw him out.

'You're not Welsh, are you?'

'No.'

'So where are you from, originally?'

'London.'

'When did you come to live in Wales?'

'Twenty-five years ago.'

'So how did you end up working for Mr Lloyd?'

'He advertised for a driver. I applied and got the job.'

'What time did you leave for Edinburgh yesterday?'

Without hesitating, Collier replied, 'Four in the afternoon.'

'And how long did the journey take?'

'Just over six hours.'

'So you arrived just after ten.'

'Quarter past.'

'Did you stop on the way?'

'We stopped at a pub.'

Ellis's voice rose in surprise. 'But isn't it motorway almost all the way to Edinburgh, except the last leg of the journey when you leave the M74? Yet you say you stopped in a pub.'

'Gavin don't like motorway services.'

'So where was this pub?'

Ellis could see Wallace out of the corner of his eye, pencil poised, ready to jot down the name and area.

Collier shrugged. 'Dunno.'

Ellis feigned bewilderment. 'Let me get this straight: you have no idea where you stopped for a drink—'

Collier interrupted him. 'I didn't say that. I know the pub was somewhere in Kendal, not far off Junction 37 on the M6. But I can't remember which pub we stopped at or its exact location. It's about six or seven miles from the junction.'

Up until now, Collier had given short answers and Ellis wondered if the man was being deliberately uncooperative, giving the impression he was taciturn.

He decided he would shift the interrogation up a gear. 'What did you and your employer talk about on this journey?'

'Nothing much.'

Ellis laughed sarcastically. 'That must have been an interesting six hours. Come on, Mr Collier, you must remember something you discussed.'

'Well, you know...'

'No, I don't know,' Ellis snapped. Out of the corner of his eye he saw the solicitor about to intervene and continued his questioning hurriedly. 'I find it difficult to believe you don't remember a single topic of conversation. You've been driving him around for twenty-five years, so you must get on with him pretty well. Did he talk to you about his wife?'

'No, we talked about the television series he's planning.'

'But he didn't talk about his wife at all?'

'No.'

'Did they argue much?'

Collier shrugged. 'How would I know?'

'Most married couples row from time to time. And don't you live with them both?'

'Not really. I've got my own separate flat.'

'Yesterday afternoon, when you left for Edinburgh, was it from the Lloyds' house?'

'No, it was from the office in Cardiff.'

'So was Mr Lloyd working in his office prior to leaving for Edinburgh?'

'Yes, I've just told you. We left from his office.'

'But what were you doing before you picked him up at his office?'

'I was at my flat, having a rest before the journey.'

'Did you see his wife or speak to her?'

Collier paused, taking his time while he thought about this, almost as if he was considering his options. 'She came and knocked on my door.'

'What time was this?'

'About one o'clock. She was going out, and she wanted to know when we'd be coming back from Scotland.'

'Have you any idea where she was going?'

'She was off to her mother's. She often went round there, to make her lunch. Her mother's got Alzheimer's disease. Sometimes a health visitor goes round, but not on a Monday.'

'Forgive me, Mr Collier, but I would have thought her mother would have been better off in the granny annex where you live, so that her daughter could keep an eye on her. Was this ever a contentious issue between Mr Lloyd and his wife?'

Collier shrugged and his head turned towards the bare wall of the interview room. 'I don't know. If it was an issue, I never got to hear of it.'

THE WRECKING BAR

Ellis said nothing, waiting for Collier to feel the discomfort of the silence and look him in the eye again. When he did, Ellis said, 'On your way to Edinburgh yesterday evening, how long did you stop at the pub?'

Disconcerted by the sudden change, Collier's mouth opened, confusion showing in his eyes. Ellis repeated the question.

'I don't think I...' He stopped and looked upwards, thinking. 'I don't think we were there very long. It was really to give me a break for a cup of coffee. It's a long journey.'

'I've driven from Swansea to Edinburgh,' DC Wallace interposed, his voice mild and conversational. 'It's just over four hundred miles. So if you broke the journey, you must have made pretty good time.'

'I don't hang about,' Collier replied, and then smiled, sharing a joke. 'You're not trying to trap me into admitting I was speeding, are you?'

Ellis stared at him, his expression serious. 'So how long did you stop at the pub for?'

'About fifteen minutes. It was really more of a toilet break.'

'Did you stop anywhere for petrol?'

Collier shook his head. 'We filled up in Cardiff. It was a BP station and Gavin had a bit of an argument with the staff in there.'

'What about?'

'Well, I sat in the car; I didn't go inside. But it was one of those petrol stations with a mini supermarket, and apparently Gavin blew his top because he had to queue behind people with loads of shopping. He reckoned there should have been a till just for petrol.'

'Unlike the pub halfway to Edinburgh,' Ellis said pointedly, 'can you remember the location of this petrol station?'

'Yes, of course. I've used it before.'

'And we'll want to check up on your Edinburgh hotel, and get staff to verify the time of your arrival.'

A short bark of laughter from Collier, whose confidence seemed to have grown. 'I don't think they'll forget us two in a hurry.'

'Oh? And why's that?'

'Gavin had a row about the service. He was annoyed the restaurant was shut. They offered us sandwiches from room service or in the bar, but Gavin wanted a proper meal.'

Ellis frowned thoughtfully.

'But you arrived around quarter past ten. Don't you think that's a bit late to expect a hotel restaurant to still be serving?'

'I hadn't really thought about it.'

'So Mr Lloyd had an argument before setting off for Edinburgh and had another argument while checking in to the hotel. Bit of a coincidence that, don't you think?'

Collier shrugged.

'Is that a question that needs answering, Sergeant?' the solicitor said. 'Or is that an observation of your own?'

Ignoring him, Ellis stared at Collier. 'Did Mr Lloyd have an argument at the pub you stopped at, by any chance?'

'No, he didn't.'

As if suddenly remembering something vital, Ellis clicked his fingers and said, 'Oh yes, something I meant to ask you, Mr Collier: do you know if Mr Lloyd owns a firearm of any sort?'

'I don't think he does, no.'

'You seem very certain about that. Does Mr Lloyd tell you everything he does?'

'Like you said yourself, I've driven him around for twenty-five years. I think I've got to know him pretty well in that time. And I've never known him to mention guns or shooting.' Collier's eyes narrowed as he stared shrewdly at Ellis. 'So if you're asking about guns, it must mean you suspect Gavin of killing Rhiannon. I'm sorry, that's bollocks. All you've got to do is check up with the hotel in Edinburgh to see where we were at ten o'clock last night.'

Ellis held Collier's confident stare. 'Don't worry, Mr Collier. We have every intention of doing that.'

∗∗∗

Following the two interviews, it was decided that Lloyd and his driver would be held a while longer, while Lambert and the other detectives drove to Cockett Police Station to compare notes in the incident room.

'There's no doubt in my mind that Lloyd went to Edinburgh,' Lambert said. 'But it's a strange coincidence. We now have four suspects with perfect alibis. There's Norman McNeil and his brother-in-law, Alan Hughes, both with watertight alibis for when the sex offenders and Yalding were murdered, and coincidentally Lloyd and his driver can account for their whereabouts when his wife was murdered.'

Ellis, sitting on a corner of one of the desks, nodded at the whiteboard where the names and photographs of their suspects were stuck, with red felt-tip lines connecting them, and said, 'It looks like one hell of a conspiracy, if they're all in it together.'

THE WRECKING BAR

'It could well be,' Lambert continued thoughtfully, 'that Rhiannon Lloyd's death is not connected to the others.'

DC Jones asked him if he thought robbery was the motive.

'Not necessarily,' he replied. 'It could have been for financial gain, though.'

'So you still think her husband had something to do with it?'

Leaning against the wall, hands in pockets, Wallace said, 'He could have paid to have her whacked.'

Kevin's American gangster jargon provoked a giggle from DC Jones.

Lambert stared at her. 'No, Kevin's got a point. We don't know what sort of gun was used yet, but it wouldn't be the first time someone has hired a professional to kill someone close to them.'

One of the desk telephones rang and Ellis picked it up. 'CID, Sergeant Ellis speaking.' He listened briefly, and his eyes flickered over to Lambert. 'He's here. I'll pass you on to him.' Holding the phone out to Lambert, he covered the mouthpiece and said, 'DC McLeish, Lothian and Borders.'

Lloyd and Collier's photographs had been faxed to Edinburgh police, requesting confirmation of their hotel arrival.

Lambert took the phone. 'Good of you to ring back so promptly, Jim,' he said. 'You checked with the hotel manager?'

The other three detectives waited quietly, watching and listening to Lambert's brief conversation.

'So the receptionist and the manager confirmed that it was them.' Listening to the reply, Lambert snorted and a grin broke out on his face. 'Okay. Thanks, Jim, I really appreciate your help. Yeah, and you.'

After he hung up, Lambert still had the grin on his face as he said, 'That was confirmation it was Collier and Lloyd in Edinburgh. And the hotel manager took an immediate disliking to Lloyd and said it was lucky the restaurant *was* shut because he'd have been tempted to piss in the wanker's soup.'

'Well, that's their alibis confirmed,' Ellis said.

Lambert's grin had become lopsidedly cynical. 'Lloyd blows his stack at the petrol station on the way out of Cardiff, and another argument on their arrival in Edinburgh. Talk about signposting their alibis.'

'Otherwise they might have gone unnoticed,' DC Jones said.

The telephone rang again and Lambert grabbed it. He listened intensely, strain showing on his face. 'Okay. I'll be there right away, sir.'

He hung up and told them, 'DCS Marden wants to see me urgently. Maybe a milk float's been stolen in Bridgend.'

***

138

As Lambert knocked and entered, he found Marden in a fidgety mood, standing to the side of his desk. He was greeted with, 'I'm not pleased with the way things are going, Harry.'

Lambert said nothing, waiting for the chief super to elaborate.

'The emails I get from you keeping me informed are, to say the least, vague to the point of...' Marden struggled to find an appropriate description.

'Of what, sir?' Lambert said innocently.

'It doesn't matter. Now I assume you've checked Gavin Lloyd's alibi by now?'

'It's been done,' Lambert nodded, being deliberately vague.

Marden's voice rose with a trace of irritation. 'And?'

'He and his driver were on their way to Edinburgh at the time of the murder. If his wife was killed just before DC Jones and I arrived at the scene, they were probably somewhere on the M6 in the Lake District.'

Marden glanced impatiently at his watch. 'So you've no evidence tying Gavin Lloyd to the murder of his wife.'

'Not yet we haven't.'

'What is that supposed to mean?'

'We were discussing the possibility of him paying someone to kill her.'

Marden laughed but his eyes were frosty. 'A hitman, you mean? Harry, this is Bridgend, not Chicago.'

'With all due respect, sir, you might have noticed the sudden spate of brutal killings in this part of the world. I've chalked up four so far, plus one drowned suicide. Soon the cops of Chicago will liken their crime scenes to ours in South Wales.'

'But it's ludicrous to put Gavin Lloyd in the frame simply because he has a motive. You could say a lot of married couples have motives. People often gain from the death of their partner. And Gavin Lloyd's a highly respected member of the community.'

Ah, thought Lambert, the truth will out. Of course, DCS Clive Marden was also a respected member of the community, mixing in those same hallowed Welsh circles as the Lloyds. The inner sanctum which Lambert had discovered was a closed door, slammed years ago in his face. It was all to do with his attitude. He could never let pretentiousness go unchallenged and more often than not it was his mouth which excluded him from those circles. Not that it bothered him. Far from it.

As if he could sense what Lambert was thinking, Marden softened his voice and added, 'I'm not asking any special favours for Gavin Lloyd because of his standing in the community. I want you to look at the evidence and the

THE WRECKING BAR

facts in this case. We know whoever shot Rhiannon Lloyd stole a valuable Augustus John painting. That alone would have been worth a small fortune. Her jewellery also was substantial, including a watch, a Patek Philippe, valued at fifteen thousand pounds. Just because her boyfriend was killed doesn't mean that the murders are connected. It could be a pure coincidence.'

Seeing Lambert about to reply, Marden raised a hand. 'Yes, I know. You don't believe in coincidences. But they do happen. And that's what makes them coincidences.' He glanced at his watch again and ushered Lambert towards the door.

Lambert tried to control his temper. One more push on the button and it would erupt. What was wrong with communicating by telephone? Why had he driven from Swansea to Bridgend for this brief meeting?

'You've got no evidence that Gavin Lloyd had anything to do with his wife's death,' Marden said. 'So I think you'd better release him and his driver. And the ACC's agreed to provide more resources. That should help you find the other three sex offenders, and I think this vigilante group needs investigating.'

'Believe it or not, sir, that was going to be my next move,' Lambert said as he walked away.

Marden called after him, 'Oh, yes, you might like to know that North Devon CID has officially identified the drowned man as Gordon Mayfield.'

Lambert stopped and turned round. 'Well, of course it was Mayfield. Who else would it have been?'

'We have to be certain, Harry. Even you know how dangerous it is to make assumptions.'

'Who else's body could have washed up in the Bristol Channel? Richey Edwards, maybe?'

Confusion mixed with disgust in Marden's expression. Lambert misinterpreted it and started to explain, 'Richey Edwards was the missing band member—'

'Yes, I'm well aware he was one of the Manic Street Preachers and his body was never found. I was just thinking what a tasteless remark that was.'

Slamming his office door, Marden turned away and stormed off in the other direction.

***

When Lambert arrived back at the incident room, he had cheered up a bit. And thinking about the DCS's remark about the Manic Street Preachers as he entered, he wore a slightly amused expression. Ellis, perceptive as he usually

Chapter Twenty

was, noticed the secret smile in his boss's eyes and asked him if the meeting with the chief superintendent had gone particularly well.

'Neither here nor there,' Lambert replied cryptically. 'Who'd have thought the chief super would have heard of the Manic Street Preachers?'

'I know what you mean,' Ellis agreed. 'Bryn Terfil, yes.'

'But not the Manics,' Lambert concluded.

Twenty-One

Because of Rhiannon Lloyd's illustrious background, and the way her life had been cut short in such a tragic way, there were many members of her family who thought the funeral should be held as soon as possible. Her older sister, Bethan, argued that the media coverage was going to dominate the proceedings and it was probably best if it was attended by only the close family, and then they could hold a memorial service two or three months later. There were other family members – uncles, aunts and cousins – who agreed and thought that perhaps Friday was not unreasonable if it could be organized in time.

But Gavin Lloyd disagreed, arguing that to go through what seemed like the entire proceedings twice would be unfair on the children, not least himself.

Bethan wanted to avoid family squabbles over what was after all a heart-rending and devastating time for the family, but she argued fiercely with her brother-in-law because she felt he was being unfeeling and callous about the memorial service. And although she wouldn't admit it, buried in Bethan's mind was a desire for a more controlled service, attended by many well-known artists, writers and opera singers, people her sister had championed during her time with the Welsh Arts Council.

But Gavin Lloyd dug in his heels; he was adamant he wasn't going to go through it all a second time. This succeeded in bringing bitter family resentments back to the surface as Bethan threw in her brother-in-law's face the loan from her father which he had never paid back.

That was when he told her about his wife's affair with Mark Yalding. At first she didn't believe him, but because she had never truly liked her brother-in-law, especially since he had callously rooked her father, she understood how her sister had sought comfort in the arms of another man. It also helped

142

CHAPTER TWENTY-ONE

her to understand, albeit resentfully, her brother-in-law's reluctance to hold a memorial service sometime later.

And when the coroner's office indicated that a Friday funeral might be difficult because of the post mortem and any complications that might arise, the funeral was put off for seven days and would be held on the following Tuesday.

Bethan had no option but to accept these plans, but it was with deep bitterness. She still argued, clinging to the wreckage, saying the circumstances of her sister's tragic death were obvious. Rhiannon had been wounded by a shot in the back as she ran upstairs, managed to crawl into the bedroom, where she was shot once in the back of the head. It didn't need a pathologist or the coroner to tell her that.

***

Following the discovery of Rhiannon Lloyd's body, the forensic team went over the Lloyds' house with a fine-tooth comb, but found no traces of fingerprints, other than those of Rhiannon and Gavin Lloyd. The handle of the back door had been wiped clean, possibly by the intruder's glove, and although small fibres were meticulously collected and bagged from various parts of the house, very little evidence seemed to emerge from their search.

When Lambert met Hughie John at the forensic lab and heard his report, he sighed and shook his head. Then he spotted a glint in the forensic scientist's eye, prior to a wide grin.

'We found grey fibres in the house that looked as if they had come from inside a car, probably came off the killer's shoe. We checked the victim's Land Rover and they didn't match. But I've been saving the good news till last.'

'Don't tell me you found a print which will match those of someone with a criminal record?'

'Not that good. But we did find this on the driveway leading up to the house.'

Hughie handed him a photograph, showing several black dollops on the gravel, about the size of a table tennis ball. 'Someone's car has a pretty bad oil leak. Again, we checked the victim's Land Rover, and it didn't come from that. So that only leaves your Merc, Harry.'

'I hope it's not from mine. The car's only two years old.'

'Yes, a nice motor. It's all right for some.'

'Recession bargain, Hughie. Couldn't resist it.'

'Still, you'll need to check that this oil's not from your car.'

THE WRECKING BAR

As soon as Lambert was outside the lab, he moved his car from his parking space and checked the ground. There was no oil spillage. But just to make certain, he took it to a garage to get it checked out.

It was clean.

***

First thing on Wednesday morning Lambert briefed his team, which had now been increased by four male uniform PCs and two female. He told them his priority was to get Alan Hughes's van checked for oil leaks, and he wanted it examined thoroughly, up on a garage ramp. He didn't think for one minute McNeil or Hughes would be co-operative, so a warrant was needed. He also instructed Wallace and Jones to revisit McNeil's house to get the names and addresses of the vigilantes belonging to PASO, who would all need to be interviewed, and the other three named sex offenders needed to be interrogated as soon as possible.

Although confident he had a good team, Lambert sensed a feeling of pessimism in them. It was something he couldn't quite put his finger on. Perhaps it was something to do with the weather. Early that morning, prior to the briefing, the weather had deteriorated suddenly, the day plunged into darkness, and the hills acquired a familiarly satanic look that was morbidly fitting as heavy rain blanketed all of South Wales. And Lambert knew how dispiriting a day like this could be to those in the team who would be knocking on doors, encountering the hostility of the vigilantes, and took pains to motivate them, explaining how important their efforts were. But Lambert realized there was a half-heartedness about his leadership that he found difficult to conquer, almost as if he was going through the motions simply to prove to DCS Marden that he had the investigation well under control.

He knew what he was doing had to be done, but he also suspected it wasn't going to achieve very much.

And the first confirmation of his doubts came towards the end of the dreary day as they discovered the fertilizer factory van didn't leak oil. Then there came the news that most of the PASO members seemed to be angry and indignant enough to lobby their MPs, write irate letters to the newspapers and send furious emails to organizations such as the NSPCC, but showed no signs of remaining anything but law abiding.

By the time the week was almost over, Lambert's team felt demoralized, even though they all knew the importance of elimination in any investigation. Just one glimmer of a result might have raised everyone's spirits, especially as the newspapers were having a field day writing their insinuations of police incompetence. Which didn't make Lambert's life any easier as far as his relationship with DCS Clive Marden was concerned, who pestered him at every juncture, demanding a greater commitment from him, and once he even made a snide comment about wishing DI Ambrose wasn't in Florida, even though on a case review basis Ambrose was only half as successful as Lambert.

What irritated Lambert most, however, was Marden referring to the other sex offenders as suspects. Lambert argued that they were far more likely to be victims, even though he himself had posited the vague possibility of one of them becoming a vengeance-seeking serial killer. And, as he pointed out, the reason it was proving difficult to discover their whereabouts was probably because they feared for their lives, knowing they were next on a serial killer's list.

One of them, a man named Peter Brown, had fled to Birmingham, and was scraping a living by working for a firm of legal migrants offering cheap car washes. It was possible he could have driven from Birmingham at night. He was able to drive but didn't own a car and there was no record of him having hired one. He was scrubbed off the list.

The fifth sex offender was discovered living in a hostel in Cardiff, and as he was technically homeless he occasionally sold copies of *Big Issue* by day. Much of his time was spent drinking cheap booze in a Wetherspoon's pub, where he talked nonsense to other problem drinkers. Although he wasn't entirely destitute, he didn't have far to fall to rock bottom. He was a highly unlikely suspect.

But the final sex offender, Randall Morris, was harder to trace. He had vanished from Tregaron, much to the relief of anyone who knew who he was and what he'd done and had not been seen for about six months.

Out of all the sex offenders, it was Randall Morris who aroused most suspicion. Although all sex offenders were well practised at deviousness, Morris took it to a higher level. The son of an accountant, he married, had a family, and owned a sweetshop in Llanelli. Whenever a lone child entered his shop, he or she would often discover it was empty, the proprietor nowhere to be seen. A child in a sweetshop, faced with the prospect of free chocolate, will nine times out of ten succumb to temptation, especially if the likelihood of being caught is negligible. And Morris had it all worked out, having singled out the most vulnerable children, the ones he knew would find the prospect of facing their parents with a shoplifting charge too difficult to stomach. That was when he pounced from behind his curtain, where he had been watching the unsuspecting child pocketing confectionery.

THE WRECKING BAR

After Morris was caught, he was given what the residents of Llanelli described as a ludicrously lenient sentence of three years. His wife divorced him and an exclusion order stopped him from seeing his children when he was released.

Morris then moved back to Tregaron, where he met and married an overweight, unattractive widow. But the attraction became apparent when social services later discovered that she had an eight-year-old daughter who Morris had abused for four years. This time he was sentenced to seven years.

And now, more than eight years later, they hadn't a clue where he was.

But on the Friday, the police press office circulated his picture to all the South Wales newspapers, and on the following Monday they had an anxious telephone call from a Methodist minister in Cardiff, saying that he thought, but couldn't be absolutely certain, that the photograph resembled one of his parishioners, someone by the name of James Randall.

When they investigated, the Methodist minister's misgivings about his parishioner turned out to be correct. James Randall was none other than Randall Morris and he was brought to Swansea for questioning. He was a tall man, over six feet tall, with thick, unruly red hair. When asked prior to the interrogation if he wanted a solicitor, Morris declined, explaining that his innocence denied any necessity for a lawyer to be present. He had, he said, nothing to hide and would answer all their questions.

It seemed that Randall Morris had got religion, and like many religious converts, had become a Bible-thumping zealot and claimed he was deeply ashamed of his past and wanted to atone for his sins. Perhaps, his interrogators thought, he wanted to rid the world of the other sinners too.

He also owned a small Fiat and had no alibi for the nights in question.

Suddenly it looked as if they had a specific suspect in custody.

But as they questioned him, frustration mounting, Morris's religious armour shone with righteousness, in spite of his tainted past. After a gruelling interrogation, a confession seemed highly unlikely, especially as the man now sought refuge in a protective madness, the same form of insanity adopted by thousands of extremists the world over. Lambert brought the interview to an end.

For once, though, he wholeheartedly agreed with Marden that they should detain Morris in custody as long as the law would allow.

As the Monday drew to a close, not a single one on the team suggested going for a drink. They all went their separate ways, Lambert to his nearest local in the Mumbles, where he started off with a couple of pints, and then switched to red wine. A lethal combination, but it had to be done.

CHAPTER TWENTY-ONE

Out of the corner of his eye, he saw a couple in a quiet corner of the bar, eyeing each other with lust and affection, giggling and sharing an intimacy inside their cosy bubble of love, and it heightened his own loneliness. Nothing but aching emptiness within, a yearning and a longing with no clear idea what it was he wanted from life. Working in a job that could change from challenging to tedious in the blink of an eye, dealing with dirty and despicable people, and yet there was undoubtedly something which motivated him, something which kept driving him on.

He hadn't been paying much attention to the pub's background music playing softly, but then his hearing adjusted as he recognized one of his favourites: John Lennon's 'Watching the Wheels'. And there was that line in the song coming up: 'There's no such thing as problems, only solutions.'

Easy enough to write as a line in a song, thought Lambert, but the reality was different. How was he to conquer the frustration of never knowing whether his father had abused his sister? Now that she was dead, there was no solution, and the problem remained unsolved, which no one in the future would ever resolve.

He had one more drink before heading back to his flat. As he walked towards the building, not for the first time he wondered if the gloomy granite had been imported from Aberdeen way back, perhaps in return for slate. The greyness of the stone seemed to be a shroud of depression about to envelop him, and he imagined a lonely heart attack one day, with no one to discover his body for days. Perhaps weeks.

The building consisted of two purpose-built maisonettes and Lambert's was on the ground floor. The upstairs maisonette had a flight of stone steps leading up from the side of the building, and outside the entrance door at the top of the stairs, an estate agent's board advertised that it was To Let.

He was almost glad it was a recession. Maybe the landlords would find it difficult to let the upstairs flat, and he could live undisturbed for a while. No pounding feet, no smoker's hacking cough, and certainly no hip-hop like the last tenant's addiction!

His flat had a tiny entrance hall, like an airlock, leading to what he described as his dreary living room, which he did nothing to improve. Since his divorce from Helen, he lacked incentive for domestic improvement. As long as he had a few creature comforts…

A rumble in his stomach reminded him that yet again he'd denied his body any sustenance. He staggered into the claustrophobic kitchen and cooked a frozen lasagne in the microwave, then opened another bottle of wine. When he returned to the living room, he sat in front of the television, randomly clicked the remote, and eventually settled for another BBC2 documentary about last year's banking fiasco and how they had squandered billions of pounds.

He watched the programme without taking it in as he forced the lasagne inside himself. His mind was bombarded with questions to do with the case. Something lay just out of reach, like the hand of a person in a film reaching for assistance before plummeting into the depths below.

What the hell was it that eluded him?

He was still none the wiser by the time the wine bottle was two thirds empty. By now his brain was fuzzy, so he took himself off to bed and was fast asleep as soon as his head hit the pillow.

***

The telephone rang and he picked it up. It was Natasha, his daughter. He could see her speaking to him but couldn't hear what she was saying. He wanted to warn her about something but she couldn't hear him either. And then he saw his father standing behind her, a metal bar raised above his head, which at any moment would come crashing down on her head. And then he heard her speak. 'Dad! Are you here?' He wanted to warn her about his father but the telephone in his hand was melting, turning to jelly. He could see the figure behind her, no longer his father. It was the Tin Man, the metal bar in his hand above Natasha's head. But, he wanted to say, the Tin Man is a woodcutter, he uses an axe not a metal bar. But Natasha had disappeared, along with the Tin Man. And then he saw her for one brief moment, climbing aboard a red double-decker bus with the Tin Man. He tried to stop her, tell her it was his father and not the Tin Man, but the bus vanished into a forest.

Twenty-Two

As if in contrast to the funereal weather of the previous day, bright sunshine and a vivid blue sky took the mourners by surprise, some of whom were renowned Welsh actors and would have welcomed rain and umbrellas, giving the ceremony a dark atmosphere and a bit of Hollywood.

The crematorium car park was crammed with expensive cars, but one vehicle stood out like the proverbial sore thumb, which got Lambert wondering. It was a scruffy red van with sliding doors, a veritable rust bucket that didn't look roadworthy. He could see a young man with shoulder-length hair sitting in the driver's seat, smoking and watching the crowd of mourners thronging the entrance to the chapel of rest.

He waited for most of the mourners to enter the chapel before getting out of his car. As he walked across the car park, he glanced at the rust bucket, and could see that the long-haired young man was showing no signs that he was about to attend the funeral as he continued smoking and staring into space.

As he approached the chapel entrance, Lambert undid the button on his dark suit, one he very rarely wore, and smoothed his black tie. He had bought the tie for his father's funeral last year but hadn't worn it, wearing a garishly patterned one instead. It was probably an ineffectual comment, cocking two fingers up at his father, rebelling against the formality of the occasion. Had he thought it through at the time, he would have realized his father would have appreciated the garish tie far more than the sombre black.

Thoughts of his father reminded him of the abrupt waking from his dream this morning. He couldn't remember most of it, elusive as dreams usually were, but there was one image which stuck in his conscious mind: his father's metamorphosis into the Tin Man. Lambert tried to analyze it over a hasty bowl of corn flakes, but soon gave up. But now, as he reached the chapel entrance, the significance of *The Wizard of Oz* suddenly hit him square on. Whereas

THE WRECKING BAR

he had previously thought the Tin Man was a symbol, he now realized it was a memory. It was a reminder of the pervert's house in Port Talbot and his collection of pornographic films. And Lambert suddenly knew why the classic MGM musical was the only normal DVD in his collection of filth, like a rose in a cesspit. It was the paedophile's dirty dream. To the paedophile, Dorothy in her white ankle socks was an innocent, the symbol of a child who can be defiled.

He found this more disturbing than any other aspect of the case so far. Probably because the film had been a favourite of Natasha's when she was a sweet innocent child, and the thoughts of what went on in the twisted mind of a paedophile were alien to him.

Jaw clenched in disgust, he was the last to enter the chapel. He stood at the back, pressed tight against other mourners who couldn't get a seat. Not a pew to be had for neither love nor money. The place was heaving. If there'd been rafters, they'd have been hanging off them. Organ music played softly, an unrecognizable dirge that was the overture to the proceedings, and there was an expectant hush as the congregation waited, and the occasional dry cough.

Along the row of pews at the front, Lambert saw Gavin Lloyd, head bowed as if in prayer, and sitting one on either side of him were two young people, a boy in his twenties and a girl in her late teens or early twenties. Sunlight streamed through the stained glass windows, catching her long blonde hair, which shone with angelic radiance as her shoulders trembled and shook with discreet sorrow, and the tableau might have resembled a scene from a Victorian painting were it not for the boy, whose dark brown hair, as long as his sister's, was unkempt and greasy, and even from the back of the chapel, Lambert could see the resentful and sullen demeanour in his troubled posture.

The organ music ground to a halt as the chaplain entered and stood at the lectern. A few dry coughs before a mighty hush. Then the chaplain spoke, first in Welsh, followed by a translation into English.

Lambert groaned inwardly. A bilingual service meant it would last twice as long.

A shuffling, scuffling sound as the congregation rose to sing the first hymn in Welsh. Someone saw Lambert without a hymn book and thrust one into his hand. He nodded his thanks, found the relevant page, and opened and closed his mouth in time to the organ music, like John Redwood when he was Secretary of State for Wales, trying to bluff his way through the Welsh national anthem.

His eyes drifted round the congregation. Although many were involved in singing heartily, many also gave crafty sidelong glances to see who else of importance might be attending the funeral. Lambert wasn't absolutely certain, but he thought he could see Shane Williams about four rows back from the front. And wasn't that Charlotte Church sitting just behind him? And further along the row, he was sure that was Max Boyce. All the great and the good in Wales seemed to be attending Rhiannon Lloyd's funeral. The only one who seemed to be missing, Lambert thought wryly, was Tom Jones. Maybe he had a prior engagement.

A booming baritone in the back row caught his attention. Lambert stared at the back of the man's head. Even from behind, there was no mistaking his avian form. Now Lambert knew why the chief super hadn't demanded an update until late afternoon. No doubt he'd be spending most of the day at the funeral buffet, stuffing his face and hobnobbing with the influential.

The service ploughed on for another hour. Thankfully, not everything was translated into English, but it was still an ordeal, and Lambert wondered if those on the periphery of grief thought the same and were contemplating the relief of the buffet and some lubrication.

Finally, with the organ thundering 'Bread of Heaven', the coffin moved smoothly towards the curtained opening as Lloyd's daughter let out a strangled animal cry. As he was nearest to the door, Lambert was first out into the welcoming fresh air. As other mourners exited, they congregated in little groups, and Lambert suddenly felt conspicuous as he stood alone.

As soon as Marden came through the chapel door, he spotted Lambert. His dark eyes like a kestrel honing in on a defenceless mouse. He darted forward and hissed, 'What are you doing here?'

'Just came to pay my respects.'

Marden moved his head back as if Lambert had said something dirty. 'You didn't know her, did you?'

'I'd got to know her slightly during the course of my investigation.'

'And that gave you...' Marden began and then corrected himself. 'You only met her once, yet you attend her funeral. You've never struck me as a religious man.'

'I'm not. But I can still pay my respects.'

Marden sniffed, as though there was something unpleasant under his nose. 'Yes, well, I hope you're not....'

Lambert anticipated what he was going to say. 'No, I won't be stuffing my face at the funeral tea. I'll be off now.' He was about to turn away but stopped and eyeballed Marden, adding cryptically, 'I got what I came for.'

Before Marden could ask what he meant, Lambert turned sharply and walked back to his car, where he sat and waited for what he guessed might happen.

THE WRECKING BAR

When Gavin Lloyd and his son and daughter eventually emerged from the chapel, Lambert saw the producer put an arm round his son's shoulders. The daughter turned away abruptly, her body language signifying irritation. Lloyd, gesturing with his free hand, seemed to be pleading with his boy, who was staring straight ahead in a passively aggressive role.

From the scruffy van nearby came several impatient blasts on the horn. The son looked over, shook off his father's arm and walked away towards the car park. Lambert saw the father calling after him but his son didn't look back. As soon as he had climbed into the passenger seat his mate's van took off with an unhealthy clanking and grinding, leaving a trail of black exhaust fumes behind.

Lambert switched the ignition on and prepared to follow. A quick glance towards the chapel told him that Lloyd's son and his friend's polluting rust bucket were already history, as mourners crowded round Lloyd offering sympathetic handshakes.

Out on the road, Lambert followed closely behind the van. He didn't think it necessary to trail them any other way. It wasn't as if they were hardened criminals expecting a police tail. They headed east along the A38, probably avoiding the M4 in case they were stopped for a vehicle check. He followed them towards Cardiff city centre, but when they reached the district of Canton, they suddenly swung left off the main road into a side street. He had no alternative but to follow, but as soon as he turned the corner he saw the van's one brake light come on as it stopped, its left indicator blinking as a precious space had been found in this overcrowded, litter-strewn street.

Lambert overtook the van and sped up the street until he found a space. He reversed quickly into it, awarding himself a gold medal for bad parking as the rear end of the car poked out into the street at an oblique angle. But having followed them this far, he wasn't going to risk losing them now.

As soon as he was out of the car, he jogged back towards their van and saw them rounding the corner at the end of the street. He put on a spurt and reached the main road just as they crossed over and disappeared into a doorway sandwiched between a kebab takeaway and a bookies. After a lull in the heavy traffic, he dashed across the road and headed straight for the doorway.

There were three doorbells, and the bottom two had small handwritten names encased in plastic. The top bell was blank, and Lambert guessed it belonged to Lloyd's son and his mate. The entrance door had been left ajar, so he decided against ringing the bell to announce his arrival as he entered the dark hallway. It was bare and bleak, apart from a small table in the hall,

152

heaving under a pile of junk mail and pizza delivery leaflets. It was a three-storey building, with a flat on each floor, and Lambert wasted no time in climbing the stairs two at a time and was seriously out of breath by the time he'd reached the top floor. Once more he promised himself a fitness regime, the same failed promise he'd been making for the past year. He heard muffled voices coming from their flat and paused for a moment to get his breath back before banging loudly on the door.

Silence, followed by a scuffling sound. A voice just the other side of the door asked, 'Who is it?'

Lambert said, 'It's me.'

Lambert, ear close to the door, thought he heard whispering. He took his ID out of his pocket as the door opened slowly and cautiously, the rust bucket driver's wary, rodent-like face peering questioningly at Lambert. But Lambert wasn't in the mood to play games and gave the door a mighty shove. The driver of the van almost fell backwards into the arms of Lloyd's son, who stood just behind him.

'Hey! What's going on?' he protested.

Lambert showed them his warrant card. 'Police. I'd like a word with Rhys.' As he pushed past the driver, he got a whiff of cheap aftershave covering a multitude of sins, and stood in the middle of the living room, looking down at a glass coffee table, so dirty it was almost opaque.

'Well, well, well. A half ounce of Golden Virginia, a rolling machine and what looks like a mini brake pad. What can that be, I wonder?'

'It's not exactly serious stuff,' Rhys Lloyd protested. 'It was downgraded years ago.'

'It's still illegal,' Lambert pointed out. 'But that's not why I'm here. I'd like a word with you – in private.' He stared at the driver. 'So if you'd like to make yourself scarce for a half hour or so.'

The driver, whose long stringy hair was like a torn curtain hanging either side of a prematurely ageing face, held Lambert's look, trying to work something out in a mind that was clogged with debris. Eventually, he said in a wheedling tone, 'Where 'm I supposed to go?'

Lambert shrugged. 'I don't care. Suit yourself.'

'I live here. You can't make me leave if I don't wanna.'

'Look, son, why don't you go to the pub? There's one just round the corner. Just so I can have a word with Rhys.'

'What d'you wanna talk to me about?' Rhys Lloyd asked.

'I'm investigating your mother's death. So I just want to ask you a few questions.'

THE WRECKING BAR

Suddenly, Rhys Lloyd's face crumpled, and he swayed for a moment before collapsing into a tattered easy chair. One small tear trickled from an eye and he dropped his head, almost shamefully, on to his chest. His friend shuffled uncomfortably, trying to look suitably concerned.

Lambert delved into his back pocket for his wallet, took out a £10 note and handed it to the driver. 'Go and get yourself a few beers.'

The young man's eyes lit up greedily. 'See you later, Rhys,' he mumbled as he snatched the note before hotfooting it out the door.

'So much for loyalty and friendship,' Lambert sighed.

With the flat of his hand, Rhys Lloyd wiped the single tear from his cheek and looked up at Lambert. 'So what sort of questions d'you wanna ask?'

Lambert looked around the spartan room for another seat, spotted a black metal folding chair lying on the floor under the window, brought it over to within a few feet of Rhys Lloyd, squeaked it open, sat down and made eye contact with him.

Now that Lambert had a chance to study him, he could see that he was quite good-looking, in an effeminate way. He had a pasty complexion and perfectly formed delicate features, with sensual lips and shoulder-length hair, giving the impression of a tortured poet who ought to be dressed in a flamboyant style of swinging sixties velvet, instead of the conventional suit he had obviously been kitted out with for the funeral at the insistence of his father.

'I'm sorry to hear about your mother,' Lambert began. 'Were you and she very close?'

'I guess. Although it was Angharad who always...'

The young man stopped, finding the memories painful. Guilt probably pounded away at his emotions, telling him he'd been too self-absorbed to get to know his mother before it was too late.

Lambert knew this questioning was going to be tricky and kept his voice soft and neutral. 'Did your mother and father get on well?'

Rhys Lloyd looked him straight in the eye and Lambert knew there was an intelligence there which you didn't get from a first impression. And, as soon as the young man spoke, Lambert knew he was right and this could be tricky.

'I hope you're not going to suggest Dad killed my mother.'

Lambert let his breath out slowly. 'No, of course not. But I need to get as much background as possible.'

'Bollocks! Why would you ask if my parents got on well if you weren't looking for a reason for my father to kill my mam?'

154

Chapter Twenty-Two

'Let me explain about police work, Rhys. It can sometimes be quite laborious and it often means we have to eliminate people from our enquiries...'

The young man clenched his fists angrily. 'Don't patronize me. I've seen enough poxy cop shows on TV to know how that works. So why d'you want to know about Mam and Dad's rows?'

'Oh, so there were rows, were there?'

Caught out, Rhys Lloyd blustered, 'Look, what... what d'you want me to say? Mam and Dad had an occasional row, so he must have killed her? Most people have rows. Angharad and I used to fight all the time... like cat and dog. You don't kill someone if you have a row. Get fucking real, man.'

Eyes blazing, Rhys Lloyd stared defiantly at Lambert.

Lambert made a calming gesture with his hands. 'Listen to me, Rhys. I'm not suggesting or even going down that route of suspecting your father. But both your parents knew many people who visited their house. The funeral today was jam packed with all kinds of people. And I'm certain most of the mourners came to give their sincere condolences to your father and to pay their respects to your mother. But there may have been a regular visitor to their house who perhaps might not have attended the funeral. I just want to know if you can think of anything unusual you can recall when you were at home.'

'I was never there very much.'

Lambert cast his eyes pointedly around the scruffy flat. 'You traded a nice home like that for this.'

'I'm twenty-two years old, for fuck's sake.'

'Yes, I understand that. You wanted your own life. So what made you leave?'

The son fell into a moody silence, and Lambert thought he wasn't going to answer. But when he looked into the detective's eyes again, they were vulnerable, as if he wanted to unburden himself.

'I was embarrassed. It used to make me cringe.'

'What did?'

'The way Mam used to speak to Dad sometimes.'

'You mean she henpecked him?'

The young man nodded slowly. 'It was usually over money. And if Dad had a great idea for a TV series or a project, Mam used to destroy it. It made me so angry sometimes, I... I couldn't stand it any more, so I left.'

Gently now, Lambert said, 'I'm trying to find out, Rhys, if there were any unusual visitors to the house.'

'There were always loads of visitors. I don't know about unusual.'

THE WRECKING BAR

'Any odd phone calls?'

Rhys Lloyd thought for a while, frowning. 'There was a peculiar phone call from this woman which Dad was angry about. I heard him asking her not to call him at the house again.'

'How long ago was this?'

'About a month ago. I'd gone home to stay the weekend and that was when she rang.'

'Any idea who it might have been?'

'I know exactly who it was.'

Lambert leaned forward, poised and waiting for the information, aware that the young man was indulging in dramatic effect.

'It was his mother.'

Lambert frowned. 'I don't understand. Why was that so unusual, his mother ringing him?'

'Because we didn't know his mother was still alive.'

'So this woman – your grandmother – had he fallen out with her years ago?'

'Yes. No.' Rhys Lloyd shrugged. 'I don't know. All I know is, all the time we were growing up, Dad led us to believe his parents were dead.'

'Let me get this straight. When your father spoke to his mother, if he had lied all those years about her being dead, why did he suddenly own up to her still being alive? He could have said it was someone else on the phone.'

'No, he couldn't. Because I was the one who answered the phone. At first I didn't have a clue who she was. She sounded pissed, slurring her words. Then she said she wanted to speak to her son.'

'So what happened after that?'

'That's when Dad became angry, and told her never to call the house again. Mam heard him, and wanted to know who it was. So I told her it was Dad's mother and she was shocked, wanting to know why he'd kept quiet about her for all these years. He said it was because she was an alcoholic and he was ashamed of her. I told Mam she had sounded drunk on the phone, and Dad explained what it was like growing up with an alcoholic. Mam said she'd still like to meet her, seeing as she was family, like. But Dad said he'd never reveal where she lived. Mam kept arguing about it but he said it was better for everyone concerned if we kept his mother out of it.'

Lambert was intrigued by the son's story. So what did it matter if his grandmother was an alcoholic? Why the secrecy? And why the hell was Gavin Lloyd so intent on keeping her out of his life?

Now he couldn't wait to get back to Cockett to delve a little deeper into Gavin Lloyd's past. Just a few more questions and he'd be finished.

'Your father came from Newtown, I believe. Is that where his mother lives, d'you think?'

'I expect so, only...' Rhys Lloyd hesitated, a puzzled frown like scars on his forehead.

'Only what?'

'She didn't sound as if she came from Wales.'

'You mean she had a different accent? What did it sound like?'

'I don't know. Like someone in *EastEnders*.'

'A Londoner?'

'Sounded like it. Because she'd been drinking, it was hard to tell. Anyway, what's this got to do with the burglary and whoever killed my mother?'

'Sometimes things hidden in a person's past....'

'Like the grandmother I've never known, you mean?'

Lambert nodded. 'You have another grandmother, don't you? Was she at the funeral today?'

'Not much point. She's got Alzheimer's. Dad went round and tried to explain about Mam, but I don't think she understood. Dad's been very good to her; he goes round there all the time.'

'Where does she live?'

'House in Porthkerry, not far from the airport.'

'Is there anything else you can remember from when you went back home? Any other strange phone calls or visitors?'

Rhys Lloyd thought about it and then shook his head. 'I don't think so. Anyway, why are you asking me about all this? Shouldn't you be talking to my father?'

'Bit too soon after the funeral.'

'Didn't stop you talking to me, though, did it?'

'I think your father's going to be tied up for a while at the post funeral tea. Any reason you didn't attend?'

'Most of the people will be using it as a kind of reunion, or an excuse to... I can't think of the word.'

'Network?' Lambert suggested.

'Yeah,' Rhys Lloyd said bitterly. 'It'll be a networking opportunity for most of them. I think it'd freak me out if I went.'

Lambert stood up. 'I'm sorry for your tragic loss, Rhys. If you'll excuse me—'

Rhys Lloyd looked up knowingly. 'So what have I told you? Bugger all, except that my father's mother is still alive. How will that help you to catch whoever it was who killed my mother?'

THE WRECKING BAR

'It won't.' Lambert said. 'But often police investigations take us down blind alleys—'

Rhys Lloyd broke in, venom in his expression. 'I hope you get the bastard who did it. And I hope they...'

Unable to think of a punishment appropriate enough to fit the crime, Rhys Lloyd began sobbing quietly. There was nothing Lambert could do or say to relieve his affliction, so he walked quietly to the door and let himself out.

***

Lambert parked near The Mountain Dew, picked up the folder that lay on the passenger seat and checked his watch. Another ten or fifteen minutes and Tony Ellis would be with him. He was visiting Sharon, who had to go into hospital early for observation because she was slightly anaemic.

As it was half seven on a Tuesday, the pub was fairly quiet, just the usual teatime regulars, who interrupted conversations to greet Lambert. Most of them knew what he did for a living, and he could tell by their eager expressions that they would be keen to bring the conversation around to the gruesome spate of murders. But Lambert wasn't in the mood for conversations about bringing back hanging, throwing away the key, or castration for sex offenders, so he took his pint and sat some distance from the bar. Besides, he needed to brief Tony Ellis about his role for tomorrow.

He sipped his pint of bitter, thinking about Randall Morris, who was still in police custody. Since a photograph and details of the wrecking bar that was purchased in Llanelli had been published in all the South Wales newspapers and several national dailies, two local Llanelli people had come forward with information. The trouble was, neither of their descriptions tallied. One of them said short and fat and the other thought the man was of average height, dark haired and thin. Randall Morris was tall with a shock of wild red hair.

The only way to settle it was to put Morris on an identity parade. But since the more recent evidence had come to light, Lambert thought it could wait another day. And he was hoping that by tomorrow it wouldn't be necessary.

He downed his pint and was at the bar getting a refill when Ellis arrived.

'I timed that well,' he said. 'I'll have the same.'

As soon as they were seated with their pints, Lambert asked Ellis about his wife.

'Sharon's fine. She's in good hands. I took her in a bar of dark chocolate and a small can of Guinness to boost her iron levels.'

'I thought pregnant women were not supposed to have alcohol.'

'They're not. But one small Guinness won't do any harm, and the benefits of the iron'll counteract the small amount of alcohol.'

Lambert patted the folder on the table beside him. 'Tony, before I give you details of where this investigation heads now, I want you to promise me if Sharon goes into labour, you'll be there. Don't think twice about interrupting the investigation. Feel confident about delegating. I think you'll find Debbie more than capable.'

'What about Kevin?'

Knowing what Ellis was driving at, Lambert smiled. 'He's improving with age. So I think you can trust them both if you're called away.'

'Thanks, Harry. I really appreciate that. But why aren't you heading the investigation?'

'I still am. But tomorrow I'm having an away-day.'

Lambert opened the folder, took out an A4 sheet of paper, and said, 'Down to business,' as he handed it to Ellis.

Ellis read from the paper, his eyes widening, while Lambert watched him, waiting for his reaction. As soon as Ellis looked up and made eye contact, Lambert said, 'He reinvented himself. There's no such person as Gavin Lloyd. Not the one we know, anyway. His name was Keith Hilden, born and bred in London's East End, and changed his name by deed poll back in 1983. The man is a phoney; a social-climbing, opportunistic liar who has even managed to fool his own family all these years.'

Ellis pursed his lips as if to make a whistling sound but stopped himself.

'So he's managed to keep his past buried for more than twenty-five years?'

'Up until now.' Lambert handed Ellis the folder. 'In there you'll find instructions for what needs to be checked tomorrow.'

Ellis opened the folder, took out sheets of A4 and read the instructions. 'Yes, I see where you're going with this. What about the chief super?'

'Up until today he still thought Rhiannon Lloyd's murder was a separate incident.'

'What's changed his mind?'

'When I presented him with the evidence about Keith Hilden's quarter of a century alias, he reluctantly agreed to my suggestions, even though he was stuffed full of the man's sausage rolls and sherry at the time. But if all this proves to be groundless...' Lambert waved a hand at the sheets of A4. 'And if I come back empty handed tomorrow, he's going to want my head on a plate.'

'What about the gun that killed Rhiannon Lloyd?'

'They think it was a Smith and Wesson .38.'

Ellis raised his eyebrows. 'Interesting. A revolver rather than an automatic is far less likely to jam. And there's no automatic ejection of cartridges. So it could have been a professional hit.'

'We can't rule that out,' Lambert said.

Ellis glanced at the sheet of instructions again and a glint came into his eye.

'So far it's been a shitty week, but now I feel confident. Tomorrow's the day for results. I just know it.'

Lambert chuckled. 'You're bound to say that, Tony, because you're so close to being a father, so I don't think it's entirely to do with the investigation.' Ellis opened his mouth to protest but Lambert continued. 'Not that I blame you. You're the one that's embarking on an exciting journey.' Lambert gave Ellis a lopsided grin. 'Mind you, I don't envy you the journey through the teenage years.'

'And what about your journey, Harry?'

'Literal or metaphorical?'

'Your away-day to London tomorrow.'

The smile suddenly vanished from Lambert's face. 'I think that's where the truth lies buried. In Gavin Lloyd's past. And I think his mother may shed some interesting light on it.'

'His mother?'

'Yes, I didn't tell you, did I? Not only has he kept quiet about his change of name, when he cunningly reinvented himself, but even his family knew nothing about his dear mother, alive and well and still living in east London.'

'Ashamed of her, you think?'

'Well, she sounds like she might have a serious drink problem. But something tells me he had another reason for reinventing himself and starting a new life here in Wales.'

Ellis glanced at his watch. Lambert could see he was on tenterhooks, his mind torn between thoughts and worries of the impending birth and wanting a resolution to the horrendous spate of murders.

Nervously, Ellis excused himself and went to the Gents, leaving Lambert to chew on his own troubled thoughts. His last remark to Tony Ellis about Gavin Lloyd having reinvented himself reminded him of his sister, starting again in another country to escape a distressing past.

But as Lambert knew, escape is never truly possible. His own past was a constant reminder of something he wanted to banish from his mind, but was always there to haunt him, a ghost of regret.

Twenty-Three

Hope triumphs over experience, thought Lambert as he sipped weak instant coffee from a plastic beaker, his third since leaving Swansea. Another hour and he'd be in Paddington. That's if there were no delays, but so far the train was running to time.

He had parked in a multi-storey close to Swansea station and caught the train just before eight, purchasing a first-class ticket which was almost what he had paid for a flight to New York six months ago. He could imagine the look on Marden's face when he put it through expenses and got a buzz of guilty pleasure from the extravagance. Marden hadn't even wanted him to travel by train, and would have preferred him to make the journey in a pool car, but Lambert had persuaded him that as he had several places to go in London which were poles apart, he couldn't risk not getting his witnesses interviewed in one day, which would then mean an overnight and the added expense of a hotel. He also explained the need to keep in touch with his team regularly throughout the day from his mobile, which would be awkward while driving. That had swung it with grudging reluctance from Marden. However, Lambert knew he was pushing his luck travelling first class. Marden would have a fit. But having witnessed the hordes of passengers heading for the overcrowded standard class, before settling into the relative quiet of the unfilled first-class carriage, where he could stretch out expansively and make one or two phone calls, any guilt about the expense of this trip instantly disappeared.

Twice during the journey he tried calling his daughter and got her voicemail on both occasions. He didn't bother leaving a message as she rarely responded. He wasn't particularly troubled by these derelictions of daughterly duty, seeing as she had only graduated from university three months before moving to London, where she was still settling into her first job with a publishing company, and was going out with a boy she met on

THE WRECKING BAR

holiday. Therefore it came as no surprise that he was low on her list of calls to return.

He settled back in his seat, picked up a copy of *The Times* and started to read when his mobile rang. It was Tony Ellis, sounding excited and somewhat breathless.

'Harry! I've got some info for you but I'll have to be quick. Sharon's waters have broken and she's gone into labour, so I'm just off to the hospital. Can you hear me?'

'Yes. Go on.'

'Gavin Lloyd, when he was still Keith Hilden, passed his driving test in 1982. The driving licence has been kept up to date in Hilden's name, one of the newer licences with a photograph. So he's perfectly capable of driving, which means—'

Lambert interrupted to say, 'Which means he can use his driving licence as an ID, and a false ID at that, seeing as he changed his name officially.'

'Exactly. And you know what the address given on his licence is?'

'His London flat? Coach Road, Hammersmith?'

'How did you know that?'

'I didn't. I'm just guessing. How are Debbie and Kevin getting on?'

'They're doing okay. That list of suggestions you gave me, they're up to speed on it.'

Lambert thought he heard his sergeant's nervous intake of breath.

'Harry, I....'

'Go on, Tony. I know you want to get away. And good luck.'

'Yes, thanks, I hope I'll have some news for you before the day is out.'

The line went dead, and Lambert was left thinking how inconvenient it was during this crucial time in the investigation for his sergeant to be off the case. But it couldn't be helped. He wanted Tony to be there for the birth, just as he had been there for Natasha's birth when he himself was a detective sergeant, and his long-since retired boss, DI Wilson, had insisted he forget about the rape case they were investigating to concentrate on becoming a father. And now, with history repeating itself, he felt good about telling Tony to treat the birth as his number-one priority. It somehow felt like the passing on of a family tradition.

And that's how he thought of Tony Ellis. He was more than just a work colleague. He was family.

As the train pulled in to Reading station, Lambert glanced at his watch. Not long to go now. And he wondered how long it would be before Debbie Jones or Kevin Wallace came up with a few more answers.

CHAPTER TWENTY-THREE

***

The Docklands Light Railway rattled out of the tunnel, climbing to its overhead height. In the distance Lambert saw the mighty towers of Canary Wharf under a leaden sky, a view guaranteed to dampen any optimism, although the central edifice did trigger feelings of admiration for the way it dominated London's docklands as an iconic landmark.

He'd never been to this part of London before and had double-checked his destination as the automatic railway branched in various directions. He caught the City airport train which didn't branch off at Westferry for Canary Wharf but took him straight on for one more station. He got off at Poplar, overshadowed on one side by the giant glass buildings, mainly banks and financial institutions, and on the other by housing estates. He walked out into the street, consulted his map, and set off along an alley, heading north.

As he neared the housing estates, he expected to find litter-strewn streets awash with the ubiquitous McDonald's milkshake cups and KFC boxes. But he was wrong. The streets were reasonably clean and free from litter, and he wondered if this was something to do with the close proximity of Canary Wharf. The power of money.

Mrs Barbara Hilden's flat was on the first floor of a three-storey block called Wordsworth House. As he approached the entrance, he found a solid security gate barring his way to the stairwell. There was a row of buttons and an entryphone system, but he didn't want to alert Lloyd's mother to his arrival, so he waited just round the corner from the entrance. After he'd been waiting for ten minutes, he heard footsteps on the stairs. When he judged they had almost reached the ground floor, he hurried round to the entrance and came face to face with a young Asian man. Lambert put a hand to stop the gate closing.

The young Asian stopped and regarded him suspiciously. 'D'you live here? I've never seen you before.'

Lambert smiled. 'I'm visiting my mother, Mrs Hilden, at number twelve.' He indicated the row of bells. 'She's a bit deaf, and she's often on the sauce.' He made a tippling gesture with his hand.

The young man shrugged and walked off without giving it another thought. Lambert went in, shut the gate and climbed the stairs. A metallic smell of cold damp concrete reminded him of his own childhood, and he questioned the temerity of the councillor who named this miserable building after the poet who immortalized golden daffodils.

Carefully avoiding a child's tricycle abandoned bang in the middle of the first-floor balcony, he found number twelve halfway along. He knocked

THE WRECKING BAR

loudly on the metal knocker beneath the letterbox and waited. Not a peep from inside the flat. Somewhere further along the balcony he heard the clatter of crockery, and guessed the kitchens were at the front of the flats.

He knocked again, louder than before. After a moment, he thought he heard a scuffling sound from inside, followed by an unhealthy coughing. And then footsteps shuffling along the hall. The door opened a crack, stopped by a security chain.

The face that peered out at him, still blinking sleep from her eyes, seemed to be suffering from the ravages of time and too much alcohol. Her leathery skin was deeply wrinkled and she looked as if she had stepped off the set of *Planet of the Apes.* Her eyes were surprisingly blue and clear, but her slept-in blue eye shadow was smudged, as was the overdone rouge of her cheeks and lipstick, adding a clown-like appearance to her ape-mask face.

Lambert showed her his warrant card. 'Mrs Hilden, I'm Detective Inspector Lambert. I'd very much like to talk to you about your son Keith.'

It took her a moment to absorb this request. 'What about?' Her voice crackled and quivered with age.

'If I could just come in and talk to you about him, I'd be very grateful.'

Another pause while she digested his words. 'My son left years ago. He ain't here.'

Lambert gave her a pleasant, understanding smile. Through the crack in the door, he smelled a sour sweetness from her breath and almost recoiled.

'I know he no longer lives here, Mrs Hilden. But I'd still like to talk to you about when he was growing up.'

'What business is that of yours?'

'If you could just let me in for a minute, I'll tell you.'

'Keith's a man now, and he's never been in trouble with the police. Never.'

'No, I know that, Mrs Hilden, but I'd still like to talk to you.'

She frowned, the creases in her face accentuating her simian features. 'But what if I don't want to talk to *you*?'

Lambert laughed and kept a lightness in his voice. 'Come on, Mrs Hilden – or can I call you Barbara? Please just give me a couple of minutes of your time.'

'I don't want to talk to you. You can't come in.'

'Now don't be like that, Barbara,' Lambert began, but she interrupted him.

'Where's your search warrant? You need a search warrant to come inside. I do know that.'

Lambert showed her an empty hand. 'We don't need a warrant, Barbara. Not to have a friendly chat. Search warrants are when people have committed crimes or have got something to hide. I just want to talk to you about…'

164

CHAPTER TWENTY-THREE

Her face suddenly contorted into a savage animal rage. 'Piss off!'

The door slammed shut, and he could just about hear her scuffling back down the hall.

***

As DC Jones put her foot on the accelerator to take a corner, a disconcerting roar from the engine made her think the car was packing up, until she realized the thunderous noise was coming from above. Of course, she was close to the airport and a jet was taking off.

She found Mrs Parry's home in a quiet cul-de-sac in Porthkerry. The house, built around the middle of the twentieth century, had a pebble-dash exterior, and looked solid and weatherproof, although the windows needed repainting. A six-foot high hedge masked the front garden from the road, and a small gravelled drive led to the front of the house through a wide open wrought-iron gate. Attached to the left of the house was an extension garage, the red tiled roof turning mildew green. The front garden was surprisingly well tended and DC Jones wondered if the old lady had help with the gardening or was capable of maintaining it.

She was halfway through the gate when she spotted another car in the drive: a green Ford Mondeo. Knowing Gavin Lloyd drove a BMW, she didn't think it was his. At least, she hoped it wasn't, because that would really scuttle her plans. And going to a magistrate to put forward a case for a warrant to search these premises might be tricky, seeing as Mrs Parry and her husband had once been influential members of the cream of Welsh society, inhabiting a cosy world of intellectuals, artists and writers, and even her son-in-law was held in high regard.

But Jones had been forewarned about Mrs Parry's condition, and wondered if the Mondeo belonged to a health visitor. She decided to risk calling, but didn't want to block the other car in, so she reversed back out and parked in the road.

As soon as she had rung the doorbell it was answered almost immediately by an enormous black woman, broad shouldered and well over six and a half feet tall, wearing a floral print frock in red and green. She gave DC Jones a broad smile and spoke with a strong South Wales accent.

'Hello, love, what can I do for you?'

Jones showed the woman her warrant card and had her story ready. 'I'm Detective Constable Debbie Jones, and Gavin Lloyd has asked me to check up on one or two things, with Mrs Parry's permission, of course. Do you mind me asking who you are?'

The Wrecking Bar

'Not at all, love. I'm Brenda from Cornets Day Care, and every Wednesday I come and collect Megan to bring her over. It gets her out of the house for a bit of mental stimulation, some tea and a change of scenery. Doesn't it, Megan?'

The woman turned and stepped aside to include the frail old lady standing in the hall, wearing a beige raincoat buttoned right up to her neck. Mrs Parry stared at DC Jones expressionlessly, although there was a glimmer of recognition behind her eyes.

'Are you and Bethan ready?' she asked. 'Are we going home now?'

Jones looked at Brenda questioningly, who explained, 'Bethan's her other daughter. I think she thinks you might be Rhiannon.' She lowered her voice and leaned close to Jones. 'That was a terrible business. Tragic. She had so much to live for. What a thing to have happened.' She turned towards Mrs Parry and raised her voice. 'This is Debbie Jones, Megan. She's come to have a look round for Gavin. You remember Gavin? Your son-in-law who's been looking after you.'

Mrs Parry looked as if this was far beyond her comprehension and gazed steadfastly at DC Jones.

'What did you say you were looking for, love?' Brenda asked DC Jones.

'Mr Lloyd wanted us to look at some old family photographs, to see if there are any strangers in the photos who might have a criminal record.'

It was an unlikely story, but the best she could come up with.

'Fair enough,' said Brenda trustingly. 'Will you still be here when I bring Megan back?'

'I doubt it.'

'Oh, well, nice to have met you. I hope you find what you're looking for.'

So do I, DC Jones thought.

'And I hope you find the scoundrel who killed her,' Brenda added.

Jones thought 'scoundrel' was rather a quaint way to describe a vicious killer, but merely nodded and mumbled her thanks.

Brenda turned towards Mrs Parry and boomed, 'Come on, Megan. We're off on our usual Wednesday jaunt.'

Mrs Parry shuffled forward obediently, giving DC Jones a glance of confusion. 'Are we going home now?' she said.

'We're off to Cornets,' Brenda boomed. 'You know you like it there.'

She gave Mrs Parry her arm, nodded at DC Jones, and walked her to the car. Jones watched while she strapped the seat belt round her passenger, gave her a wave, and went inside and shut the door. She waited until the car had driven off before opening the front door, clicking it on to the latch, and walking to the

166

garage. She tried turning the door handle but it was locked, as she suspected it would be. She returned to the house, knowing she needed to work quickly to see if she could find the key to the garage and get the information she was looking for, just in case Gavin Lloyd suddenly turned up.

***

After having Mrs Hilden's door slammed in his face, Lambert walked to Poplar station, cursing and muttering, his mood sinking with every step. To talk to Lloyd's mother, he felt, was crucial. But he'd caught her at a bad time, waking her from a drunken stupor. Maybe she'd be more responsive later in the day, especially if she was given that shot of alcohol her body craved.

But first there was someone else he needed to interview. He caught a Jubilee Line tube at Canning Town and changed at West Ham for an eastward-bound District Line train. By the time he got to Hornchurch, it was nearly one o'clock, and he felt the first pangs of hunger from a complaining stomach. As soon as this interview was out of the way, he promised himself he would take a break and eat something.

But when he came out of the station and saw the rows of semi-detached houses that greeted him in this quiet suburban limbo, he knew the food would have to go on hold until later.

Fortunately, when he stopped to study his Google map, he saw the address he wanted was quite close to the station. He had just crossed the road when his mobile rang. It was DC Wallace.

'What have you got for me, Kevin?'

'It's about the credit card that was used by Mark Yalding to download child pornography off the internet.'

'What about it?'

'For a start, it was a new credit card and the pornography was the only transaction made on it. And it wasn't registered to his address in Cowbridge.'

'Go on,' Lambert said, waiting for Wallace to confirm what he had already guessed.

'The card was issued to his supposed address, Asquith Mansions, Coach Road in Hammersmith, London. The flat that belongs to Green Valley Productions.'

'So it looks like he was set up.'

'Exactly, sir. It's doubtful he ever saw that credit card; never even knew he had it.'

'Which would explain why Yalding's wallet was stolen after he was murdered.'

'Yeah, whoever killed him didn't want the police to find out that the debit card wasn't in his wallet.'

'Did the credit card company tell you the date it was issued?'

'Yeah, it was issued in September. Last month.'

'And at that time he no longer worked for Green Valley Productions,' Lambert said. 'Now listen, Kevin, we need to present the chief superintendent with as much written information...'

Wallace knew what he was about to say and cut in, 'It's okay, sir. The credit card company have confirmed it in writing. It took a while to get them to play ball, but when I told them it was urgent they agreed to fax the information over. And there's a hard copy in the post.'

'Thanks, Kevin. Well done. Has Debbie gone to the old lady's at Porthkerry yet?'

'Yeah, she should be there by now.'

'And has she got the uniform back-up as I suggested?'

'There's a patrol car just round the corner from Gavin Lloyd's house, keeping an eye on the place. He's got the BMW registration, and if he sees it heading in the direction of Porthkerry, he'll ring her. She should have about ten minutes to get out of there.'

'Good. Although I don't suppose Lloyd will rush round to visit his mother-in-law the day after the funeral.'

He heard Kevin laughing.

'Unless it's to evict the old girl and lay claim to the house. How are things in London, sir?'

Lambert told him what had happened with Lloyd's mother, saying he planned to return later in the day.

Wallace laughed again and said, 'Take some booze with you, and don't let her have a drop until she talks to you nicely.'

'I have a feeling that's highly unethical. But I think in this instance, the end justifies the means.'

***

Debbie Jones hurried into the living room, taking in at a glance the dust on the furniture, the general untidiness of the room, and an expensive carpet that was almost threadbare in places. Obviously Mrs Parry's children hadn't considered refurbishing their mother's house, for it wouldn't be long before she would need to be packed off to a residential home.

The first thing of importance to catch Jones's eye was a writing desk in an alcove directly opposite the door. She knew she had to work quickly in

CHAPTER TWENTY-THREE

case Lloyd decided to visit, so she ignored the top part of the bureau, which opened out into the writing desk, thinking it probably contained invoices, receipts, bills and the usual array of stationery, and pulled open the top one of three drawers. It contained mostly family photographs, monochrome mainly and yellowing with age, and also some diaries from the 1980s. She shut the drawer and pulled open the second one down. This was packed with cardboard folders and documents. She raised the flap on the top folder and felt a surge of excitement deep inside her chest. She knew she had struck gold as she opened the vehicle log book for a Vauxhall Nova, colour red, first registered in 1989, and acquired by Megan Dilys Parry in 1991.

Opening the handbag she wore diagonally strapped across her shoulder, Jones fumbled hurriedly for her notebook and pen, and made a note of the registration number. Now, if only she could find the key to the garage.

She slammed the drawer shut and turned away from the writing desk. And that was when she knew she had got lucky for the second time that day. To the right of the of the door, which she hadn't noticed when she first entered, was a small occasional table on which stood a telephone with extra large letters on the dial pad, and above it, fixed to the wall, was a heavy board with the family's phone numbers printed in large font. But the board also had hooks on which hung four keys and three of them were labelled. There was one for the front door, back door and garden shed. The fourth key was unlabelled and looked like the sort of key that would fit a garage lock.

She grabbed it, dashed out into the hall, put the front door on the latch again and strode over to the garage. She slid the key into the lock and turned it clockwise.

It fitted, and she turned the handle. She was about to pull the door upwards when her mobile rang.

Damn!

She grabbed it from her bag and answered the call. It was PC Swift in the patrol car, telling her Lloyd was on his way over and she had ten minutes to get out. Maximum!

She glanced at her watch. It was 1.32.

She thanked PC Swift hurriedly, cut the call, and yanked open the garage door. Her drug-like rush of excitement suddenly plummeted. The garage was empty. Well, not empty exactly, but there was no car. She walked inside, knowing she still had plenty of time before he arrived, but wasn't really expecting to find anything of interest. Until she looked down at the concrete floor and saw the pool of oil. And it looked like a fresh leak. Whichever car

THE WRECKING BAR

had been parked here recently had a bad oil leak, just like the one that had parked at the Lloyds' house the night Rhiannon Lloyd was murdered.

Knowing she needed to take a trace of this oil so that forensics could match it, Jones fumbled through her handbag for anything into which she could scoop a sample. She rummaged through the untidy contents of her bag but found nothing suitable. Then she remembered the plastic bags in the glove compartment of her pool car, and as another glance at her watch told her she still had seven minutes left, she decided she had time to run and get one.

Ducking under the garage door, she ran down the driveway and out through the front gate. She had parked the car hurriedly a few feet from the kerb, and as she lunged towards the door on the passenger side, her foot missed the edge of the kerb, twisted sideways and she felt hot and cold needles of pain shooting through her nervous system. Her eyes watered as the freezing pain scolded her ankle. She leant over the roof of the car, cursing her luck. Everything had been going so well up until now.

She put pressure on the foot, testing the pain. It was pretty bad, but would be nothing as bad as the trouble she'd be in if she was caught going through Mrs Parry's house unwarranted. Any defence lawyer would claim evidence obtained in this way was inadmissible.

As she leant over the car's roof, trying to recover, her watch showed that it was now 1.37. She had only five minutes left to get her evidence, and return the garage key to its rightful place.

As she hobbled up the drive, shards of pain shot up her leg like broken glass. She stopped halfway for some respite, but another glance at her watch told her she now had less than four minutes left.

But because of the urgency of the situation and the fear of what would happen if Lloyd caught her, she found a way of overcoming the pain by sheer determination and managed to limp hurriedly to the garage. Taking a nail file from her handbag, she leant over and used it to scoop traces of oil into the bag.

As soon as she had what she wanted, she shut and locked the garage door and hobbled painfully back to the house. Another quick glance at her watch told her she had less than three minutes left.

Using the hallway wall for support, she limped back into the living room and replaced the key on its hook. By the time she reached the front door, took it off the latch and shut it behind her, over nine minutes had passed since the PC's call.

Although she couldn't see the road because of the high hedge, she heard the car approaching. Ten minutes maximum, PC Sweet had warned. There was no way she was going to be able to limp back to the road before Lloyd pulled in to the drive, so she turned towards the house and pressed her finger to the doorbell. She heard the car pull up, and could feel eyes in her back like laser beams. As if she'd not been expecting him, she turned round as he was getting out of the passenger seat.

'What the hell are you doing here?' he demanded. A trifle defensively, she thought. His driver, Jack Collier, remained in the car, staring at her expressionlessly.

Putting on a bored, acting-under-orders, expression, she said, 'It's just a routine enquiry to ask your wife's mother if there was anyone she could remember who might be able to help with—'

'You're wasting your time. You won't get anything from my mother-in-law.'

Playing dumb, she asked, 'Oh? And why's that, Mr Lloyd?'

'She has senile dementia. She doesn't always know who I am. Talks to me sometimes as if I'm her husband who died fifteen years ago.'

Jones sighed pointedly. 'Another wasted journey. I wish I'd known before driving over here. In any case, it doesn't look as if she's in.'

'She's at a day care centre this afternoon. When she gets back, I've somehow got to try to explain to her what's happened to Rhiannon. It won't be easy.'

Jones's left ankle was throbbing like mad and she dreaded the walk across the drive. 'I don't envy you the task.'

Lloyd relaxed and smiled pleasantly, showing her how much he wanted to help. 'You can always come back and talk to Mrs Parry if you wish. But I promise you, I'm not exaggerating about her condition.'

'I don't think that'll be necessary,' she said. 'I'm sorry to have troubled you.'

As she began to walk across the drive, her ankle almost gave way, and she was unable to disguise her limp.

'Are you all right?' he called. 'What happened?'

'Getting out of the car, I twisted it on the edge of the kerb.'

'A wasted journey and a twisted ankle. Not your day, is it? You okay to drive?'

'I'll manage.'

She could feel him watching her as she walked lamely to the gate. When she reached the car, in spite of the pain, she felt waves of relief for having got away with the search, hopefully without arousing his suspicion.

Hot and cold stabs of pain from her foot brought tears to her eyes as she pushed the clutch down and put the car into second gear. It was fortunate it was her left ankle, leaving her right free if she needed to slam on the brakes; and if necessary she could do most of the journey in second gear.

THE WRECKING BAR

As she drove away, she thought about Mrs Parry's Vauxhall Nova, which the old lady hadn't been able to drive for years. And Keith Hilden, who in his new identity had led people to believe he was unable to drive, looked as if he had access to her car. But where was the car now? Had he managed to get rid of it? And even if forensics found that the sample of oil from the garage floor was identical to the oil on the Lloyds' drive, was it enough to connect him to his wife's murder? Not unless they could find someone he had paid to do the killing, because his presence in Edinburgh on the night of her murder was a perfect alibi.

And how did any of this tie in with the sex offender murders?

As she turned left out of Mrs Parry's road, she glanced to her right and glimpsed the sea, choppy and grey, a view that she might have appreciated when she wasn't in such pain.

As she drove along towards the Cowbridge Road, she heard another roar as a jet took off and she saw the plane banking as it changed direction and headed north.

North! Of course! Why had none of them thought of it? It suddenly became clear how his watertight alibi might fall apart now. If there was an evening flight from Cardiff, he could have got to Edinburgh within the hour.

The car's engine whined and protested as she drove at speed in second gear, heading for Swansea where she intended checking the flights from Cardiff to Edinburgh.

Twenty-Four

The semi-detached house was identical to the others in the street in an area that was well behaved and insipid, and light years way from civilization, unless the most welcoming pub in the British Isles was just round the next corner. Lambert doubted it. The district was a secure enclave, where the natives only ventured out into the world at large from necessity, and rarely at night.

He thought he saw the net curtain twitch as he walked up the path, and when he rang the doorbell, the door opened almost immediately, as if they were looking out for him.

'Mr Farleigh?'

The retired teacher smiled and offered his hand. 'We've been expecting you. Detective Inspector Lambert, isn't it?'

He was ruddy complexioned and looked as if he'd walked out of a joke shop wearing a disguise of a ragged moustache, thick, black-framed glasses and a bulbous nose. He was tall and broad shouldered, with a slight stoop, as if he suffered from back trouble.

Standing behind him, his wife, ample busted and wearing a smart twin-set as though she had dressed especially for his visit, beamed at Lambert, and he got the impression they were both excited about being interviewed by a detective. She had one of the biggest busts he had ever seen and he wondered how she didn't topple over. He was introduced to her before being ushered into the front room; a room so tidy it would have been a sacrilege to leave a newspaper on the floor near your chair. Lambert stared at the walls as he entered, which were festooned with framed watercolours.

'Rita's the artist,' the ex-teacher explained. 'I keep telling her she should hold an exhibition.'

Mrs Farleigh blushed shyly and quickly changed the subject with an offer

THE WRECKING BAR

of coffee. Then, seeing Lambert hesitate, she gave a nod in her husband's direction and said, 'I can make some fresh. Don likes a good strong cup.'

Lambert smiled at her. 'I'd love some. Thank you.'

She shuffled out to make the coffee as Lambert and Farleigh sank into easy chairs.

'You wanted to talk to me about one of my pupils,' Farleigh said. 'Only I've been retired for eighteen years now. I'm seventy-eight, you know.'

'You certainly don't look anywhere near that,' Lambert lied as he unzipped his document case. 'I hope you have a good memory, Mr Farleigh. The boy I want to talk to you about would have been at your school somewhere in the mid seventies.'

'Well, I can't promise I'll remember someone that far back, but you never know.'

'The boy's name was Keith Hilden. Ring any bells?'

Farleigh tilted his head and looked up at the ceiling. 'It does vaguely. I'm trying to picture him but…'

Lambert slid a photograph out of his case, leant across and handed it to Farleigh. 'This is him in his mid-forties. His hair would have been dark then.'

Farleigh stared at the photograph for a long while, biting his lip. He seemed tense, and Lambert realized he was afraid of letting him down.

His wife entered and said, 'Coffee's just started to filter through,' and hovered in the doorway, clearly afraid to miss out on whatever Lambert was investigating.

Her husband turned to her and said, 'The inspector wants to know about a boy in our school, going back to the seventies. This is a recent photo of him. The chap's face seems vaguely familiar but…' He shrugged helplessly.

'Why, if you don't mind me asking,' his wife said, 'are you investigating this man from when he was a boy? It's a long time ago.'

Lambert gave her a vague answer. 'He's part of an ongoing investigation.'

'Oh!' Mrs Farleigh exclaimed. 'I don't think he wants to tell us, Don.' She laughed to show she was joking, but Lambert could see she was irked by his noncommittal reply. Needing her husband's cooperation, he decided he'd offer her a bit more information.

'Keith Hilden has disappeared. And we're trying to trace him.'

Which was true in a way. The boy had vanished years ago and become someone else.

Mollified by his answer, she excused herself to fetch the coffee.

'Still no luck?' Lambert asked.

Farleigh stared at the picture, frowning and concentrating before shaking his head. 'Sorry. I just can't place him. Name's familiar, though.'

And then, on a sudden impulse, Lambert removed Lloyd's driver's photograph from the document case and handed it to Farleigh. 'Have a look at that. See if his face means anything to you.'

It was a long shot. He hadn't considered this before. But now it made sense. Perhaps Lloyd and his driver went back a long way, back as far as their schooldays. And what if Jack Collier wasn't his real name?

Farleigh stared closely at the photograph. 'What's this chap's name?'

Lambert hesitated. He was reluctant to give Farleigh a name that might be false. Instead, he said, 'We don't know. We think he's a criminal associate of Keith Hilden.'

Suddenly, the air was electric as Farleigh, eyes gleaming with excitement, sat up straight and tapped the photograph with the back of his fingers.

'I know this chap, and he was a friend of Keith Hilden's. Yes, yes, it's all coming back to me now. Con O'Sullivan. I'm sure this is Con O'Sullivan.'

'How is it you can remember this man so clearly?'

'Because we were always talking about him at school; we were worried about him. We thought he might have been abused at home.'

It was Lambert's turn to sit up straight. 'Why d'you think he might have been abused?'

'He was always withdrawn. Hardly spoke to anyone. There was obviously something going on at home.'

'When you say at home…' Lambert began.

'His father,' Farleigh explained excitedly. 'We think his father abused him. He was being brought up by his unemployed father.'

'And you say Hilden was his friend?'

Farleigh nodded. 'Yes, I remember the other chap clearly now I can lump them together. He was a bright lad, Hilden. And none of us ever understood what a bright kid like him saw in O'Sullivan, who was always so sullen.'

'Perhaps he liked to have someone he could manipulate,' Lambert suggested.

'Yes, I'm sure there was an element of that in it.'

Mrs Farleigh pushed a hideous gilt tea trolley into the room. 'Coffee's ready,' she said. 'How are you getting on?'

Pleased with himself, Farleigh grinned at her. 'I've remembered them.'

'Oh good,' his wife said, more interested in serving the coffee now. 'Sugar, Inspector?'

'No, thanks. And I'll have it black.'

THE WRECKING BAR

He waited for her to pour him a cup, and offer him a biscuit, which he declined, before turning his attention back to her husband.

'If most of the teaching staff thought the boy was being abused, was anyone going to contact social services or do anything about it?'

'Oh, we were just about to, but something happened.'

Farleigh's eyes became distant as his mind scrolled back to 1975. Waiting for him to continue, Lambert's breathing became shallow and tremulous, as though he was poised on the edge of a cliff.

'So what happened, Mr Farleigh?'

'His father was murdered.'

Lambert was aware of the heavy silence in the room, apart from the faint clink from the crockery in his hand.

'Can you remember any of the details? Who killed him or anything like that?'

'I think it was a burglary. He was robbed, I think. I don't know any of the details.'

'And what happened to Con O'Sullivan after that?'

'He was taken into care, until they found him a foster home in the same area.'

'And did he stay on at your school?'

'Yes, and after his father had gone, he seemed to improve – marginally. So naturally all the staff thought they'd been right about the abuse.'

'And did he remain friends with Keith Hilden?'

Farleigh screwed his face up as he tried to recall. 'I think so. Yes, I really think he did.'

Sitting on the edge of his seat now, Lambert stared at Farleigh, hoping he could answer the key question.

'Mr Farleigh, I know you probably don't remember details of the burglary and the murder, but have you any idea how his father was killed?'

Farleigh clicked his cup down positively in its saucer. 'Oh, I can remember that all right. He was bludgeoned to death – with some sort of metal bar.'

***

When DC Jones arrived back at the incident room, Wallace had his back to her, spooning instant coffee into a cup. He glanced over his shoulder and didn't notice how badly she was limping.

'You timed that right,' he said. 'Kettle's just boiled. Tea or coffee?'

'They say you should drink strong sweet tea after a shock, but I'm not going to start drinking it with sugar now.'

CHAPTER TWENTY-FOUR

That got his attention. Turning to face her, he asked, 'Why? What's happened?

Groaning, she limped over to a chair near a desk. 'Sprained my bloody ankle, that's what's happened. Make me a tea no sugar, will you? I've just got to check something online, then bring your coffee over and I'll tell you all about it.'

She moved the computer mouse and waited while the screen reignited. She knew Flybe was the main carrier from Cardiff to Edinburgh, went straight to their website and typed in tomorrow's date for a single journey to Edinburgh. It came up with several scheduled flights, and the latest one left at 8 p.m.

'Bingo!' she cried. 'Got you, you bastard!'

Wallace brought their drinks over, and she told him what had happened at the old lady's house, ending the account with her idea of how Lloyd could have murdered his wife before flying to Edinburgh to be met by his driver, which would explain why he wanted to make certain the staff at the hotel remembered him.

Impulsively, Wallace stood up and said, 'I'll get to the airport right away and get the CCTV checked for that evening.' He rummaged in one of the folders on the desk for a photograph of Gavin Lloyd. 'I'll take this as well, and see if someone can ID him.'

'Why don't we both go?'

'I think you need to see First Aid and get that ankle seen to. I can probably get a copy of the CCTV on disk and we can both go through it here.'

As DC Wallace hurried to the door, Jones clicked her fingers as an idea struck her. 'Hang on, Kevin! You might not need the CCTV. He still holds a driving licence in the name of Keith Hilden, remember. He could have booked his ticket in that name, and if ID was required going through security, his photo driving licence would have been acceptable.'

Wallace grinned at her. 'You're not just a pretty face. Thanks, Debbie.'

'Not so fast, Kevin! You might need this.'

He came back into the room as she delved into her handbag for her notebook, scribbled something on a scrap of paper and handed it to him.

'What's this?'

'It's the registration number of a red Vauxhall Nova. You might try looking for it in the long stay car park.'

Wallace pulled a long face. 'Thanks a bundle. I take that back about the pretty face.'

As soon as he'd left, DC Jones moved her left ankle in a circle to test how painful it was. She winced. Now that the excitement had died down, the pain was back with a vengeance. She started to rise, bracing herself for the walk to First Aid, when her mobile rang. She sat down again and grabbed it from her handbag.

It was DI Lambert, wanting to know what had happened at Mrs Parry's house. She repeated her story, ending with her theory about the possible air travel to Edinburgh.

'Christ! How come none of us thought of that sooner?' he groaned.

'It was a conjuring trick,' she replied. 'I believe it's called misdirection. He drew attention to himself with his bad behaviour, at the petrol station in Cardiff and at the hotel, fooling us into thinking he really had been driven to Edinburgh, and letting us think he employed a professional killer, knowing we'd never find anyone, because that person doesn't exist.'

'Well done, Debbie. Good work. You know, something tells me you could be right, and Kevin will find that Hilden was booked on that flight to Edinburgh. Fingers crossed that's what happened. Now you need to get that ankle seen to. But if you can delay that just a minute longer, there's something I'd like you to do.'

He told her about what he'd learnt from Mr Farleigh, the retired schoolteacher, and asked her to contact the Metropolitan Police to find out about the father's unsolved murder, and see if she could find out who worked on the case, even though it was thirty-five years ago.

'Harry!' she called, as he was about to hang up.

'What?'

'Mind if I ask you something?'

'Go on,' he answered.

'Earlier on, Kevin found out the London flat of Green Valley Productions was the address for Mark Yalding's credit card. And at least ten days ago, as we were going to meet Rhiannon Lloyd at that pub, you said how easy it was to learn my mother's maiden name. So you must have had some idea back then of how Mark Yalding's card was obtained.'

'But that's all it was then, Debbie, a vague idea; a hunch.'

'Still, it's one that's paid off. Just like you must have had some sort of idea of what I might find in Mrs Parry's garage.'

'I was hoping you might find the car.'

'We still might. Kevin's going to search the long stay car park at the airport.'

'Good. But now let's hope you can find me one of the officers who investigated the death of Con O'Sullivan's father.'

'I'll get straight on to it and call you back.'

***

CHAPTER TWENTY-FOUR

Less than an hour later, Lambert got off the District Line at Embankment, and had just stepped out into Villiers Street when his mobile alerted him to a text message from DC Jones, asking him to call her. He turned into the Victoria Embankment Gardens, walked past the bandstand, found an empty bench to sit on, and called her back.

'Hi, Harry,' she greeted him. 'Where have you been? I tried to get hold of you ten minutes ago.'

'I was on the underground train. I'm in central London. Any joy with the Met officers?'

'The DI on the case died of a heart attack in 1990, and the detective sergeant now lives in Canada. But there was a Detective Constable Martin Dyson, who retired five years ago and is still around. I've got his phone number and address for you.'

When she finished reading it out, Harry said, 'Shit! Big mistake!'

'What is?'

'He lives in Barking, Essex. I thought by coming into central London I could branch out in any direction, to any one of the hundreds of districts. And what happens? Barking's not that far from Hornchurch and I've just come from there.'

He heard her stifle a giggle. 'Oh well, at least you've got a good transport system where you are.'

'Yes, and I'm helping to pay for it. Any news from Kevin at the airport?'

'I was just coming to that. Kevin phoned fifteen minutes ago to confirm that Keith Hilden was on the passenger list for the eight o'clock flight to Edinburgh on the night his wife was murdered. He paid cash for his ticket early that morning, and two of the Flybe ground staff identified him from his photo. It looks like we've got enough evidence for an immediate arrest, Harry.'

'Except that Clive Marden wants it all done up in a neat package with pink ribbons to hand to the CPS. Don't worry, by this time tomorrow we'll have that bastard behind bars. Did you get that ankle seen to?'

'I'm just about to hobble over to First Aid.'

'Good work, Debbie. I'll ring you later when I have some news.'

After ending the call, Lambert immediately tried the retired Metropolitan police officer but got an answering machine giving a mobile number. He made a note of the number and rang it. It was answered after a couple of rings, and judging by the background noise, Martin Dyson was speaking from somewhere crowded like a shopping centre. The ex-police officer had difficulty hearing, but managed to explain to Lambert that he worked as a

THE WRECKING BAR

security guard at Lakeside Shopping Centre and wouldn't be home until seven. But he would be quite happy to speak to him then.

With some reluctance, Lambert agreed and disconnected the call. It was just gone three, and he had almost four hours to kill.

At least now he had time to eat a proper meal.

***

Martin Dyson lived in a small, cramped, untidy flat. The walls were dotted with framed photographs of children at varying stages of growing up, and Lambert guessed he was divorced, saw his children once in a while, and spent his nights down at his local, adding even more weight to his enormous midriff. His face was damp with perspiration and his hair was dark and slicked back with a middle parting. He was still wearing a brown security uniform, with an American cop-style badge on the lapel, and there were dark sweat patches under his arms.

'Why do you want to know about a crime going back thirty-five years?' he asked.

'It was an unsolved crime,' Lambert said. 'Do you remember a man called Frank O'Sullivan who was murdered in the docklands? He had a young son of thirteen – Con O'Sullivan.'

Dyson stared down at the carpet. 'Let's see now,' he began, 'O'Sullivan… O'Sullivan.' He clicked his fingers. 'Oh yeah, now I remember. That was the guy who was bashed on the head.'

'Could you tell me what happened?'

Dyson smirked as if digging up an old case was trivial. 'The guy left the door on the latch for his son. But he had a visit from an opportunistic burglar who beat him over the head with a heavy instrument. His wallet was found a few streets away with no money in it.'

'And did you and the other investigating officers accept robbery as a motive, Mr Dyson?'

'Please! Call me Martin.'

'Martin.'

Dyson hesitated, and Lambert could see his reluctance to answer the question straightaway. Eventually, he exhaled noisily and said, 'Although I was one of the officers, I was a rookie. Most of the investigation was carried out by DS Jimmy Lennon.'

'What about the DI on the case?'

'There was a lot going on at the time. So he left most of the investigation to Jimmy.'

180

Chapter Twenty-Four

'Who found the body?'

'The son did. He stayed the night at his mate's house, went to school the next day, and discovered the body when he got home.'

'Was he interviewed soon afterwards?'

'Well, at first he was traumatized. In a state of shock. When we did eventually get round to talking to him he told us he spent the night at his friend's house watching TV.'

'And did you check that?'

Dyson suddenly bristled with indignation. 'What do you take us for? Yeah, of course we checked.'

'I'm sorry,' Lambert said. 'I didn't mean to imply your investigation was anything but thorough.'

'We questioned his friend, and his friend's mother. She was in the pub most of the night, but she remembered they were there when she got home. And she remembered them both going off to school the next morning.'

'Can you describe the murder weapon for me?'

Dyson frowned deeply, unnerved by Lambert's change of thought.

'A murder weapon was never found.'

'Didn't that strike you as strange?'

'Not really. The killer could have disposed of it by throwing it in the Thames. The river weren't far from O'Sullivan's house.'

'Whereabouts was his friend's house?'

Dyson jerked a thumb at one of the walls, as if the building was nearby. 'That site was redeveloped. I think it's a big Asda supermarket now.'

'I mean, how far away from each other did they live?'

'Oh, less than a quarter of a mile, I'd say.'

'And you visited the Hilden house, did you?'

'Yeah, it's funny, I can remember their house quite clearly. It was an old house – Victorian, probably – and part of the front garden had been paved over, and there was an old Hillman Hunter outside, a real old rust bucket. No tax, but it was parked off the road. Jimmy asked the mother if she had the keys, but she said they'd got lost over the years. She was a widow, and the car used to belong to her husband.'

'Did you search the house?'

'Yeah, we had a quick shufti but we never found nothing.'

'Did you speak to Con O'Sullivan's teachers?'

The question caught Dyson by surprise, and Lambert saw the guarded look in his eyes, like a shutter rolling down. After a moment's pause, he said, 'I didn't speak to any of the teachers. But I think Jimmy did. I was busy doing

THE WRECKING BAR

door-to-door with some uniforms to see if anyone spotted anything that night.'

'And did the sergeant tell you what the teachers told him?'

Dyson shrugged. 'Nothing very much, I don't think.'

Lambert feigned surprise. 'Didn't the sergeant tell you about the possible sex abuse Con O'Sullivan may have suffered from his father?'

Dyson found a small threadbare spot on the arm of his easy chair and examined it. 'I don't think he did,' he muttered. 'If he did, I don't remember.'

Lambert snorted. 'Oh, come on, Martin. The teachers were about to call social services. They would have done had the father not been murdered. And if the boy was being abused, doesn't that give him a motive? He'd have been a specific suspect.'

'We found no evidence linking him to the murder. So Jimmy was convinced it was a burglary gone wrong. And DI Grant backed him up.'

Lambert stared pointedly at a portrait of a primary schoolgirl in a blue-gingham blouse, smiling sweetly to camera. 'You're a family man, I see.'

Dyson scowled with suspicion. 'What's that supposed to mean?'

'I just think it's commendable to love one's children. There's something spiritual about that sort of love.'

Dyson's scowl uncoiled and he nodded his agreement. 'Although the missus and I split up about eighteen years ago, and the children are grown up now, I still see them regularly. I've got a good relationship with them.'

'And what about DS Lennon? Was he a family man, too?'

'He was devoted to his kiddies. Do anything for them.'

'So when he suspected O'Sullivan was seriously abusing young Con, he didn't look too hard for evidence linking the son to his father's murder.'

Dyson's face darkened and he lumbered to his feet. 'I think I can safely say this interview's over.'

Lambert also stood up. 'That's okay, Martin. You've told me everything I need to know.'

Dyson moved a step forward, his chin jutting forward confrontationally. 'Well, I'll tell you something else for nothing: if it turns out that Con O'Sullivan's been killing those paedophiles in South Wales, I hope he finishes the job and gets away with it.'

Lambert smiled thinly. 'How did you know?'

'You don't have to be Einstein to work that one out. It's still in the news, and you sound like a Taff.' Dyson glanced at his watch. 'Now if you don't mind – it's pub quiz night.'

As he swung open the flat door, Lambert thanked him and started to exit.

182

'Me an' a mate went on holiday to Wales a couple of years back,' Dyson said, and Lambert noticed a malicious glint in his eye as he turned to face him. 'Would have been all right if it weren't for all them Taffs. Fucking sheep shaggers, the lot of them.'

'I've never heard that before,' Lambert said, but the door had already slammed in his face.

Twenty-Five

As Lambert walked towards Wordsworth House, a plastic bag containing vodka and cans of Pepsi in one hand, and his document case under the other arm, his mobile rang. He shoved the case hurriedly under the arm carrying the plastic bag and struggled to extricate his mobile from his pocket.

'Hi, Kevin,' he said as he pressed answer. 'You're not still at the airport, are you? It's gone eight o'clock.'

'I don't think the car's here, Harry. I've been over every square metre of the long stay car park – twice!'

'Maybe that's not how he got to the airport. He might have parked the car somewhere else and taken a taxi.'

'So where's the old woman's car now then?'

'I've no idea. But at least Debbie got that oil sample off the garage floor. Presumably forensics will have it by now.'

'I think so, but I haven't heard if they've got a result and matched it yet. Are you on your way back?'

'No, it looks like I'll be catching the 10.45 train. Gets in to Swansea at 2.15. I've yet to talk to Keith Hilden's mother. She's a dipsomaniac, so that could be tricky, and I think…'

He stopped, unable to hear any sound from Kevin's end. 'Hello? Kevin?'

'Shit!' he uttered. Last night he'd forgotten to charge his mobile, and with all the calls he'd made throughout the day, the battery had just died. Not that it made much difference now. Once he finished questioning Hilden's mother, he could head for home. And first thing tomorrow they would meet with DCS Marden and present him with all the evidence and make the arrest.

When he arrived at the gloomy building, he pressed the buzzer for Flat 12. After a while a croaky voice asked who it was. Taking a deep breath, he replied, 'It's me, Mum. Keith.'

Chapter Twenty-Five

He thought he heard an excited intake of breath and the door buzzed as it was released. He pushed it open, hurried up the stairs and along the balcony. He thought she might be out on the balcony, waiting to greet her son, but her door was shut. He knocked loudly and waited. From further along the balcony he could hear the cheers and then the disappointed groans from the crowd as a striker failed to score in a televised football match.

Perhaps she hadn't heard him. He knocked again, twice as loud this time. And then he saw her form through the mottled glass on the top half of the door. When she opened the door and saw it wasn't her son, she screamed at him.

'Who the fuck are you?'

'It's Harry?'

'I don't know any Harry.'

'Barbara! Just unlock the chain and let me in, I want to talk to you.'

'Well, I don't want to talk to you.'

'I thought we could have a nice drink together. I've brought a bottle of vodka with me.'

He saw the cogs grinding slowly in her addled brain while she thought about this. After the smallest of pauses, she unlatched the security chain and stared up at him, like a small chimp hoping for a handout.

He smiled reassuringly and showed her the vodka. Her eyes lit up and her hand reached out to grab it, but he held it out of reach.

'No, no, Barbara! I just want a quiet talk while we have a few drinks together. There's no harm in that, is there?'

Reluctantly, and still eyeing his bag of temptation, she stepped aside to let him enter. 'Door down the end,' she said.

He walked into the living room, expecting to find filth and untidiness. What surprised him was the chaotic neatness of the room. Piles of old newspapers and magazines had been stacked in bundles. The dining table contained three neat stacks, each about a foot high, and there were also piles of books on the floor, but they were positioned carefully, like building blocks. Lambert imagined, during her more sober moments, she was obsessively compulsive, and had a misguided need to create order in her life. But the room smelt musty and damp, and the one-bar electric fire gave out little warmth.

An oak sideboard had a fruit bowl on the top, containing one black rotting banana. Lambert nodded towards the sideboard cupboard. 'You got any glasses for our drinks?'

She darted across the room, waving him out of the way, opened the door and grabbed two crystal glasses. 'We'll have the posh ones.' She placed them carefully on top of the sideboard. 'Waterford,' she explained.

THE WRECKING BAR

After he'd poured the drinks, taking a smaller measure himself, he settled into a garishly patterned two-seater sofa with wooden arms. She scurried across and sat in a tattered easy chair close to the fire. He watched as she sipped her vodka and Pepsi, and saw the relief, followed by a return of sociability as she turned towards him with a smile.

'What's this in aid of?' she said.

'I just wanted to have a talk with you about Keith.'

She raised the glass to her mouth for a sip, rather too quickly, and the drink spilled out of the side of her mouth. She wiped it with the back of her hand and looked Lambert in the eye, defying him to comment on the accident.

'So why did Keith choose to go and live in Wales?' Lambert asked.

'Who said anything about him living in Wales?'

'I know where he lives, Barbara. He's married and he has children, and they have a big house.'

Like a parody of a drunk, she put a finger to her lips, covering a secret smile. 'Shh! It's private. I'm not supposed to tell no one about him.'

'But I know all about him, Barbara. Where he lives, what he does for a living. And he's got a flat in London. Did you know that?'

She stared at the bottom of her glass, which was now almost empty. 'Course I did. I've been there. Nice flat it is too. He's very good to me is Keith; looks after me when he comes to London. He won't let me go to Wales though. He said if I ever do, he—' She stopped and examined her glass again.

'He'd what, Barbara?'

Confusion clouded her gaze, and she shrugged.

'Let me get you another drink.'

Lambert poured her another generous measure of vodka with a small top up of Pepsi. As he handed it to her, she looked up at him trustingly, as if he was the only person who understood her problems.

'It's good to have—' She searched for the words '—congenial company.'

'So you've never been to Wales to visit Keith, Barbara. But you rang him at his home there a few weeks ago.'

'Did I?'

'Don't tell me you've forgotten.'

She smirked. 'Oh yeah. We had a long chat.'

'He wasn't angry you rang then?'

'Was he? I don't remember.'

'Didn't he wonder how you'd got the number?'

A crafty smile as she tapped the side of her nose. 'It was when I went to his flat in… somewhere in London.' She waved a hand at one of the walls. 'Keith

186

was in the bathroom, and I found a letter with his address on it. So I copied the number.'

Her grin widened at the memory, proud of her alcoholic deviousness.

'Do you know who Gavin Lloyd is?'

Her smile vanished and she looked like a cornered animal.

'He made me promise never to tell anyone. You won't ever tell anyone, will you?'

Lambert shook his head and said, 'No reason to,' before asking her some more questions, this time in a light conversational tone, plying her with a few more drinks, until he thought she had reached the stage when she might remember what happened in 1975. Her long-term memory, he guessed, would probably be sharper than the short term.

'When you lived in your other house, when Keith was still at school, do you remember his friend, Con?'

'Oh, him! Didn't have two words to say for himself. I can't think why my Keith was his mate. Keith was bright. But Con was... he seemed a bit thick.'

'Do you remember the night he came round to stay at your place, and his father was attacked and killed?'

'Yeah, they was in watching a film on the telly. The police came and had a look round my house afterwards. Dunno what for. They didn't find nothing.'

'Did they ask about the car?'

She screwed up her face in confusion. 'What bleedin' car?'

'I thought you had a car belonging to your husband parked outside. Did the police search the car?'

'No, we never had no keys. Keith said we lost 'em.' She tapped the side of her nose again, as if she enjoyed the gesture. 'But I think he had 'em all along.'

'Why would he want to keep that a secret?'

She shrugged hugely. 'It's kids, innit. I mean, what did it matter if he did have the keys? I couldn't drive. And neither could he. He was probably just playing games.'

'Did he ever keep things in the car?'

'He might have done. But it didn't bother me.'

'What happened to Mr Hilden, his father?'

Her mouth contorted into a grimace, and Lambert watched as she struggled with a painful memory.

'Did he leave you?'

She shook her head violently. 'No, not in the way you mean. He was doing so well at first. Started his own business in East Ham. He poured his heart and soul into it, working all hours.'

THE WRECKING BAR

She paused, lost in her memories.

'What sort of business did he run?' Lambert prompted gently.

'He used to design and fit kitchens for people.'

'And what went wrong?'

'What didn't go wrong? He had a couple of people working for him, and they was ripping him off. And he got cancelled orders and then the suppliers wanted paying. He was going bust when it happened.'

There was a silence, even though Lambert was aware of the strident football commentary through the paper-thin walls.

'When what happened?'

Her eyes became distant. 'Dennis went out early one morning – I thought he was going to work. Instead, he went to that park by the river – near where the tunnel to walk to Greenwich is. I can't understand what made him do it. He should've thought of his family first.'

'How did he kill himself?'

'He stuck his head in a plastic bag so he couldn't breathe no more. Just lay down in the park and stopped breathing.'

She knocked back her drink and held it out for Lambert to refill. After handing it to her, he said, 'How old was Keith when this happened?'

'He was ten.' She laughed bitterly. 'That's why I thought it was funny Keith growing up and going off to live in Wales. Maybe he wanted to be like his dad.'

Lambert, more alert now than at any time during their talk, remained standing. 'When you say he wanted to be like his dad, you mean what exactly?'

'His father was Welsh.'

'And he had a strong Welsh accent and everything?'

She looked up at him, a puzzled expression on her face. 'Of course he bloody did. He was Welsh, wasn't he?'

Deep inside, Lambert felt a small vibration of satisfaction. 'So Keith grew up listening to his father's Welsh voice.'

'Yeah. He really used to enjoy talking with his dad. And then Dennis went and killed himself. It took Keith a while to get over it. At least a year, and then he became – well, whenever I talked about his father he became angry. Said he'd never be like him. Keith used to upset me by calling his dad a failure. Keith reckoned he was going places. Not like his dad, he said, who just ended up sticking his head in a bag.'

She looked up at him, pleading, eyes brimming with tears.

'Keith is successful, isn't he? Not like his dad.'

Like one of his suspects, Lambert broke eye contact with her as he lied.

'Keith's done all right for himself. He's a very successful television producer and he's won all kinds of awards.'

It was what she wanted to hear. When he looked at her again, he saw the smile of gratitude, and the tears which had threatened to become a torrent had miraculously vanished.

He glanced at his watch. 'I've got to catch the 10.45 to Swansea. And that doesn't get in until 2.15 in the morning,' he said. 'So if you'll excuse me, I've got to get across to Paddington.'

He noticed the alcoholic desperation as she stared at the vodka bottle, hoping he wasn't going to take what was left with him, and he felt deeply sorry for the woman.

'I'll see myself out,' he said as he picked up his document case.

As she watched him move away from the sideboard, and more importantly the bottle, she relaxed. She could enjoy the remaining vodka during the rest of the evening, while she watched *The Apprentice*. She liked that programme, and there was a young man in it who reminded her of Keith.

Keith! She needed to tell this bloke not to tell Keith what she'd said.

'Wait!' she said as Lambert was about to leave. 'You won't tell him, will you?'

He stopped at the door. 'Keith, you mean?'

Her brain fuzzy, she struggled to find the words. 'His name,' she slurred. 'I didn't tell you his name. Gavin... that's his name... he... he'll get angry with me if he knows I told you.'

Lambert patted her on the shoulder. 'Don't worry, Barbara. It never came from you. We already knew his name.'

With barely a backward glance at her, Lambert moved swiftly to the front door and let himself out.

As soon as she heard it close, she refilled her glass, without the Pepsi this time, and knocked back the neat spirit with one swift gulp. Confused now, she wondered who that man was she had spoken to. Something to do with Keith, she thought. And then, through the thick fog of her mind, she saw an image materialize. Christ! He was a copper. She'd been speaking to a copper. And what was it Keith had told her? It was something to do with his name.

Jesus Christ! She had told that copper his name, and after she'd promised him she wouldn't.

Don't tell anyone I'm Kevin. Not anyone. Understand? I'm Gavin Lloyd.

'Yes, Kevin,' she mumbled drunkenly, and then corrected herself, 'Gavin! That's it! Gavin! Oh Christ! I shouldn't have told that copper your name, Gavin. I'd better ring you.'

The Wrecking Bar

But where had she put his number? Her misty eyes surveyed the bundles of newspapers and magazines stacked neatly on the table. It wasn't there. She could remember having a clear up earlier in the day, restacking the bundles so there was barely an untidy overlap with the pages, but where was his number?

And then she remembered the kitchen! The noticeboard! Carefully tacked to the cork, all the things she needed to remember, all in neat rows with coloured tacks.

She thought she remembered putting Keith's number in a row of red tacks.

She staggered out to the kitchen and lurched towards the noticeboard on the wall above the mottled green work surface. She narrowed her eyes and focused on the noticeboard. And there it was, in big, bold letters. Keith stroke Gavin.

She unpinned the number from the board, rushed back into the living room and picked up the phone. After several attempts to dial, knowing she had pressed the wrong digits numerous times, she eventually heard the phone ring at the other end. She slumped to the floor and sat cradling the phone, humming a tune as she waited.

'Keith!' she shouted when it was answered. 'Is that you?'

It was. It was him. Her Keith. She hadn't misdialled after all. She felt pleased about that. But she wanted him to know how sorry she was.

Speech slurring heavily now, she said, 'A man came here to see me. I think he was a copper. I'm sorry, Keith! I'm sorry! What? Yeah, I think he said that was his name when he first came round. I think that's what it was. Yeah! Lambert! Yeah, I'm sure of it. And he's just on his way back to Swansea on a late train. Oh, Keith. I'm sorry. I never meant to tell him you was Gavin. He knows you're two people. Keith and Gavin. I'm sorry – I didn't mean to tell him who you are. Keith! Listen! I know what we'll do...'

But her son had already hung up. After sobbing for a bit, she got up off the floor and poured the remaining vodka into her glass.

Twenty-Six

Two shifts and different staff during fourteen hours of labour and still there was no sign of the baby being born. Twice Ellis had been told there was nothing happening because Sharon's contractions were still too far apart and he was advised to take at least an hour's break to get some food inside him. On both occasions, scared that something might happen in his absence, he grabbed a coffee and sandwich and took only half an hour.

He had returned to Sharon's side well over three hours ago, when the nightshift staff came on duty. He'd been at the hospital since ten that morning. Now that it was almost midnight, he was nervous and jittery, feeling something was wrong.

He held Sharon's hand tightly, squirming in its claw-like grip, trying not to wince at the pain. It was trivial compared to hers. But worse than her fingernails digging into the back of his hand was the rancid smell from her breath, putrid like drains. He tried not to think about it and concentrated on giving her encouraging smiles and weak words of comfort. But, apart from her grip, she was unaware of his presence, and he saw the desperation in her eyes, like an animal in pain, incapable of rational thought.

And then he noticed the urgent way the staff exchanged looks and he knew something was wrong. A strange feeling of disorientation overwhelmed him and he wasn't sure if time had speeded up or gone into slow motion.

The consultant entered hurriedly, worried about the foetal distress and the baby passing meconium which, he explained, was the infant's first stool, and if it was expelled into the amniotic fluid there was a danger that the baby could inhale the contaminated fluid which could lead to respiratory problems. He strongly advised what Sharon was afraid of hearing – an immediate caesarean birth. For the baby's sake, he stressed, they needed to act quickly. That was when Ellis saw and admired Sharon's decisive calm,

The Wrecking Bar

her guts and determination as she insisted on an epidural caesarean. It was explained to him by one of the staff that she would be anaesthetized from the waist down so that she would be aware of what was happening and could hold her baby as soon as it was delivered.

***

Neck aching from where he'd been lying back with his head twisted uncomfortably, Lambert woke, yawned and stretched. The train braked as it approached a station and the announcement gave Cardiff as the next stop. He had drifted off into a fitful sleep just before Bristol Parkway, weaving in and out of consciousness, unclear whether his thoughts were dreams or vice versa.

When he'd boarded the train at Paddington, he'd bought himself a toasted sandwich and two small bottles of overpriced red wine, but he'd been too tired to eat the sandwich and left most of it. Now his mouth felt sour and stale from the wine and he needed to drink some water, but he doubted the buffet would still be open.

As the train completed the last lap of the journey, he thought about Dennis Hilden, whose suicide set up a chain of events culminating in a series of brutal murders. Had the man been given the benefit of foresight, would he still have contemplated taking his own life? But there were hundreds of suicides each year, and the relatives of those suicides, after having survived the traumas of the deed, carried on living normal lives, their heartbreak eventually healed with the passage of time.

It still didn't absolve Dennis Hilden from his act of self murder and its effect, and had Lambert been a religious man he would have liked to be a witness for the prosecution on Hilden's judgment day.

As the train neared Swansea, Lambert sat up and blinked the sleep from his watery eyes. He was exhausted and would be lucky if he got three hours' sleep as he had to be up early to present the case to Marden prior to the arrest.

When the train pulled in to Swansea, Lambert felt the early morning cold blowing through the draughty station as he stepped down on to the platform, and for a moment it seemed to revive him after the heat of the sleep-inducing carriage. He hurried to the car park, and raised the collar of his leather coat as he climbed the freezing stairwell to the second floor where he'd left his Mercedes. Because of his tiredness, he thought he saw demons lurking in the shadows, waiting to attack him. He smiled at the foolish notion, knowing the only thing likely to jump out at him was made of flesh and blood, but as it was almost 2.30 in the morning, it was unlikely that even the most desperate mugger would be lying in wait.

As soon as he settled behind the wheel of his car and turned the ignition key, his tiredness returned. By the time he had driven carefully out of the multi-storey, he was fighting to stay awake. He was so tired he failed to notice the car that pulled away from the kerb and followed his Mercedes out of the city centre and along the sea front towards his flat.

***

As he cradled his baby daughter, smiling at her as she looked up at him, Ellis could have sworn she instinctively recognized him as her father.

Sharon was now asleep, exhausted after her ordeal but ecstatically happy. After the delivery she had cuddled her daughter and wept tears of joy, the baby had then been checked and weighed and found to be perfect, and Sharon had one more cuddle with her before allowing herself to lose consciousness.

After ten minutes of gazing into his daughter's eyes, a nurse came and told him he ought to go home and get some sleep, offering to look after the baby for him. He was reluctant to part with his daughter, but also relieved after such an emotionally draining experience.

Once he had handed the nurse his child and saw her looking down at his baby with such loving care, he felt reassured about leaving. And he knew as soon as he got home, and his head hit the pillow, he'd be spark out.

But as soon as he stepped outside the hospital into the cold air, he snapped awake with an elation he'd never known before. He was desperate to share his news with someone, but no one would thank him for being woken at three in the morning.

On the other hand, what did it matter? And he suddenly knew who to contact; who might be finding it hard to sleep.

***

As soon as Lambert walked into his flat, the telephone rang. He had been so involved in the investigation, he had forgotten all about Tony Ellis and the birth, and he wondered who on earth could be ringing at three in the morning. He grabbed the phone.

'Harry, sorry to ring so late,' Ellis began.

'Tony, what's happened?'

'Sharon was in labour for over fifteen hours, but she finally gave birth to a baby daughter.'

'Congratulations, Tony! That's fantastic news.'

THE WRECKING BAR

'I know. It's brilliant. I'm sorry to ring so late, but I've just come from the hospital and I felt I had to tell someone.'

Lambert smiled, flattered he'd been chosen as the first to be told.

'If you want to wet the baby's head, I've got a bottle of Courvoisier sitting in the kitchen cupboard.'

'Are you sure you don't mind?'

'I've only just got back on the late train, and I was debating whether or not to have a nightcap, so we'll make it a celebration instead.'

'Thanks, Harry. By the time you've poured the drinks, I'll be there.'

Grinning, Lambert went into the kitchen, opened the cupboard, grabbed the cognac and two glasses, and was about to pour when the doorbell rang.

He laughed and said, 'That *was* quick!' Presumably Tony had driven over to give him the good news but decided to ring before calling.

He walked across the living room, out into the small hall and opened the door. He was still smiling as the fist caught him on the cheekbone and he fell back, cracking his head on the living-room doorframe.

Twenty-Seven

When he turned into Lambert's street, Ellis couldn't find a single space to park his car, unless he blocked someone's drive. As it was the middle of the night, and he only intended stopping for one drink, half an hour at the most, he didn't think it would matter. He parked his Fiat with two wheels on the kerb, squeezing in behind a BMW.

He was about to cut his headlights when he realized something was trying to grab his attention. He stared at the BMW's number plate for a while, until it clicked into place.

It was the registration number of Gavin Lloyd's car. He was sure of it. And he remembered it from earlier in the day, when he'd delegated Harry's instruction to use a patrol officer to watch out for the car while Debbie was at Mrs Parry's house. So what was Gavin Lloyd doing at his boss's flat?

***

Lambert's head throbbed with pain. He knew he was dazed and not unconscious because he could hear voices, although he couldn't make out what they were saying. Hands grabbed him roughly under the arms, pinching and pulling his skin, and he felt himself being dragged into the living room and turned over onto his stomach. With a massive effort he opened his eyes and struggled to turn over, but something hard slammed into the back of him and his head hit the floor.

Stunned and choking on carpet dust, he felt a rope being squeezed tight around his wrists. Hands grabbed him under the arms again and lifted him into a sitting position against the edge of the sofa. He forced his eyes open, and Gavin Lloyd's face swam into focus, sweating and desperate. Lloyd fumbled in the pocket of his fleece, pulled out a roll of gaffer tape, peeled off a strip and gagged Lambert with it.

THE WRECKING BAR

Over Lloyd's shoulder, Lambert saw Collier, a metal bar in his hand, standing erect like a statue, his face a mask as he watched his boss. They both wore latex gloves and were clearly intent on committing another murder.

Lloyd, who had been bending over to secure the tape over Lambert's mouth, straightened and stepped back several paces, surveying his handiwork. Still Collier hadn't moved a muscle and Lambert sensed a reluctance to participate in this crime. If only he wasn't gagged he might have a chance to negotiate with Collier. But Lloyd wasn't going to give him that opportunity.

Lloyd turned towards Collier. 'Let's get it over with.'

An almost imperceptible shake of the head from Collier.

'Just one hard crack,' Lloyd urged. 'He won't feel a thing.'

'It ain't that. All the others deserved to die. This guy's just a copper doing his job.'

Lloyd's face reddened and his eyes blazed. 'You're forgetting my wife. She was no child molester. But I had to kill her. And whether you like it or not, you helped me. If she'd had her way, she'd have divorced me, and I'd have got fuck all. And you'd have ended up selling copies of *Big Issue* on the streets. So don't start getting squeamish. We've come this far and this bastard's not going to ruin everything I've worked for all these years. So if you won't do it, I will.'

Lloyd walked over to Collier and reached for the crowbar, but Collier pulled his hand away like a child resisting a parent.

'Don't be stupid, Jack. D'you seriously want to lose everything?'

The doorbell rang. Lloyd's startled head swivelled towards the door, but Collier hardly moved, his reactions deadened over the years by psychological damage.

Lloyd stared at Lambert. 'Are you expecting someone?'

Lambert nodded. Lloyd froze, his brain trying to cope with the notion of Lambert having a visitor in the middle of the night.

The doorbell rang again, long and insistent.

'It's not going to go away,' Collier told his boss, and moved to answer the door.

Outside the flat, Ellis had second thoughts about his actions. Perhaps he should have called for the armed response unit and waited. He was taking a great risk going it alone like this. Especially now he had everything to live for. He saw a morbid headline flashing through his brain, news of a young detective killed in the line of duty and leaving behind a wife and newborn baby.

But by now it was too late. He held his ID in front of him as the door swung open and he was confronted by Jack Collier, a crowbar in his hand.

196

'I've got back-up,' he bluffed. 'An armed response unit will be here in less than ten minutes. So you may as well give it up.'

Collier turned his back on him and went back into the living room. Ellis closed the door and followed him. When Lloyd saw him, he must have known it was all over, and sank into an easy chair, his face drained of colour now.

Ellis, one eye on the metal bar in Collier's hand, eased past him, went over to Lambert, peeled off the gag and untied his hands. Lambert, feeling dazed from the bang on the head, was helped to his feet by Ellis, and both men stood facing Collier.

'I know all there is to know about you,' Lambert said to Collier. 'Con O'Sullivan, in 1975 Keith Hilden helped you murder your father. All these years he's had a hold over you because of it. What did he do? Keep the murder weapon in that old banger outside his house, threatening to use it against you if you didn't toe the line? But you went along with his recent plans because you thought he was helping you avenge all the abused children by killing those paedophiles.'

'They were just like my father,' Collier broke in. 'Poisoning young children's souls; destroying their childhood. When I was just seven years old my father started on me. The pain was… it stays with you for the rest of your life. I have no regrets about killing my father or those men.'

'And what about Mark Yalding?'

'What about him? He was downloading child pornography. How long would it be before he began abusing young children?'

'I'm sorry to have to tell you, Jack, but Mark Yalding's only crime was in having an affair with another man's wife.' Lambert stared pointedly at Lloyd. 'And the husband stood to lose everything, seeing as how he had never paid back his father-in-law for a loan. Mark Yalding was having an affair with Rhiannon Lloyd, and she was about to leave her husband for him. That was why he used you, contrived this whole sordid affair, so that you would think Yalding was a potential paedophile.'

'But he was. The police found out he was downloading child pornography.'

'Wrong. He was set up by your employer, who got a credit card in his name, found his wife's key to his cottage and downloaded the porn on his computer.'

Lambert noticed the panic in Collier's eyes, the look of a mistreated mongrel.

'Your boss knew his marriage was over and needed to get rid of Yalding, and so he used your revulsion of sex offenders as a way of getting rid of him. Even the idea of the TV programme about the sex offenders came from

THE WRECKING BAR

him, as did the leak to the press. He used you to kill an innocent man, first torturing him for a crime he never committed. And when that didn't work, when he discovered his wife still intended divorcing him, he decided to kill her, using you as his alibi. He used you, Jack, to murder an innocent man, and also to conspire in the murder of another innocent victim. Unless you think infidelity is grounds for murder.'

In retrospect Lambert almost wished he hadn't pushed these accusations at a man yielding a crowbar. But he couldn't wind back time, and it all happened so quickly they didn't have time to react.

Eyes burning with white heat, Collier turned to look at his boss. Lloyd looked up at him at that moment, and smiled as if to say 'so what'.

Collier swung the crowbar in a great arc and brought it down on Lloyd's head. They heard the sickening crack. Ellis was the first to react, and dived for Collier's waist, bringing him down on to the floor with a mighty crash. But it was all over. Lloyd's chauffeur sobbed uncontrollably, and the cries of pain that came from deep inside him were like the torments of tortured souls condemned to an eternity of suffering.

Twenty-Eight

Clutching a Sainsbury's carrier bag, Lambert stood at the head of the bed, staring down at Lloyd's unconscious form, his head swathed in bandages, a ventilator tube in his mouth, his eyes closed as if he was sleeping peacefully instead of in a coma, being kept alive by medical technology. The heart rate on the monitor appeared to be steady, and Lambert stared at Lloyd's eyes, willing them to open. He hoped and prayed the man would recover so that he could arrest him.

He heard the door opening but ignored it, thinking it was a nurse coming to check up on the myriad tubes and intravenous drips of the life-support system.

'You feel cheated, don't you, Harry?'

It was Ellis. Lambert turned and gave his sergeant a half-hearted smile. 'I guess that's one way of putting it. On the other hand, why don't I just unplug him? Not much point in keeping him alive, seeing as he's costing the NHS about £750 a day to keep him in this state.'

'I think once his children find out he killed their mother, they'll probably give their permission to switch him off.'

Lambert exhaled noisily and shook his head. 'I wouldn't want to be in their shoes for anything.'

'What about his driver?'

'We got a full confession out of him, which led to the arrest of McNeil and his brother-in-law.'

'I always knew those two had something to do with it,' Ellis said.

'Yes, but little did they know how they were being used by this bastard.' Lambert pointed a finger at Lloyd. 'They were convinced they were avenging abused children instead of subscribing to a plot to rid Lloyd of his wife's lover. They were the ones who gave Collier the information as to the whereabouts

THE WRECKING BAR

of the two sex offenders. And Hughes left the white van at the factory, unlocked and with the keys in the ignition, plus a supply of sulphuric acid. They switched the number plates for a scrapped vehicle, Collier drove to the factory to pick up the van, and McNeil and Hughes made certain they had perfect alibis on the nights he killed them. And it was Lloyd who persuaded them Yalding had to die, telling them he was a child abuser but had never been caught.'

'What d'you think will happen to those two?'

'Well, they've conspired to murder, and once they learn one of the victims was innocent, let's hope they enjoy their time at Her Majesty's pleasure.'

Lambert stared at Lloyd's unconscious form for a moment, his jaw clamped tight, frustration and tension showing in his strained expression. And then Ellis noticed him relaxing. The change was rapid, as if a drug had kicked in.

Lambert raised the plastic carrier bag and a glint came into his eyes as he grinned at Ellis. 'Come on, let's go and see Sharon. I've got a little something for the baby.'

As they walked along the corridors, following the signs for Maternity, Lambert asked, 'You got a name for her yet?'

'We decided on Lucy.'

'Lucy Ellis. Sounds good to me.'

They walked along in silence for a while, and just as they reached the maternity ward, Ellis stopped Lambert with a hand on his arm.

'Just a minute, Harry. You didn't tell me about Mrs Parry's car.'

Lambert smiled, knowing his sergeant's curiosity had to be satisfied before the visit.

'It was at the airport. Collier drove him over to pick it up just after they bumped into Debbie at Mrs Parry's house, and they got there before Kevin did. Lloyd returned it to his mother-in-law's garage, and we've found it complete with the burgled items in the boot.'

'What about the murder weapon?'

Lambert shook his head. 'The gun wasn't there. I'm only guessing, but Lloyd may have chucked it into the sea or river immediately after the murder. And, unless he comes round, we'll probably never know.'

'Thanks, Harry. Shall we go in now?'

When they went into the ward, they saw Sharon sitting up in bed, peering into the cot, which was within arm's reach.

'Hello, Sharon. Congratulations!' Lambert said. 'A little Lucy, I believe.'

'Thank you, Harry. Did Tony find time to tell you she took fifteen hours to come into the world?'

Chapter Twenty-Eight

'I think he may have mentioned something like that.' Lambert stood over the cot, pretending to admire the baby. 'She's beautiful, Sharon.'

'Don't lie. All men think babies look the same, except their own.' She giggled, and then clutched her stomach. 'Ouch!'

Lambert handed her the carrier bag. 'Sorry, I was too busy to wrap it properly. It's for Lucy.'

Sharon took out a collection of crazy shapes joined together with string and metal parts. She looked at Lambert quizzically.

'It's a mobile,' he explained. 'I remember Natasha had one hanging over her cot. Hours of endless fun.'

'Thank you, Harry. That was very thoughtful; especially as you've had a busy time of it yourself.'

'It has been a bit hectic,' he mumbled. Ellis came and stood next to him and he patted him on the back. 'Congratulations to both of you. Now if you'll excuse me. I'll let you have some time together.'

It was stifling hot in the ward, and Harry needed to get out into the fresh air before he fell over. The recent events were starting to take their toll. And he always liked to make a clean exit even though it might seem abrupt. After one cursory 'cheerio', he marched briskly away from the ward and along the corridors.

As he left the hospital he looked up and saw the sombre clouds hanging over the city, black and sagging, and knew the deluge would come pretty soon. But he didn't care. There had been so much death to contend with recently, but now the birth had revived him, and he made up his mind that he would spend some time in London soon and take Natasha out to dinner and to a few shows.

His brightness lasted as long as the weather remained dry. As the rain pelted down, a taxi pulled up outside the hospital entrance, and out of it got Lloyd's son and daughter, both clinging to each other for support. As they went inside the building, Lambert guessed that they had been told their father was in a coma and had been hit on the head by Collier.

But what they didn't know was that their father had murdered their mother. They would hear it on the news that evening, which was not the way they ought to find out.

He shivered as the rain soaked his hair, trickled under his collar and down his spine. As he went back inside the hospital, he wondered how he was going to tell them. But someone had to do it, and it might as well be him.

~

Inspector Lambert's next case is found in...

Missing Persons

Chapter One Preview

It was almost 3.30 p.m. and Jimmy Harlan was on his eighth pint on an empty stomach. He had reached that drinker's point of no return, everything a blur, a hazy weaving in and out of reality, and he had no idea that his binge drinking on that fateful Tuesday afternoon was about to lead to his downfall and set in motion a sequence of violent and lethal crimes.

He leaned, almost collapsed, over the pool table and attempted to pot the final ball, lunged forcefully, missing the white, and his cue shot forward and fell to the floor with a clatter. The landlord of the pub, an establishment not renowned for catering to the cream of Swansea society, would have asked Jimmy to tone it down a bit or diplomatically suggest he might have had sufficient, but he was upstairs having a snooze before the evening session and had left his son Daryl in charge; and Daryl, not yet twenty, still plagued by teenage acne, feared Jimmy, whose reputation as a hard man was more than bluster, so he tolerated the stream of foul language spewing out of Jimmy's mouth without a break.

Jimmy's pool partner, his old school chum, Jason Crabbe, was slightly less bad for wear, having had the man-sized breakfast in Wetherspoon's just before twelve. When Jimmy decided it was time to move on, Jason was sober enough to persuade his mate to leave the car at the rear of the pub. But Jimmy was having none of it. He was sober enough to drive. Even made a joke of it, saying he was too pissed to stand up but was steady enough to get behind the wheel.

Fortunately for Jason, he lived nearby and could legitimately refuse a lift, even though Jimmy insisted. But it was difficult arguing with a belligerent drunk like his mate who had always been the leader. During their schooldays Jason obediently accepted his role as sidekick.

And over the years, without realizing it, he began copying his mate. His speech patterns and the things Jimmy said were unconsciously repeated in the company of others. And when Jason got his hair cropped fashionably short, bordering on total baldness, Jason adopted the same cloned bullet-head, so they started to look more like brothers than friends. The only difference was, whereas Jason could eat and drink without putting on an ounce of fat, Jimmy was chunky with a beer belly.

Although Jason faithfully accepted his mate's orders, perhaps he had some sort of sixth sense warning him of the events of that gloomy February day. Perhaps he sensed the tragedy that was about to unfold, giving Jimmy his allotted fifteen minutes of fame. No, not fame. Notoriety. Even though Jason couldn't foresee that his mate's arrogant and cocky face was soon to become one of the most reviled on television, he knew better than to accept a lift from him, even the short distance to his house.

He excused himself by saying he had to go to the Gents to take a dump, leaving Jimmy to reel out to the car park, where he fumbled for his bunch of keys, dropped them several times, but eventually managed to fit the car key into the ignition of his BMW.

***

Now she was in sixth form, Alice Mason actually looked forward to going to school. No more school uniform; now she could dress like a young adult. Outgoing and bright, a popular girl with many friends, Alice was pretty much a star pupil and was destined to do well in further education.

As she stood at the bus stop with her friend Amy, slightly apart from a great knot of younger pupils from the same school, they chatted and giggled about the boys they did or didn't fancy, and then something Amy said prompted a sudden reminder in Alice's mind. It was her brother's birthday tomorrow and she had forgotten his card, which she had left in her locker at school and she needed it to catch the last post.

She embraced her friend briefly and then hurried back to school to get the card, which was an outrageously funny one. It wouldn't take long, although she would probably miss the bus and have to wait 15 minutes for the next one, which meant missing the frantic, girlie noises that was part of the fun of the homeward journey. As she dashed back through the school gates, she checked her watch. It was just after 3.30 p.m.

At 3.32 p.m. Jimmy pulled out of the pub car park and his hands slipped on the steering wheel. He over-compensated by yanking the wheel the other way and the BMW swerved with a squeal of tyres. A pedestrian stared at the car, glaring judgementally, which Jimmy took as criticism of his driving skills, so he accelerated, going much too fast for his inebriated state, zigzagging along the narrow street like Jason Bourne escaping an assassin.

At 3.36, having collected her brother's birthday card, Alice came out through the school gates and saw her bus, the one with Amy on board, flash by. She couldn't see her friend, the bus was too far away, but she waved in any case, because she thought Amy could probably see her. There was no one at the bus stop now. It was cold, and she turned her coat collar up. Somehow, when she was with her friends, the cold was less noticeable. Now that she was on her own, she shivered, and anticipated getting home to warmth and a welcome purr when she stroked their tabby Moggs.

At 3.38, tearing down the hill towards the bus stop, Jimmy's head swam as he tried to focus on the road. He was on automatic pilot now and the messages his brain was sending to the rest of his body were as blurred as his vision.

As Alice watched out for the next bus, she saw the BMW hurtling down the road towards the bus stop. She had no reason to be alarmed at this stage – plenty of drivers drive too fast. But in a split second came the change, the sudden realization that your life is in danger and out of your control.

Jimmy had driven too far to the right of the road and a heavy lorry was coming up the hill towards him. He swerved massively and the car skidded. Unable to hold the wheel, he wrestled and tugged helplessly as it spun in his hands. Everything was a blur in Jimmy's head as he lost control and the car screeched towards the bus stop. With a massive impact, the car hit Alice head on.

And that was what saved Jimmy from any serious injury. He was braking as the car bumped and rumbled over her body, which slowed it down. That and the privet hedge of the house behind the bus stop. Although he wasn't wearing a seat belt, he only suffered a bruised head from where it hit the windscreen.

On the other side of the road a passer-by recorded the accident on his phone camera. Alice Jessica Mason, aged 16 years and five months, was killed at precisely 3.39 p.m.

After the accident, it was said that Alice would have died instantly. But how can anyone really know that?

Also from David Barry...

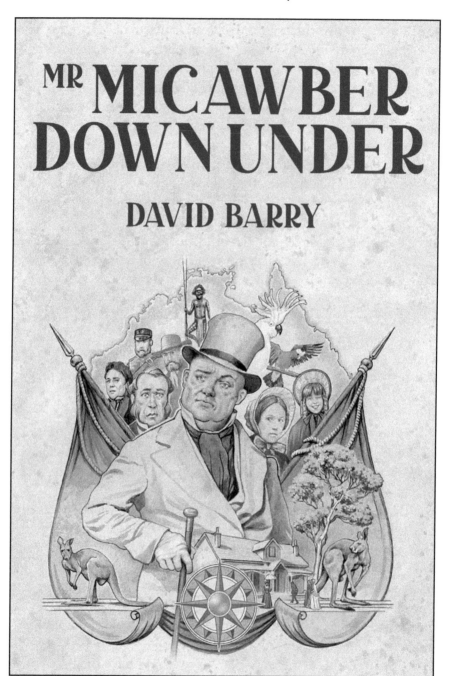

Ingram Content Group UK Ltd.
Milton Keynes UK
UKHW041124210423
420562UK00001B/26